On the Edge

On the Edge

BY

Julie Coulter Bellon

spring creek
BOOK COMPANY
Provo, Utah

ISBN 13: 978-1-932898-30-9
ISBN 10: 1-932898-30-1
e. 1

Published by:
Spring Creek Book Company
P.O. Box 50355
Provo, Utah 84605-0355
www.springcreekbooks.com

Cover design © Spring Creek Book Company
Cover design by Nicole Cunningham

Printed in the United States of America
10 9 8 7 6 5 4 3 2 1
Printed on acid-free paper

Library of Congress Cataloging-in-Publication Data

Bellon, Julie Coulter, 1969-
  On the edge / by Julie Coulter Bellon.
      p. cm.
  ISBN-13: 978-1-932898-30-9 (pbk. : acid-free paper)
  ISBN-10: 1-932898-30-1 (pbk. : acid-free paper)
  1. Intelligence officers--Fiction. 2. Bioterrorism--Fiction. I. Title.
  PS3602.E648O5 2005
  813'.6--dc22
                                    2005006789

Dedication

For Brian, my best friend, partner, and eternal companion.

Acknowledgments

I couldn't do any of this without the love and support of my family, Brian, Jeffrey, Lauren, Jared, Jayden, Nathan and Brandon. You guys are my world.

Thank you to Dore Elmer and Sara Parcell for their comments on the early version. You helped me find my direction.

Dennis and Connie Gleason graciously agreed to read the completed manuscript and through their thoughtful suggestions, the book was much improved. Thank you for that.

I also want to thank my parents, Bob and Renee, who taught me about love, forgiveness, and what a testimony of the true gospel of Jesus Christ is really about.

I'd also like to thank my mentor through the entire process, Rachel Ann Nunes, and the staff at Spring Creek Book Company for being so incredibly wonderful to work with.

Chapter One

Dylan Campbell walked along the side of the Kampala road, his feet aching and his camera bag slapping against his hip. Of all the times for his jeep to have engine trouble! With each step his boots ground into the road, his frustration evident. The last two intelligence gathering missions—or to be more politically correct, threat assessment directives—had been just like this, with one thing going wrong after another and he was tired of it. Tired of the whole business. It definitely wasn't the smooth James Bond lifestyle he'd thought it would be. He absently rubbed the scar just underneath his collarbone and above his heart. Getting shot had changed his perspective on his career with the Canadian Security Intelligence Service. He knew it wasn't what he wanted to do in life anymore and he needed to get out and find something else. He planned to tell his boss, Andrew Blythe, as soon as he got home from Uganda. Dylan couldn't remember the feel of his own bed beneath him, and he wanted to go home, to regroup emotionally, something that every good agent needed to do once in a while—to get in touch with their emotions.

He sighed and adjusted the camera bag over his hip again. His cover for this mission had been that he was a photojournalist capturing the medical failures and successes of private hospitals in Kampala, the capital city of Uganda. The only drawback was carrying around the blasted camera bag. It was awkward against his hip and making it sore, but walking was his only option at this point. The road was empty and would probably remain so at this time of night. In the daytime it was teeming with people, vehicles, and animals. When Dylan had first arrived he was amazed at the number of people driving small herds of goats and Ankole cattle on such a busy road. Especially among the chaotic driving—on the wrong side of the road for a Canadian driver—that included not only buses, slow-moving trucks with men lounging on top of the loads, taxis and the like, but also had carts, bicycles, mopeds, and bodabodas, a type of motorbike. Near midnight, however, it was dark and silent.

The nighttime darkness in Africa never ceased to amaze him, the inky blackness consuming everything but the millions of stars twinkling across the sky. The only light on the earth was the occasional candle or kerosene lamp in a hut, but even they were usually extinguished when he came near. The Ugandans outside of Kampala were a cautious people and he couldn't blame them. The country was in turmoil and had been for many years. It just paid to be cautious. He pushed the luminescent light on his watch and saw that it was 10:30 p.m. As he crested a small hill, he could see the lights of Kampala in the distance and knew that if he were to reach the Mulago hospital before midnight, he had better pick up the pace.

As the long grass near the side of the road brushed his ankles, he could hear the rustling of the nocturnal wildlife as they began their hunt for food. The lush greenery that abounded in the hills surrounding Kampala provided well for the wildlife it supported. Plants and animals were found in plenty in this part of Uganda. On the Kampala road however, the animals didn't seem to stray too close, but they did let their presence be known.

Dylan was careful to stay on the road, watching for any animals that might mistake him for a snack. He patted his shoulder holster, under his light jacket, reassuring himself that his gun was still there if he needed it. The shoulder holster and the camera bag would make it awkward to run, but he started jogging at an easy pace. He didn't want to miss this appointment.

—◦—

Elizabeth glanced at the clock for the millionth time, knowing she had nursing duties to attend to in the hospital, but not able to help herself. What could be keeping Dylan? She'd told him he needed to be at the hospital promptly at midnight so he could take pictures of the truck unloading the new medical supplies. It was nearly midnight and he wasn't here yet. Each time the door to the stairwell opened she turned, hoping it was him, his green eyes and confident smile coming toward her. Her heart fluttered a little thinking of him. She had been hoping he would come a little early so she could take a break from her duties and they could talk.

Being with him the last six weeks had lifted her spirits. He had been easy to talk to from their very first meeting, his relaxed manner and quick smile attracting her immediately. He had a light about him, she couldn't pinpoint what it was exactly, but it drew her to him. Her usual walls of suspicion had come down as she intuitively felt she could trust him, something that rarely happened in her line of work, since she dealt with so many criminals.

She had been given a difficult assignment in Africa, trying to win the confidence of the hospital administrators and become a member of the inner circle. As a CIA agent her job was dangerous, but she was good at it and prided herself on that. She'd worked hard over the years to prove she could do the job and usually she could blend in and feel in control of her surroundings quickly. Uganda had been different, though. It had taken several months before the owners of the private hospital would even speak to her, much less trust her, and the conditions she faced every day in the hospital ward were heartbreaking, especially watching the suffering of the children.

Dylan had come at a time when she'd needed a friend, but she had to be careful that he didn't interfere with her job. The first few times he asked her out she'd refused, citing her duties as her excuse. He'd taken on the challenge and offered to help her around the hospital. It was a gallant gesture and she had taken him up on it, immediately leading him to the triage area. A child with a cut on his head was bleeding profusely, waiting for stitches, and Dylan was asked to hold a compress over it. He'd been all right until the child threw up and then he'd almost lost his own lunch. Elizabeth had taken over for him, instructing him to sit down. After the child was taken care of she'd gone back to find him. He looked so forlorn that she had agreed to go out with him.

She smiled at the thought of the time they'd spent together. Smoothing her shirt and trying to straighten her ponytail, she remembered how he'd playfully pulled on it last night right before he kissed her for the first time. It had been so long since she'd let a man into her circle of trust it had been disconcerting for her, but exciting at the same time. She couldn't wait to see him again. When he was around all thoughts of her dangerous assignment were thrust aside. She was playing with fire, but told herself that since nothing was happening right now anyway it would be okay to spend time with someone. She knew she was rationalizing, but it helped to ease her conscience.

She walked back to the nurses station and watched the seconds tick by on the large clock behind the table. She hoped he'd hurry so they could have a few moments alone.

⊱━◈━◯━◈━⊰

An hour and a half later Dylan entered Kampala. It was a big city, but the buildings were somewhat dilapidated with a run-down, inner-city feel, the once colorful signs and facades on the shops worn and faded. Some "shops" were made of corrugated metal, most had living quarters in back and a small yard with corn or bananas growing in the front. Dylan had to walk carefully and squint in the dark to make his way through since there were no streetlights in this part of town. During the day there were always large amounts of people around, some ready to sell you something or other—trinkets, piles of fruit, or paintings. But at night, people mostly stood together talking or were trying to go home.

He zigzagged around several buildings and clubs, finally arriving at the hospital, tired and out of breath. He immediately climbed the long flight of stairs to the ward where Elizabeth worked. He smiled at the thought of her. She had been the one bright spot on this trip. His job took him away so much he'd never really had time for a relationship, and he definitely didn't want to date anyone in his line of work. Elizabeth was a breath of fresh air, and had been from the moment he'd met her six weeks ago. She was warm and friendly, always ready to lend a helping hand. That's what made her a great hospital worker because she was knowledgeable, people were drawn to her, and she seemed to instinctively know how to make those around her feel at ease. Everyone he'd talked to in the hospital praised her and she was looked up to for her innate leadership abilities, evidenced by the fact that the hospital administration had recently asked her to be their public relations coordinator.

Her new job had made it an easy decision to use her as his inside contact at the hospital. But as he befriended her and spent time in her company, she became more than a contact. He truly wanted to be around her. Dylan had invited her out several times before she finally said yes, as if she was giving in to something she knew she shouldn't do. He reached the top of the stairs, out of breath, but excited to see Elizabeth again.

Opening the door that led to the ward, he immediately saw Elizabeth standing in the middle of the large room, surrounded by several African women. Her bronze skin still contrasted with their black skin, making her appear pale, though at home she would have a healthy tan. They were all trying to look at the paper in Elizabeth's hand and she was pointing to several different rooms on the floor, apparently dividing out some nursing responsibilities for the night. Her long brown hair was tied back in a ponytail, her glasses slightly slipping down her nose each time she looked up from the paper. He smiled nostalgically, remembering the night before when he'd gently pulled on that ponytail, tipping her face upward so he could kiss her. The memory warmed him.

During their conversations, Elizabeth had told him how she'd come to Africa as an aid worker. She said she felt out of her element here, but it didn't seem that way. Most people were drawn to her and Dylan thought it was probably her happy spirit that made everyone want to be with her, including him. She looked up from the women, pushed her glasses back onto her nose, and turned to smile at Dylan. "You made it," she said. "I was beginning to wonder."

He stepped toward her, the other women scattering as he did. "The Jeep broke down again so I had to walk. Sorry I'm late."

She shrugged. "Don't worry, it seems everyone is running late tonight. The trucks aren't here yet either."

He put his bag on the floor, happy to get rid of its bulk. "Can you take a break then?"

Elizabeth leaned over a large table to a woman sitting behind it and told her she'd be taking a break in the lounge and to let her know when the shipment arrived. She turned back to Dylan. "I'd like that. Let's go down to the lounge."

Dylan took her hand. "Why do you call it that when it's a room with three metal chairs and a tilted table? The word lounge implies to me that there would be a couch and a television."

"Well, we lounge there, so we call it a lounge. It's not what's in a room that counts, it's the spirit of it, right?"

He squeezed her hand. "It's sort of like saying, it's the

thought that counts, eh?"

Elizabeth smiled, squeezed his hand back and led him down the hall, her ponytail swinging, walking past what looked to Dylan like several delivery rooms where women were in various stages of labor. Elizabeth seemed unperturbed by the moans and screams, but it was upsetting to Dylan.

"Shouldn't someone be in there with them?" he asked, his tone worried.

Elizabeth shrugged. "There are only two doctors here tonight. They do the best they can."

Dylan walked behind her, meeting the eyes of several men sitting in the hall. They looked hollow and lifeless, the whites of their eyes magnified by the darkness of their skin. Dylan smiled as he walked by, but it was not returned, until his gaze lit upon a young boy about ten. The boy returned Dylan's smile and gave him a little wave as he watched Dylan and Elizabeth move through the crowd in the hallway. Standing on his tiptoes so the boy could still see him, Dylan waved back.

Elizabeth had stopped walking and Dylan noticed her eyeing a small, well-dressed man coming down the hall toward them through the wave of people. She nodded her head toward the older man, then led Dylan to a doorway. "Wait in here," she said. "That's the man in charge of the shipment. Looks like we'll have to take a rain check on our lounge date," she said, laughing and touching his arm briefly, then turning to shut the door.

Dylan gently rubbed his arm where the warmth of her hand had been and stepped further into the sparsely furnished room, sitting down in an old metal chair. He opened the bag and picked up the camera, adjusting its weight and moving the lens different ways as if to put it into focus. He put it on the table and sagged in his chair. Dylan pinched the bridge of his nose, his head aching and his body tired. *All I have to do for this mission is verify the information and make the threat assessment. Maybe take a few pictures for proof and I can get out of here*, he thought to himself. *I'm going to tell Andrew it's time for me to leave Africa and the CSIS.* The only sadness he felt was the thought of leaving Elizabeth.

He closed his eyes briefly, his legs still having small muscle spasms from his ten-mile jog. Telling Andrew would be hard. Andrew Blythe had been his mentor at the Canadian Security Intelligence Service. Dylan knew the CSIS had been Andrew's home for most of his adult life, especially after his wife had died, but Dylan realized he didn't want an all-consuming career for himself. He felt he was ready for a new direction in his life, one that included a wife and a family. He wanted to settle down, find the new direction he was looking for and he didn't know if Andrew would understand that. He looked at the camera lens on the table and wished his life could be that easy to focus. Stretching his neck, he hoped Elizabeth would hurry.

Chapter Two

Elizabeth stepped away from the door, feeling a little bereft without Dylan walking by her side. His height and confident stride made her feel small but protected. She hadn't had those feelings since she was a child, walking next to her father. And she was now a field agent, perfectly capable of protecting herself.

She turned and watched Dylan for a moment through the small window in the door, his dark hair probably longer than he normally kept it, curling below his collar, his sideburns blending with the beard he had grown. Africa had brought out the bushman in him, as he hadn't seemed concerned about shaving or cutting his hair since she had known him. But even with the longer hair he obviously cared about his appearance and was always neat and clean. She wondered what he would look like clean-shaven, if the small cleft in his chin would be more pronounced on his jawline. His beard was slightly lighter than his hair, the warm brown tones mixing with dark caramel highlights, probably from all the sun exposure he'd experienced since coming to Africa, she surmised. It contrasted with the green of his eyes, and every time she looked in them, they reminded her of the vibrant green carpet of plants and trees in her native Oregon.

She watched him pinch his nose, his shoulders sagging, and realized he was likely tired from the long walk. Pulling her gaze away, she turned around and stepped out into the hallway, attempting to keep her balance as she was jostled by several medical aides—most of them women she had become attached to, who were trying to attend to the sick and ease the suffering. She murmured hello and said she would be there as soon as she could. Making her way through the crowded hallway, she waved and walked toward her undercover partner, David Kanu. He looked tired, his powder black eyes ringed red, his salt and pepper curls disheveled. He was of medium build, but was wiry and strong both physically and in his moral convictions. He deplored the conditions found in many African countries, but was even more disgusted by those who would take advantage and try to get gain from the suffering. Whenever he could, he helped the United States intelligence community in rooting out those who would cause more chaos and suffering.

Elizabeth walked quickly toward him feeling the need to get things going so Dylan could take his pictures and she could get back to work. Of all the assignments she had been given, she felt a deep satisfaction at being a medical aide, helping people and being needed. She especially loved making the children feel as comfortable as possible and trying to console them through their suffering. It reminded her of why she had started medical school before becoming an agent and it was times like these that she wished she had finished her studies.

She finally reached David, smiling at him, and heaving a sigh at making it through the crowd. She was glad to see him, that he was safe, and had been able to deliver the long-awaited trucks with their precious goods to the hospital. It had been a difficult two weeks as David had been incommunicado while he'd gotten this shipment. He was being tested, to see if he was loyal to the cause and worthy to be let into the terrorist cell's inner circle. Something big was going to happen and these shipments seemed to be the key. The risks were great and they didn't want to arouse anyone's suspicion at this stage in the game. Not being able to communicate with him had worried her, but there was nothing she could do about it. All her worrying was a moot point now as David was next to her apparently none the worse for wear. But every agent had seen too much death and destruction to take anything for granted.

She pushed her glasses back onto her nose, annoyed that they kept slipping. It was one part of her cover disguise she could do without. "David," she greeted the older man. "How did the trip go?"

He took her arm and walked back the way she had come. "Who was that man with you? Do you know him?" He looked furtively around, but no one paid them any attention, anyone within earshot wrapped up in their own duties.

Elizabeth smiled. "That's Dylan. He's a photographer doing a piece on the hospital."

He shook his head slightly. "That's a Canadian operative. I met him last year in South Africa during a diamond smuggling operation." Elizabeth gasped audibly at the news. "Have you given him any information?" David asked, his voice low.

"No, none. I . . . we . . ." Elizabeth stammered. She absently touched her lips, where Dylan had kissed her. "We've spent time together, that's all. Who would have thought we were both here for the same reason . . ." She looked back at the room where Dylan was waiting and her heart sank. This definitely changed things. "I believed him when he said he was a photojournalist so I asked him to come here to take pictures of the shipment tonight. It was a great opportunity to see how well the hospital is doing and help my job as the hospital administration's public relations coordinator, not to mention my cover as an aid worker."

David gripped her arm. "We have the virus with us tonight and all the materials we need to alter it into a biological weapon. Bumani has guards everywhere. You'll have to tell him to leave."

"You're right." Elizabeth eyes widened and she took a deep breath. This is what they'd been waiting for. "It's definitely too dangerous to have Dylan around. But won't he be suspicious?

If he's an operative, he probably has some idea of what we're doing." She shook off David's fingers digging into her arm.

"He'll have to be eliminated Elizabeth, you know that. Especially if he knows too much. If Bumani even gets wind that he's here . . ."

Elizabeth swayed slightly. "You can't eliminate him, David, we have to help him . . ." her voice trailed off, and David grabbed her arm again to steady her.

Sighing deeply, he looked at her in disappointment. She turned away. "You should know better than to give in to your feelings, my friend." David shook his head. "I will do my best to keep him alive, but I don't know how much good I'll do. Bumani . . ." David stopped speaking as another man joined them. He towered over Elizabeth, his shirt stretched tight across a massive chest, and his arms were folded as he came to stand beside the pair. Elizabeth watched him, his intense gaze following David's every move. It was a cold stare. David's body stiffened and his entire countenance changed. "Elizabeth, this is Lizige. He's here to help me with the shipment." His eyes showed a sense of desperation and Elizabeth wondered what Lizige's true mission was.

"Lizige," Elizabeth greeted him, extending her hand. Lizige just nodded, barely looking at her, his arms remaining folded. The dim fluorescent lights hanging from the ceiling reflected off Lizige's bald head and gave him an eerie aura. Elizabeth felt a shiver of fear. At that moment, the door to the stairwell opened and several men came through, shouting to David that the trucks needed to be unloaded immediately.

"We should go tell Dylan that the photo opportunity is off," Elizabeth said, waiting patiently while David finished giving instructions to the men. He didn't hear her, the men were talking so loudly, but Lizige watched her carefully, his dark eyes hooded and brooding. She felt uncomfortable under his gaze, but returned it with a smile.

Dylan heard a commotion outside and opened the door. Elizabeth was talking to two men who had their backs turned to Dylan. They were pointing another group of men back toward the stairwell, talking loudly. When the smaller man turned and met Dylan's eyes, Dylan thought he saw a flicker of recognition, but as quickly as it had appeared it was gone. Dylan squinted and looked harder, but couldn't place him at all, so he dismissed the thought. He met so many people in his profession that each face was starting to have familiar characteristics. Elizabeth began to walk toward him motioning for the men to follow.

After skirting around a small crowd in the hallway, they finally reached him. "Dylan, this is David Kanu," she introduced the smaller man. "He is in charge of the shipment tonight." She pointed to the taller man towering over David. "This is Lizige, David's assistant."

Lizige barely acknowledged Dylan, nodding slightly, but saying nothing. Dylan turned to David and shook his hand. "You must be very proud to be able to help so many of your countrymen," he commented.

David did not look up to meet Dylan's eyes, and he seemed quite anxious, stealing glances at both Elizabeth and Lizige. After a moment he looked up at Dylan, trying to make his face passive, but his jaw was working and he licked his lips several times, giving away his apparent nervousness. He finally gave up and bowed slightly to Dylan before turning toward Elizabeth. "I must help the men unload the trucks. It is best to work at night when it is cool and we have not time to spare." He nodded to Dylan. "It was very nice to meet you." His English was well-spoken, but clipped, and it was obvious it wasn't his native tongue.

Dylan held up his camera. "So you don't mind if I take a few pictures do you? My magazine is doing a spread on medical conditions here in Uganda."

David shook his head, nodding toward Elizabeth. "There will be no pictures. Elizabeth will explain," he said curtly, motioning to Lizige to follow him.

Dylan doggedly continued after him. "It's just a few pictures. Maybe you'll be famous if your picture is in my magazine. We publish all over the world you know."

At that comment, David's head whipped around. "Have you taken any pictures of the supplies at all?" He turned to look accusingly at Elizabeth.

Dylan furrowed his brow. "Yes, just a few pictures of your previous shipment." *Why would that upset him?* he wondered.

David started back up the hallway muttering something unintelligible under his breath. "I must go," he called to Elizabeth. Lizige's gaze lingered on Dylan, his eyes hard, then he finally turned to follow David.

Elizabeth was happy to see him leave, the hairs on the back of her neck prickling as he watched Dylan. She started to follow in David's footsteps. "You'll have to excuse David, he seems a little stressed out tonight. He's usually the picture of politeness," she said over her shoulder. Turning back to face Dylan for a moment, she continued speaking. "But I've never seen him act *this* stressed out." Her eyes were drawn to Lizige who was following David close enough to see over his shoulder. No wonder David was stressed. "His assistant looks like he takes his job seriously," she said thoughtfully.

"Did he say why I couldn't take pictures tonight?" Dylan asked, coming around to face her and blocking her view of David and Lizige. One hand touched her shoulder as if to pull her back from her thoughts.

"No, just that it wouldn't be possible and you'll have to come back another time." With an almost imperceptible shake of her head, she started for the stairwell. "I'm so sorry you came all this way for nothing."

Dylan smiled, stuffed his camera back in his bag and followed her. "I got to see you, so it wasn't for nothing."

Elizabeth found a small path through the masses of people and walked ahead of Dylan, reaching the stairwell door before him. "Are you coming? I could walk you out," she said as she turned, realizing she had left him behind.

"Right behind you," he said and caught up to her, putting his hand at her back to guide her down the stairwell. "How long have you known David?" he asked casually.

She seemed preoccupied, reaching down in her pocket for a stick of lip balm which she applied. "Ever since I came here. He was one of the first people I met at the hospital. He was an orderly, helping out wherever he could. Then he disappeared for a while." She started down the steps, no longer noticing their steepness or the peeling paint.

"Where did he go?" Dylan asked, watching the stairs carefully so he didn't fall. They were set at an odd angle making his footing unsure.

Elizabeth shrugged her shoulders. "I don't know. It's not uncommon for someone in this area to be gone for weeks in the bush, go north to visit family, join the army, who knows. He came back about two months ago and said he wanted to help the hospital. He's gotten supplies for us almost every week since then. Stuff we really needed."

Dylan let this sink in. David had to have access to some big money from somewhere for the last two months in order to afford the magnitude of these supplies. "Is he the middle man or is he using his own money?" he asked. Elizabeth didn't respond and he wondered if she heard him or pretended not to. He made a mental note to do a background check on David when he got back to his room.

When he and Elizabeth reached the main floor and went out into the courtyard of the hospital, he was amazed at the manpower unloading several trucks. The wooden crates they carried were marked "Medical Supplies" and seemed very heavy, some taking two men to carry them.

"I wonder why he doesn't want me taking pictures?" Dylan mused.

"Maybe the publicity makes him uncomfortable," Elizabeth offered. She walked toward the street, pulling him along with her.

He stopped and held her at the waist. "Can I take your picture?" He smiled and tilted his head toward his camera. "It would make my trip worthwhile."

Her face looked stricken for a moment, and she shook her head, looking at the ground. "No, I'm not photogenic," she said firmly, finally looking him in the eye. Her mouth was set, but her eyes seemed to be asking him to understand.

"You're beautiful. What do you mean you're not photogenic?" He reached down for his camera bag, but she grabbed his arm.

"I really don't want my picture taken, okay?" She started back toward the hospital. "I've got to go."

He took two strides and caught up to her, catching her by the arm and turning her to face him, her ponytail brushing his arm. "Can I see you tomorrow?"

She hesitated. "I'm not sure what my schedule is. I'll have to see," she shrugged as she spoke.

Dylan was disappointed. He thought she'd been as excited to see him as he had to see her. What had changed? "Okay. I'll come by and see if you're busy then."

She nodded. "I've got to get back to work," she said, as she continued on, walking quickly toward the hospital.

"See you tomorrow," he called to her retreating back. She waved, but didn't turn around. Dylan was puzzled by her behavior. He'd never seen Elizabeth act this way. Something wasn't right here, and he was going to find out what it was. She seemed nervous and anxious to get rid of him. Or was it his agency training to be suspicious of everything and everyone getting in the way? Walking carefully back to the courtyard, he watched Elizabeth stand next to David Kanu who was directing the men to the basement of the hospital. Dylan took out his camera and began surreptitiously shooting the volunteers, the crates, the trucks, trying to be as inconspicuous as possible.

When David and Elizabeth went inside the hospital, he went into the courtyard and grabbed a small crate, hoisted it on his shoulders and followed the line of workers into the storage rooms in the basement. When Dylan got into the last room he set his crate down and looked in amazement at the wooden boxes that were already stacked several layers high. The medical supplies in those boxes represented thousands of dollars worth of materials that these people desperately needed. That was one thing that had shocked him so much when he'd arrived in Uganda; the great disparity in the people— the poverty among the riches, the shacks among the walled gardens, and the AIDS virus which struck all classes. The majority seemed poverty-stricken and in dire circumstances. And from what Elizabeth had said, the hospital was constantly full.

Several workers were beginning to eye him, so he left the storage room and slowly walked down the long, concrete hall toward the stairwell, the line of workers ahead of him. When they had all gone through, he turned to go back to the storage room to open one of the crates and take pictures. He hoped to find a clue as to whether a weapon was being hidden in this hospital and he thought these shipments might be the key. Chatter on the terrorist network had only hinted as to what could be in such large shipments of supposed medical supplies. He tried to step quietly so he didn't call any unnecessary attention to himself if anyone else was still down in the basement, but it was not an easy feat with heavy boots on. The buzz overhead from the fluorescent light was pulsating like a heartbeat, matching his own. Looking around at the dim yellow light reflected off the gray, narrow walls surrounding him, he began to feel claustrophobic and quickened his step toward the storage room, wishing it wasn't the furthest room away from the stairs.

He finally reached his destination and was just about to open the storage room door when the large metal handle of the stairwell clicked behind him, signaling that someone was about to open it. Something inside him told him to hide. Dylan had learned long ago to trust those instincts and quickly ducked into an empty room across the hall, propping the door slightly ajar. Two men walked noisily down the corridor and came to stand right in front of the storage room door where Dylan had stood moments before. Through the crack in the door of Dylan's hiding place, he could see that it was David talking quietly on a cell phone, Lizige standing next to him unashamedly listening. David was obviously listening to someone on the other end speaking, and nervously took a long drag on his cigarette. He blew out a large amount of smoke which wafted throughout the hall, and Dylan resisted the urge to cough.

"Lizige should not have called you. I can take care of this myself." David turned away from Lizige and paused, his finger in one ear as if he was having a hard time hearing. "Yes, I may know this man from somewhere." He glanced sideways at Lizige and from what Dylan could see, he was angry at the man who was listening to the conversation. "He could be a liability, but I have everything under control," David said, his jaw clenched.

Dylan strained to hear as the men moved away, back down the hallway. Were they talking about him?

"No, no one here knows anything," David paused to listen again. "Yes, the shipment is all here. The doctor arrives in two days and we can begin our work," he said into his phone. "Not to worry, Jimon. No one will find the weapon until we are ready." He shut his phone, took another long drag on his cigarette before dropping it to the floor and squashing it.

"Mr. Bumani is pleased that everything is in place but we must double the guards. We don't want anyone snooping around," he told Lizige, who nodded at him with a satisfied smile on his face. David looked anxiously around, then led the way back to the stairway.

Dylan waited a few moments before emerging from his hiding place. His stomach was in knots. If what he had just heard was true then the CSIS's intelligence had been correct. Jimon Bumani had a weapon in this hospital and was planning on using it. He would have to notify Andrew immediately, so the threat assessment could be made and the Prime Minister appraised of the situation. Dylan ran his fingers through his hair. His mission was complete, he'd verified the information and could go home and start the process of getting out of the Canadian Security Intelligence Service. As his heart and breathing slowed, he left the hospital dreading the long walk home. It was just one more indication that the job had lost its draw for him and it was time to get out.

Chapter Three

Dylan woke up in his room in a small household just outside of Kampala. He laid there for a moment, but the heat of the day was already creeping in. He got up and dressed in khaki cargo shorts and a navy blue T-shirt, grabbing his Toronto Blue Jays ball cap before going into the main room of the boarding house. Nabulungi, the lady who ran the house, had left a small breakfast for him on the table. He was grateful because he knew how hard it was for her. Ovens were a luxury the boarding house could not afford and all the cooking was done outside over an open fire. Since Dylan had come to Uganda his diet had consisted of a lot of fruits and vegetables, and since it was mango season, Dylan had them at least once a day. For breakfast was *posho*, a type of porridge made from maize flour and water. Sometimes he added millet or cassava, a tropical plant that had edible, fleshy roots. Dylan had also grown accustomed to the roasted sweet potatoes at his dinner meal and ground peanuts had become his favorite snack.

He moved to the small window and watched Nabulungi in her garden for a moment as he ate. Her red dress and turban stood out against the lush green of the garden and trees. He guessed her to be in her early fifties. Her smile was quick and her indented crow's feet near her eyes showed that she smiled often. She was a wonderful woman, but he knew her life had been hard. A few weeks after his arrival, he had sat on the small porch with her, talking about family, and she had told him how she had lost her husband when he had politically opposed Idi Amin thirty years before. Secret police had come to their home in the middle of the night and taken him, and she had never seen him again. She was told only that she should keep quiet and never speak of her husband again.

After that she could only eke out a living to support her two sons by growing a garden and opening her home as a boarding house. Her reputation for providing clean accommodations was well-known and she had sheltered several Canadian Security agents. Her sons were a favorite among the agents who had stayed with them, their rambunctious antics and need for a father figure apparent. But as the years passed her sons had come of age and made Nabulungi proud by marrying well and becoming contributing members of society. Unfortunately, they both had moved away to the birthplace of their wives, one to the city of Mbale, near Mount Elgon on the border of Kenya and the other moved near Kle to work at the Nsambya Catholic school. Her loneliness had only been eased when her nephew Serapio had come to live with her just before he turned two. His parents had died of the AIDS virus and he was left alone in the world. Nabulungi had eagerly taken him in, wanting to ease any suffering she saw, including her own loneliness.

Serapio was a good boy, but he couldn't sit still for long. Nabulungi tried to channel that energy by teaching him how to work. The boarding house was made with walls of red clay supported by branches of trees, elephant grass, and a tin roof. The entire house was made up of one large room divided into sections and several smaller rooms. The walls and roof on the house required many repairs and Serapio was always eager to help, but was really too small to do much. Currently it was his job to keep the floor as clean as possible, however with so many people in and out of the house that was sometimes difficult for him. Still he took pride in his work. Since there was no electricity or running water, the little family gathered water from a river a mile away from their home, requiring several trips a day. Serapio thought of it as a great adventure to go to the river and perhaps see a crocodile. He was also given the task of caring for their rabbits and chickens, which he did well from what Dylan had observed.

This morning Serapio was dancing around Nabulungi. "I am a wild hunter," he cried. She smiled at him, handing him a stick and then continuing on with her work.

"Go make yourself a spear, and hunt for the family," she told him, her eyes sparkling. Serapio smiled back, and went off to make his spear. Nabulungi noticed Dylan watching her. "Good morning," she called. "Oli otya?"

Dylan raised his hand in greeting, replying to her question in Lugandan as well. "Bulungi, I'm fine. Can I help you today?" he asked.

She shook her head. "No, I am fine. Your pronunciation is getting better," she complimented. "Don't worry about me. You go about your business."

Dylan nodded and returned to the house to get his laptop. He'd have to walk into the central part of the village to use the phone line and electrical outlets. Cell phones were hit and miss in this part of Africa and getting a secure line was almost impossible so he was limited to the computer. He had tried to contact Andrew last night, but had no success. He'd try again this morning.

He walked the small dirt path, arriving at Akiki's hut. Akiki had been part of the Village Phone Project that gave access to phone lines and communications in rural villages. He had been chosen as the village phone operator and was very proud of his job. It had allowed their village to take phone orders for the produce from the village farm and it made Akiki somewhat of a celebrity. There was a three year waiting list for anyone else to get a phone line, so Akiki's access allowed him an elevated status in the village. Before Akiki's phone line, if anyone had wanted to make a call they had to walk just over five miles to the nearest telephone and had been charged outrageous fees.

Now they had one in their own village that they could use for a small usage fee. Dylan had been amazed at how much he was able to access with a booster antenna, a battery and a solar power panel, but of course the wireless handset, and fixed line helped, too.

When he reached Akiki's hut, he was on the porch, almost as if he were waiting for Dylan. "The telephone has been acting crazy today, just so you know," Akiki told him. "Munyiga was here earlier and when the phone went dead he would not pay me!" He put his hands on his hips indignantly, his small hands balled up in fists, his stance reminding Dylan of one of his little sisters right before they had a temper tantrum.

Dylan smiled and tried to soothe him. "I'm sorry about Munyiga, but don't worry about me Akiki, it's okay if the phone line goes down. I'm used to it now and I'll still pay you," he reassured the smaller man. He followed Akiki into the modest home to the "telephone room" and Dylan sat down on the tightly woven chair. He waited for a moment until Akiki was out of the room, then got his laptop up and running and started the protocol. He heard boys laughing just outside the window and looked up in time to see Serapio dressed in a leopard skin, demonstrating for his friends how he would hunt with his spear. Dylan went to the window and called to him.

"Serapio, be careful," he cautioned. At Serapio's scowl, he toned his advice down a bit. "Maybe if you kill a wild pig or an antelope, the men of the village will light a bonfire for you," he winked.

The girls in the group giggled and Serapio stuck out his small chest. "I'm going to provide for my family," he announced to Dylan. "The men of the village *will* light a large bonfire for me and then they will know I am a man." He started off on his hunting trip, several other boys following him. "Welaba, goodbye," he called to Dylan, looking over his shoulder and raising his spear.

Dylan watched the eight-year-old disappear into the bush before he turned back to his computer. He logged on to the agreed site and tried to send a contact message encoded to Andrew. He was anxious to get this done, typing in the codes as quickly as possible. Dylan wanted to report what he'd overheard with David and Lizige last night and get a background check on David. Once that was done, he'd probably be able to go home. He stopped, the screen asking for his name, the cursor blinking expectantly. Dylan ran his fingers through his hair trying to remember the alias he was using this time. He'd had so many aliases it was hard to remember his own name sometimes. But for this mission he'd insisted on using his real first name. They'd given him one of his first aliases from when he was a brand new field agent. Dylan Fields. It was sort of an inside joke for him. Someday he would live his life with his real name, Dylan Campbell, but here in Africa he was Dylan Fields.

He finished entering in all the codes and clicked on Andrew's signature. So many agents would do anything to work with Andrew Blythe. He was the consummate professional—a legend at the CSIS. He had chosen Dylan, taken him under his wing, trained him, taught him the tricks of the trade and then let him be his own man. He was like a father to Dylan in a business where you didn't get close to many people, and Dylan was grateful.

He got past the signatures and checked his own section of the website for any confirmation his message had been received, but nothing was there yet. Their dummy website provided the opportunity to communicate with the head office of the CSIS without anyone realizing it. The website was for an exclusive worldwide Public Relations firm that proclaimed it could make over your professional image. When agents logged on, they could access their image databank and get their mission orders. It was clever and unobtrusive. Dylan rubbed his unshaven beard. He could probably use a real make over since he hadn't shaved in a month. His hair had grown over his collar, and his clothes were smudged and stained with the clay dirt that seemed to be everywhere. But it wasn't like there was a laundromat on the corner, he consoled himself. Nabulungi did what she could with what she had and he was thankful for her service.

He closed his computer, thanked Akiki and gave him a small fee, then started back to the boarding house. He climbed the gentle slope of a hill and hadn't gone too far when he noticed several children in the trees picking the mangoes. He smiled at them and they smiled back, shouting to him in Lugandan, their native tongue. He waved and kept on walking. When Dylan was a small distance from Akiki's house, he heard a blood-curdling scream of fear. Running toward the sound, he saw Serapio scrambling down a tree as fast as he could, scraping his arms and legs against the harsh bark as he slipped toward the ground. "Serapio," he called.

Serapio ran toward him screaming. Dylan didn't understand why until he got closer and saw the large black mamba snake following close behind. Serapio threw himself into Dylan's arms and Dylan lifted him onto his broad shoulders as they started to run back toward the house with Serapio shouting, "Fastah, fastah," the whole way. Dylan struggled to carry his laptop and hold on to the boy on his back.

When they reached the garden Nabulungi opened the gate for them her eyes wide. "What happened?"

Serapio jumped off Dylan and ran to her arms. "Mama, mama," he sobbed. "I climbed a mango tree to get some fruit for us and I saw the biggest mango on the highest branch. I climbed for it and when I got to its branch I reached out my hand for the mango and a black mamba snake stretched its head toward my hand I climbed down and it chased me." He buried his head in Nabulungi's neck. "Mr. Fields saved me."

Nabulungi looked at Dylan who was breathing hard, bent

over with his hands on his knees. She smiled. "A black mamba chased you?" she said disbelievingly. "And you ran all that way with Serapio?"

Dylan nodded, perplexed as she started to laugh. "It was a big snake," he breathed.

"A snake would not chase you. It was probably more scared of you." She patted Serapio's head. "Now go inside and sweep the floor."

Dylan straightened, still struggling to catch his breath. "I saw the snake, and it was following Serapio," he defended himself.

Nabulungi nodded and smiled before she turned back to her work. "Webale. Thank you for bringing him home," was all she said.

Serapio ran into the house and slammed the door. Dylan slowly followed him and peeked in the window to see him sitting at the table breathing heavily. He'd been scared today, but he'd be all right. Dylan picked up his laptop and decided to go into Kampala. Maybe he could get some more information on the doctor that David had mentioned. *And see Elizabeth*, he thought, smiling to himself.

⊱─⊰⊱─○─⊰⊱─⊰

Dylan walked the same road he had walked the night before, alone with his thoughts, but not alone on the road. It was the exact opposite of what had been on the road last night. The people, animals, and vehicles all came together in cacophonic chaos. He stopped by his jeep on the way and tried to start it again with no success. Nabulungi had told him the name of a man who knew cars and Dylan had made arrangements for him to look at it. Until then he would be forced to walk everywhere or try to figure out the public transportation. He chose to walk.

His feet pounded the crudely paved road that was flanked on both sides by overgrown elephant grass that seemed to be trying to take back the land the road had been built on. The long, wavy grass made a foreground in the landscape that Dylan had before him, with the background of colorful fields that were dotted with gardens and huts. But the line in front of him on the road that consisted of barefoot women carrying children who were too sick or malnourished to walk bore testament to the plight of the people in this breathtaking land of extreme contrasts. When he knew he'd been assigned to Uganda he'd studied up on the country and its people. It definitely had a rich history and was as beautiful as the pamphlet said it would be, but politically it had suffered and its people had paid a high price. The rulers from Milton Obote down to Idi Amin had pillaged and murdered throughout the country and Uganda had once been known for all its human rights abuses. Each new president ordered the execution of anyone who opposed them. The riches of the country were soon squandered. Hospitals and health clinics could close at the drop of a hat, roadways were generally in disrepair and the inflation was outrageous.

It wasn't until a guerilla army, led by Yoweri Museveni, took power that the country begin to flourish again. As president he tried to introduce democratic reforms and improve the economy, but did not allow multi-party politics. The country still struggled with war and the safety of its citizens. Dylan knew he had to be on his toes every minute.

He wiped the sweat from his brow and replaced his hat, feeling weighted down with not only his thoughts and his camera bag, but also his own struggle with the uncertainty of where his life was going. Dusting off his hands on his cargo shorts, he shielded his eyes to estimate how much longer he had to walk, feeling the humidity and wanting a rest both spiritually and physically.

He walked on, his mood reflective. Dylan had known for a while that something was missing in his life, but when a mission had gone badly and he'd been shot, the close call made him realize he needed something more. Coming close to death had given him a new perspective on his life and he felt like he'd just been floating along day to day. He needed a new direction. He started reading the Bible again, and looking at different organized religions. His parents had been careful to expose their children to many different religions so they could make their minds up when they came of age, but Dylan had never really felt comfortable with any of them.

As he struggled to find the spirit he was looking for, Andrew had confided in him how his daughter Emma had gotten caught up in capturing international terrorist Juan Carlos Miera. Dylan had asked how she'd made it through such a horrible ordeal and Andrew had told him that since she'd joined the LDS church she'd had a strength, a glow about her that he'd never realized was there. The church hadn't changed her, he said proudly, it just added to and confirmed what was already there inside Emma. Dylan had heard of the LDS church, but not much of it had been good. However, after seeing Andrew's reaction to his daughter becoming LDS he decided to look into it further.

He started his research on the internet finding thousands of sites about Mormons. There were sites for Family History, LDS products, LDS singles, as well as the negative tirades decrying the LDS church as a cult or at the very least not Christian. Dylan finally went to the official church site, carefully reading the material about their beliefs. After several days of thinking about the things he'd read, he finally ordered a Book of Mormon, just to see what it really was all about. When he'd finished reading the book all the way through he got down on his knees and asked God to know if what he'd read was true and if it was what he should do. After several moments he'd received the strongest impression he'd ever had and he knew what he had to do.

He followed protocol and contacted the missionaries, asking to join the church. They wanted to make sure he was ready so they asked him to take what they called "the discussions." He enjoyed discussing gospel principles which were so new yet so familiar to him with the young missionaries. But it was a busy time for him professionally and he could only take the discussions when his job permitted, which was frustrating. He didn't want to wait to be baptized because he knew he'd found his faith, but his job seemed to get in the way so often and it ended up being several months before he could make it through all of the discussions. He tried to be patient, spending his time memorizing scriptures that he could recite to himself while on assignment.

The day finally came and Dylan was ready to be baptized. He'd been a little nervous about telling his parents and sisters his plans, and they were surprised but supportive. All of them attended his baptism. His new ward had also been welcoming and Dylan had briefly explained the nature of his job to his bishop and why he would be absent a lot. The Bishop had been very understanding, giving him a fatherly hug and telling him how proud he was that Dylan was serving his country and to be careful.

When Dylan knew he'd be going to Uganda, he'd looked up on the internet where the nearest LDS meeting place was located in Kampala and found an address not too far from the hospital. He knew he wouldn't be able to attend because of the nature of his mission, but Dylan consoled himself that he would have gone under normal circumstances. Attending church and being able to take the Sacrament probably would have helped his flagging spirits and possibly given him time to reflect on what direction the Lord thought his life should take. He needed the comfort and guidance that the Spirit could give him that would help ease the restlessness he was feeling. He knew it was there, but somehow it seemed just beyond his reach. Dylan had been given the knowledge that he had a divine purpose, he just didn't know exactly what it was for this time in his life both personally and professionally.

He stopped by the side of the road to let some vehicles pass and got out his water bottle. He took a long drink of the now warm liquid that still quenched his thirst despite its lack of icy temperatures. The heat of the day combined with the humidity was so oppressive he wondered how the people of the country stood it. It was definitely a big change from the climate of Canada that he'd left not too long ago. He followed the stream of people entering the capital city and decided to walk by the building the church had rented out for the small Kabowa branch that met there. Maybe just being close to it would help him. He saw two men outside the building who smiled at him as he approached. The one consistent thing he'd noticed about church members was that they seemed to be happy. It had attracted him from the start. His parents and sisters had mentioned it to him as well and here he was half a world away and it was still true. He smiled back at the two men, wanting to stop and talk, but knowing it just wasn't possible.

As he walked toward the hospital he recited the thirteen articles of faith to himself, finding it gratifying that he knew exactly what his beliefs were and could find the answer to any question he had in the scriptures. He'd cultivated the habit of memorizing scriptures while waiting for his baptism and had continued the practice since then because he couldn't take any identifying personal things on agency missions. It helped keep him close to the truths of the gospel of Jesus Christ. Sometimes late at night in Uganda he could hear the lions roar and gnash their teeth. He first thought of Daniel in the lion's den and with actually hearing them outside, he realized how frightening that experience truly must have been. While he knew he was safe with the men of the village keeping the prowling lions in check, he then thought of the scripture in Mosiah 16:2, "And then shall the wicked be cast out, and they shall have cause to howl, and weep, and wail, and gnash their teeth." He chuckled at how even the most ordinary things could remind him of scriptures he'd memorized and it confirmed to him of how far he'd come since he first started investigating the church. He looked back at the building that was used for the chapel, feeling the happiness well up inside him, knowing that despite his trials his testimony was growing every day.

Chapter Four

After zigzagging through the makeshift markets and saying "Sagala," or "no thanks," to countless vendors, Dylan finally made it to the hospital, but Elizabeth was nowhere to be found. He went down into the basement and saw two guards in a small office near the stairwell door. They were bent over some papers so Dylan seized the opportunity, squatting down to slip by.

He walked quickly down the hall and went to the storage room door he'd been through the night before but it was locked. He pulled out his lock pick set and got down to work. After a few moments he eased the heavy door open and went inside, locking it again behind him. Several of the crates had been opened, and a large one stood gaping in the center of the room. Dylan looked inside and saw only heavy duty hazardous materials protective gear. He fingered what looked like heavy rubber gloves. *What would they need this for?* he wondered. Cards that told how much radiation a person had been exposed to were hanging on the side. Dylan got out his camera and took several pictures. Were they dealing with a radioactive weapon? Was it a bomb? He continued clicking away. Maybe it would make sense later, or Andrew could analyze the pictures with the lab technicians. Just as he finished taking a picture, he heard the door creak and he crouched down beside the large crate, quickly drawing his gun.

"I thought I heard something in here," a low voice said.

"You're imagining things," his partner returned. "How could

anyone get into a locked room without us seeing them?"

The two voices faded as they left the room. Dylan put away his gun, trying to calm his breathing. He put his camera away and half-crawled to another large crate. He cased the room, making sure it was empty, then stood. Going to the door, he put his ear to it, to see if he could hear anything in the hallway outside. The heavy metal of the door prevented any sound at all so he eased it open a crack. All looked quiet so he slipped through the door, hearing it click loudly as it shut, then he started walking back toward the stairs as quickly and silently as possible, hoping the guards were still busy. About halfway down the hall, one of the guards came out of the office and spotted Dylan. He strode quickly toward him, as fast as his large build would let him, the medals on his military uniform bouncing with each step. He did not look happy at all and Dylan could plainly see the gun on his belt. He smiled and willed his insides to be calm.

"What are you doing here?" the guard demanded. "This is a restricted area."

Dylan tried to look nonchalant. "I'm looking for an aid worker. Maybe you know her? Elizabeth Spencer."

The guard shook his head. "No, I do not know her. You'll have to move along."

Dylan nodded and pointed toward the doors lining the hallway. "What's down here anyway, that needs a military guard?"

The guard looked at him sternly. "None of your business. It's a restricted area."

Dylan held up his hands. "Okay, okay, thanks anyway. I'll find Elizabeth myself." He walked toward the stairway and did not look back, but could feel the guard's eyes on him. Going back upstairs to Elizabeth's floor he went down the hallway near the lounge and saw the little boy who'd been sitting with his father the night before. He now sat all alone near a doorway to a hospital room. He smiled when Dylan walked by.

"Hello," he said.

Dylan stopped. "Hello. What's your name?"

"I am Balondemu," he said simply, as he stood up to talk to Dylan. "What's your name?"

"Dylan. Are you waiting for someone?"

"Yes," he motioned toward the door. "My mother is inside. We are waiting for her, but I think she will die."

Dylan moved closer to the boy. "Why do you think that?"

"No one will tell me what is going on, and this morning my father looked awful after he'd visited her." He stopped. "I have many brothers and sisters at home. We need my mother."

"I'm sorry," Dylan said. "What happened?"

"My mother was worried about her family in Gulu because of all the rebel fighting there. She went to bring them to our house." The young boy shifted his weight from foot to foot as he talked, his eyes bright with tears. "The truck she was on was ambushed and many were shot. Some of the women ran away into the bush and the soldiers fired on them. My mother was shot in the back. The next day some villagers found her and brought her to the house of my father. Then we brought her here. They say she has lost much blood." The boy glanced toward the door and repeated. "I think she will die."

Dylan's heart went out to this boy who was having to grow up way too fast. He put his hand on his shoulder. "Maybe if you pray for a miracle, God will save her. I will pray for your mother, too."

The boy nodded. "Thank you."

"Can I take your picture?" Dylan asked. When the boy nodded he set up his camera and took several shots. "If one turns out well, maybe I could send it to you and it will bring you luck." He pulled a slightly melted chocolate bar out of his bag and offered it to the boy. He seemed hesitant for a moment, then took the offered candy, rewarding Dylan with another smile as he sat back down to unwrap the chocolate and wait for his father.

Dylan's step was a little lighter as he walked toward the makeshift nurses station which was only a table and a few chairs. The woman behind the table looked up at him. "Yes?"

"Have you seen Elizabeth Spencer?" he asked.

"Elizabeth is sleeping in the last room on the right," she informed him, then turned back to her work.

Dylan walked toward the room she pointed at, noticing the hospital seemed much quieter today than it had last night. He gently opened the door and spotted Elizabeth on a small cot in between some crates. She looked so peaceful with her hair fanned out across her arms which served as her pillow. She wore no makeup, but her tanned complexion still contrasted with her dark brown hair, and the dark circles under her eyes testified of the long hours she kept. She wore the same sort of tan cargo pants that he did, and a white shirt. Her ID tag was hanging over the cot at a crazy angle, but he could see it stated her name and had her picture. He stared at her for a few moments longer, then started to back away and close the door when she called out. "What's wrong, do you need me?"

"No," Dylan replied. "Go back to sleep."

Elizabeth immediately sat up. "Is that you, Dylan?"

Dylan sighed. "I'm sorry I woke you up. You look pretty tired."

"I am," she said, rubbing her eyes. "But I should probably go home if I want to really sleep."

Dylan moved closer to her, making a path around the boxes, and sat on the edge of the cot. "How much sleep have you had lately?"

Elizabeth tilted her head and smiled at him. "Are you worried about me?"

Dylan smiled back. "Well somebody has to."

"What about you walking for three hours last night to take pictures? You couldn't have had much sleep yourself."

"You got me there," Dylan chuckled.

"Can I interest you in a cup of coffee?" she asked. "That

might help wake both of us up."

Dylan jolted, remembering his new commitment not to partake of caffeine, but covered well. "No thanks," he said. "I'm trying to be more healthy."

"Yeah, that's why you have melted chocolate bars in your knapsack," she teased.

"Hey, when were you snooping in my backpack?" he shot back. "A man can't have any secrets."

As soon as he said it, Elizabeth's face changed, her smile faded, her eyes searching his. "Do you have secrets, Dylan?" she asked him seriously.

"What do you mean? We've only known each other a few weeks. Of course I have secrets." He stood up, quickly changing the subject. "I could buy you some lunch," he said smiling at her, reaching out his hand to help her up. She took it, standing up next to him and running her other hand through her hair.

"How do I look?" she asked.

He looked down at her. "Believe me, you never have to ask that question."

Elizabeth blushed and let go of his hand. She started for the door, pulling her hair into a ponytail as she walked. "Come on, I'm starving. You can take me to the Fang Fang. They have the most incredible Chinese food there."

After negotiating three busy road crossings and going down several alleys, Elizabeth stopped in front of what looked like a hotel. They went inside and she crossed to the back of the building. Above the door was a simple sign that said Fang Fang. Elizabeth seemed to be familiar with the woman who greeted them and asked to be seated outside. The waitstaff led the couple to the roof. Dylan looked over the city, listening to the hustle and bustle on the markets and roadways below. "Wow, I didn't even know this was here."

"Wait until you taste the food."

The waiter brought them a watermelon bowl filled with fruit and took their order. Elizabeth ordered the sweet and sour chicken and recommended the almond chicken to Dylan. "You'll love it," she reassured him.

"After eating in the village for a month, this will be a treat," he said lightly. "How did you find this place?"

Her face clouded over for a moment and Dylan was puzzled by her expression. "Just exploring," was all she said. "So did you get home all right last night? I felt bad you came all that way."

Dylan nodded and made a mental note to ask her about her exploring expeditions later. "It's okay. I have some pictures from the week before and most of the information I need for the story. I'll be going home soon."

Elizabeth looked thoughtful. "Really?" She stopped for a moment as their food arrived. When the waiter left she continued. "I would think your boss would need more than that."

"Why do you say that?" Dylan asked cautiously, wondering if he'd given something away.

Elizabeth shrugged. "I would think there are so many things in Uganda to take pictures of and more than one hospital. I thought you'd be going to several hospitals." She sipped her drink. "Besides, a hospital is so ordinary. Don't you get bored?"

Dylan relaxed. "I found it quite . . . interesting," he said pointedly.

She looked away. "Well you certainly upset David last night. He was muttering half the night about being on a schedule and how you'd messed it up. And he even thought he'd seen you before in South Africa." Her eyes met his in a steady stare as if she was asking him a question.

As soon as the words left her mouth it all came back to him. A year ago he'd been in the liaison office in Johannesburg and met at a local restaurant with an informant to get his report on a diamond smuggling operation. The guy thought he'd been compromised and wanted out. As they were talking a man had come to their table and warned them that they were being watched and should leave. That man was David Kanu. But that didn't make sense. What was he doing helping Jimon Bumani with a weapon?

"Did David say anything else?" he asked Elizabeth.

She chewed her food, her eyes never leaving his. She swallowed and wiped her mouth daintily with her napkin "No, just that he didn't want you around taking pictures anymore."

Dylan smiled and forced himself to appear nonchalant. "Most people like their picture taken. Maybe I should stop by and tell him I'm sorry," he said. *And find out what's really going on*, he thought.

They finished their meal and Dylan escorted her back to the hospital, weaving in and out of the small streets, passing the men talking under makeshift canopies and the vendors calling out their wares. One man squatted on the ground drawing pictures, his small display next to him. Dylan leaned closer, the images calling out to him. There were several landscapes, but also some breathtaking, lifelike pictures of the Savior. It had amazed him how many artists in Kampala painted pictures of Jesus Christ and he wondered if it was personal or something just for the tourists. Some artists were better than others, but the ones in front of him were phenomenal. He tried to appear as if he was interested in the landscapes, but it was as if the eyes in the pictures of the Savior were watching him and he couldn't draw away from it.

Elizabeth looked over his shoulder. "What are you looking at?"

He hurriedly picked up a lush landscape, but she pulled the picture of the Savior up from underneath it. "Wow, I've never seen a picture that seems to really look at you before. His eyes are so amazing. Very unique in color and expression."

Dylan agreed. "They are beautiful, eh? I've never seen anything like it."

Elizabeth smiled. "Your Canadian accent is showing,"

she teased. "Where in Canada did you say you were from?"

"Toronto," he said absently, studying some of the other drawings in front of him. "How much?" Dylan asked the man.

He scratched his head and held up two fingers. "Two dollah."

"One dollar," Dylan argued.

Elizabeth punched him lightly on the arm. "Dylan, just pay him two dollars."

He looked at her and smiled. "You have to dicker or they don't respect you," he whispered conspiratorially. "Every man should know how to dicker." He turned back to the artist and handed him the equivalent of five dollars. "Keep it," he said.

The vendor smiled and handed the picture to Elizabeth. "He watches over you," he said, and took the money from Dylan's outstretched hand.

Elizabeth studied the picture for a moment, then handed it to Dylan. "Here you are."

He pushed her hands back. "I bought it for you. Besides, the guy said he watches over you." He looked at the picture over her shoulder. "It does seem like his eyes are following you. I've just never seen a picture so lifelike. His expression is so . . . loving."

"I've always thought that God watched over me. There have been several times in my life when I've felt like I had been protected." She stopped, looking thoughtful. "Did he mean God is watching over me or you are watching over me?" Elizabeth asked lightly.

Dylan took her hand. "Probably both of us. Heaven knows you need it." His expression became serious, his green eyes capturing hers. "I do think God is aware of and loves all His children here on earth, just like any father."

Elizabeth's gaze fell on the small child sitting beside his father who was the artist. "If God loves all his children why does he allow such great suffering?"

Dylan followed her stare to the small frame of the child

who was obviously malnourished. "I don't know all the answers, Elizabeth, but I do know that God has a plan for all of us." He looked into her eyes, wanting to share his newfound testimony with her, but was required to hold back because of rules and regulations.

She looked up into his eyes, squeezed his hand and smiled up at him. His heart skipped a beat and he wished he could be completely honest with her. He wanted to tell her he was an agent sent to see if a weapon was being stored in her hospital and protect her from Jimon Bumani ever coming near. But he couldn't.

They walked back to the hospital in silence. He felt an air of sorrow settling over them as they both seemed to know their time together was coming to an end. All too soon they were in front of the hospital and it was time for her to go back to work. They stopped in the small courtyard, and Dylan sat down on a stone bench, pulling her with him. "I'm pretty sure I'll be leaving tomorrow. Can I see you before I go?"

She sighed. "I don't know if that's such a good idea, Dylan." She fingered the edge of the picture he'd bought her. "It's not you, it's just that I have a job to do here and I don't want to neglect my duties." She stared at the picture, not meeting Dylan's eyes. "Thanks again for the beautiful drawing."

He turned her toward him and ran his finger down her cheek, marveling at how smooth her complexion was, the only thing marring it was a small scar near her chin. His thumb lingered on it, wondering how she got it. "You should keep that picture close to you. Especially if he watches over you, like the artist said." Dylan took a deep breath, not wanting to leave her. "If I promise not to get in the way of your job can I see you tomorrow?"

Elizabeth closed her eyes for a moment and the expression on her face was if she were warring with herself. Finally she nodded yes.

Dylan grinned. "Well, I better get going then. Do you know

where I might find David? I want to apologize before I go." They stood together and he cupped her chin, tilting it upward and running his thumb over her bottom lip, mesmerized by her face.

"He's in the main floor office, I think," Elizabeth said, pulling back from the contact. "Thanks for lunch." She reached up and gave him a soft kiss on the cheek laughing as she drew back. "You need to shave," she commented, touching his beard. "That tickles." She stepped closer, her face suddenly serious. "Don't leave without saying goodbye, okay?"

Dylan took her hand and held it for a moment longer than necessary. "I won't," he said. They stood there as if memorizing each other's face, then Elizabeth stepped away and Dylan watched her go. The time they'd spent together had been the highlight of his trip to Uganda. He would really miss her.

He made his way to the front office near the courtyard. David was there with Lizige. They both looked up when he entered.

David immediately raised his hand. "No pictures today either."

Dylan smiled. "Yes, I heard I had upset you last night. I came to apologize." He looked at the other man. "Can I talk to you in private?"

David nodded and dismissed Lizige, who left reluctantly. "There is no need for apology. I heard you were down in the basement today. If you know what's good for you, you will stay away from this hospital from now on."

Dylan leaned in close. The small timid man he'd met yesterday was gone. The man before him was oozing confidence which made Dylan wonder what had changed. "Don't I know you from somewhere? Didn't you help me in South Africa?"

David was thrown off his guard and looked surprised for a moment, then masked his reaction. "I don't know what you're talking about," he said.

"Don't you remember the restaurant in Johannesburg?"

David leaned close, his full lips enunciating every word. "You need to leave now." He poked his finger into Dylan's chest. "I know who you are, and the people I work for do not like your presence here. The only reason you are not a dead man right now is because I care about Elizabeth and I know she has some feelings for you, misplaced as they may be. If you do not want to cause Elizabeth pain, just leave and don't look back."

Dylan backed up, surprised by the ferocity in David's eyes. He lowered his voice. "Are you threatening Elizabeth or protecting her?" David stood mute before him. Dylan pulled himself up to his full height, towering over the smaller man behind the desk. "Answer me!" he ground out between clenched teeth.

David didn't give an inch. "Make no mistake Mr. Fields. I will be forced to kill you if you do not leave. Please leave now."

Dylan turned and put his hand on the door handle, turning back to face David. "You leave Elizabeth out of this. If you want to come after me, you do that, but leave Elizabeth out of it," he warned, his eyes hard. "Remember that."

He passed Lizige outside the door and wondered if he'd been eavesdropping. He nodded as Dylan went by, a small smile on his lips. Dylan's instincts told him something wasn't right, but he didn't know what. *I'm leaving anyway*, he thought. *I'm just overreacting*. But his mind was churning. How was this David Kanu really connected to Elizabeth? What had she told Kanu about him?

As he walked out of the hospital he turned back and noticed a movement in the second floor window. It had looked like Elizabeth with her dark hair and white shirt. *Just wishful thinking*, he told himself. He'd taken a chance reminding David where he knew him from. But why would he have helped him in South Africa and be his enemy here? *I know better than that*, he chided himself. *People change sides in this business, more than I change socks.* It all comes down to money. Well if they knew who he was, the sooner he got out of Uganda the better. *Maybe I should take Elizabeth with me, if she is in danger,* he thought. He made up his mind to ask her the next time he saw her.

Chapter Five

Elizabeth stepped back quickly from the window, hoping Dylan hadn't seen her watching him. Her emotions were mixed as she watched him leave. It was the first time she'd had a connection with anyone for so long and she'd indulged herself in letting Dylan get close to her. It was difficult for her to remember that he was an agent also, and apparently in danger, when she'd let Dylan see so much of her heart already. Sometimes her job carried too high of a price and she wondered if it was worth it. She sighed and leaned against the window sill.

All of her training to compartmentalize different aspects of her life didn't seem to be working. She generally had no personal life to speak of anyway and hadn't had to worry about it since she put her heart and soul into her job. It had taken all of her strength to prove herself in a man's world and she had never wanted to give that up.

But lately, she'd found herself wanting more, feeling unfulfilled in her job as an agent. Being here in Africa, helping to ease the suffering all around her and being with Dylan had seemed to fill that void for a while. He was fun to be with, and she felt like she could tell him anything. *Except who you really are*, she thought. It still seemed strange to her that he was an agent as well. She lifted her head when David Kanu entered the room.

"What did you tell him?" he demanded.

Elizabeth lifted a shoulder, rubbing her arms as if a chill

had suddenly entered the room. "What do you mean? I didn't tell him anything."

"He remembered me from South Africa. He confronted me with it."

"So what?"

"So what? It's dangerous for him to get too close, you know that. Do you want to get him killed?" He walked to the window and stood in front of her. "Lizige would probably make me kill him as a test of loyalty." At her stare, he sighed and scratched the top of his head. "I don't want to hurt you, Beth, but Lizige is looking for anything to prove I'm not loyal to Bumani so he can get rid of me. Just stay away from the Canadian, for both our sakes, please?" His dark eyes bored into hers, as if begging her to understand his position. "If you don't, it could get us both killed, or at the very least compromise the mission."

Elizabeth schooled her expression at the grimness of David's tone, not willing to let him see how transparent her emotions were. "He's gone." She stood up straight, facing him head on. "He told me today he got all the information he needs and he's leaving. We're in the clear." She folded her arms across her chest. "Besides, it looks like this was only a fact-finding mission for him and from what I can tell he has no idea what's really in this hospital. He probably just gave up and is going home. There's no way he could have seen the weapon with all the guards Bumani's had crawling around here."

David took a deep breath. "Good. His snooping around does nothing but put us all in danger. The doctor arrives tomorrow and we've got a lot of work to do." He pointed a finger at her. "You know Sam will not be happy."

Elizabeth shook her head, not caring what her brusque, super-efficient task force chief would think. "Sam isn't happy about anything these days. She's breathing down my neck every chance she gets for a report on this or a report on that. How am I supposed to do my job? She's even threatened that she's going to take over on this mission." She rolled her neck, the stress obviously getting to her. "If she could do a better job than I can in infiltrating Bumani's organization, more power to her," she said, her voice lowered

Sighing, Elizabeth tilted her head all the way back and let the anger wash away. She wished things were different. Sam Fowler had somehow maneuvered herself as the sole person over this mission and she only reported to the director of the CIA. She had handpicked Elizabeth to infiltrate the hospital and gain Bumani's trust, gave her David Kanu's name to recruit him for his ability to blend in and provide backup. Other than that, though, Elizabeth was on her own and it was unlike anything else she'd experienced in her years with the agency. Sam seemed to instinctively know that Elizabeth wasn't as sure of herself on this mission and preyed upon it, demanding that she report her every move. After years of agency service, it was demeaning and Elizabeth was starting to chafe under Sam's command.

The way things stood now, the mission was high priority and Elizabeth reported only to Sam and there was nothing she could do about it at the moment. Speculation was that Sam was bucking for a big promotion, but Elizabeth didn't care about that. She only knew that Sam's actions were affecting her job when she demanded detailed reports more often than normal. It was annoying. Elizabeth planned to complain about it when she got back to the States, even if she had to go to the director himself.

"I'm having trouble doing my own job." David expelled his breath in a long, frustrated sigh as he paced behind her. "Lizige never leaves my side. Bumani is suspicious of any outsider, so he put Lizige on me like a dog, until I've proved myself a loyal follower of his organization." At the mention of his name Lizige appeared at the door. "I'll see you later," David muttered, as he joined Lizige in the hall. "I think all the public relations work is taken care of," she heard him say to Lizige.

Elizabeth turned back to the window watching the

courtyard where Dylan had been. She was going to miss him, but would never admit that out loud. Her forehead touched the glass and she felt a coolness for a moment before the heat permeated her skin. The rational part of her was saying to forget about Dylan. He was just another agent that had passed through her life on a mission. She pulled the small picture of the Savior that he had bought for her out of her pocket and ran her fingers gently over it. She had been thinking quite often about their discussion of God being aware of his children and having a plan for them. What would her life plan be? Would it include Dylan, or maybe someone like him? She hoped so. Quickly putting the picture away and wiping the lone tear from her face, she stood and straightened her shoulders. For now, Dylan was gone and she needed all of her wits about her to get through the rest of the mission alive. *Goodbye Dylan*, she said silently in her heart. *Be safe.*

><+>+<>+<>+<

When Dylan got back to the village, he immediately went to Akiki's, fired up his laptop and went to the website. His make over profile had been updated and his instructions were clear. After decoding the message it said that he was to bring the information and board a plane to Lusaka, Zambia. From there he would board a bus to the Chirundu border and meet his contact there for a brush pass of all pictures and information he'd collected. *A job well done*, was all it said. *We'll talk more when you get back.*

Dylan closed the laptop, his feelings mixed. He'd enjoyed the weeks he'd spent here, getting to know Elizabeth better, and was relieved to have finished the mission he was sent to do. He wanted to go home and get on with his life, but he was sad to say goodbye to Elizabeth. Maybe he wouldn't have to if she came with him, or if not, maybe he could look her up when he got back.

When he arrived at Nabulungi's home, darkness was just setting in. Nabulungi sat on the porch as if she was waiting for him.

"Hello there," he called.

"Hello," she answered. "Jangu." She patted the seat next to her. Dylan sat down. They sat in a comfortable silence for a few moments, watching the last rays of the sun before it sank under the horizon. The magnificent oranges and reds made it seem as if the horizon were slowly sinking into a fire of gold. It was breathtaking and Dylan had never seen anything like it. Nabulungi shifted in her chair and cleared her throat. "Do you believe in God?" she asked softly.

"Yes," Dylan said immediately, surprised.

"Do you believe in a loving God?"

"Yes." He remembered his earlier discussion with Elizabeth and wondered where Nabulungi was going with her questions.

She pulled a small book from the folds of her dress. "Two Americans came to the village today and gave everyone a gift. They said it was very important."

Dylan took the proffered book. It was the Book of Mormon. He tried to contain his excitement. "Did you look at it?"

Nabulungi shook her head. "I opened the first pages, and I could not understand what I read, but the words made me feel good here." She pointed to her chest. Reaching for the book back from Dylan, she turned to a specific page. "It says here that "*I told the brethren that the Book of Mormon was the most correct of any book on earth, and the keystone of our religion, and a man would get nearer to God by abiding by its precepts, than by any other book.*" Nabulungi was silent for a moment as if letting the words sink in.

Dylan held his breath and waited for her to comment. He didn't want to appear too eager, but as a new convert himself it was difficult not to jump in and share his own newfound feelings about the Book of Mormon. Through sheer willpower he stayed quiet and listened for Nabulungi's thoughts.

After a few seconds she spoke again. "It astonishes me that someone could say that this was the most correct book upon the earth. It is a very bold statement." She paused. "We don't have greater books than this?"

"What kind of book do you think it is?" Dylan asked.

"It is a book about Jesus, I suppose," she replied. "The young men said they would come back to answer any questions we had." She stood and put the book back into her pocket. "Yes, I will listen and study it further."

Dylan wanted to shout for joy, but he nodded and bid her good night. He sat on the porch for a few more minutes, thinking of his own feelings when he'd first seen and read the Book of Mormon. It was as if a light had suddenly permeated the darkness as the words on the page became true and living testimonies of the divinity of Jesus Christ. The depth of his feelings had shocked him, prodding him to learn more. He was like a sponge wanting more and more information, analyzing and finally praying about the book. He knew it was true. Without any doubt at all, Dylan knew the book was from God. He hoped Nabulungi could also receive such a witness.

He stayed a few moments longer to watch the last of the sun's rays dance off the landscape before finally succumbing to the darkness. Going into the house, he dressed for bed, the night closing fast around him as he lay down, alone with his thoughts. When he got home, what did he want to do for a career? Being a CSIS agent was all he'd known. He wanted something he could enjoy that would support a family, but also be able to serve others in some capacity. Maybe he could be a teacher or something. Maybe he'd go back to school. He just didn't know what the Lord had in store for him. He ran a few scriptures through his mind and settled on one in Words of Mormon 1:7: ". . . and now I do not know all things, but the Lord knoweth all things which are to come; wherefore, he worketh in me to do according to his will." The thought brought him comfort.

Dylan got out of bed and knelt down, praying fervently for an answer as to what direction his life should take, but the heavens seemed closed. He lay down again, wondering what the feeling might mean. It was as if the Lord were waiting for him to figure it out on his own, without His help. But Dylan knew that wasn't true. How many times had the Lord been there for him lately, witnessing to him that he was a beloved son of God. No, it would just take time and Dylan would have to be patient. With that settled, he finally fell asleep.

The next morning was rushed for Dylan, packing his things, saying goodbye to Nabulungi and Serapio. The small boy had given him a carving of a lion he'd made for him and Dylan gave him his Toronto Blue Jays ball cap. When he'd said his goodbyes, he made his way to the Mulago hospital in Kampala, but when he arrived Elizabeth wasn't on duty. He didn't see David either and that worried him. His last conversation with David had given him pause about Elizabeth's safety. He really wanted to at least warn her and give her the option of coming with him. Dylan tried to find the address where she lived, but to no avail. The disappointment of not being able to find her was crushing, and he sent a quick prayer heavenward that she would be safe.

He went to the Entebbe airport and quickly made it through the security checks and boarded his plane. As it lifted off and he looked at the green fields and hills, he knew he'd miss Uganda. He'd made some great memories here.

>-+-<+>-0-<+>-+-<

Elizabeth sat in the small basement laboratory, the heavy rubber suit she was wearing making her feel sticky and wet as the sweat dripped down her face. The absence of air conditioning made the heat in the room palpable and she was ready to get out, but couldn't leave. She watched the doctor directing the men as if in a choreographed dance.

Developing a biological weapon had a lot of logistical challenges that she hadn't been aware of. Not only did they have to transform a deadly bacterium into a weapon but they also had to figure out a way that it could be effectively dispersed. Her first impression was that they would just be dropping a "dirty bomb" filled with the bacterium. But Bumani had informed her that a bomb carrying a biological agent would just destroy the germ as it exploded. So the challenge was to not only make the weapon, but figure out a way to infect as many people as possible.

The more she worked with Jimon Bumani the more she realized how truly driven he was. He wanted power, and the more he got the more he wanted—it was like a drug to him. But more than his love of power was his hatred for the United States. Even in her very first meeting with him he told her that the U.S. government was criminal and tyrannical, having committed unjust acts in their quest to take over the world. He felt it was his duty to bring them to justice. His brand of justice.

His aura when he walked in a room spoke volumes. He commanded respect not only by his size, but by the way he carried himself. He was tall, probably about six foot two, Elizabeth guessed, with long limbs and big, strong hands. He dressed well, usually immaculate in a suit, his hair perfectly arranged, the curls tamed. He was a smart man, enlisting the help of professionals whenever he needed it. He'd decided that he wanted to make the world and the United States listen to him, to feel the power of the world stage and achieve the ultimate prize of being the most powerful man on the earth with all the trappings of money and weapons behind him. He'd mapped out his plan and put it together almost effortlessly. It didn't surprise Elizabeth. Apparently, a lot of people in this world that had an axe to grind against the U.S. and violence was the easiest way to seek release.

When Bumani had introduced her to Dr. Bruder, he'd been like a little boy with a new toy. Dr. Bruder was well-known for his work in the field of biological research and he had developed a genetically engineered virus, something that had never been seen before. When it was announced to the world, several governments had clamored for more information, but Bruder had conveniently disappeared. Jimon Bumani had bought the virus, the doctor, and his future services to develop the virus further and find just the right size of spore for the maximum infection of humans. With a new virus and a scientific genius at his disposal, Jimon Bumani was in an excellent position for engineering it as a biological weapon.

Dr. Bruder had started his work to alter the virus immediately. It had taken years to engineer the virus itself, but they expected it would only take a few days to make the viral spores the right size to attach to and infect a human host. In order to attack and kill as many people as possible, the spores had to be breathed in and then attach themselves to the lungs. If the spore were too small, a person would exhale them and not become infected with the virus. If too large, the spores would fall to the ground and become unusable. Dr. Bruder's job was to alter them to the perfect size. Once that was achieved, Dr. Bruder could make just the right dosage for an antidote and the weapon would be ready.

Bumani was obsessed with the idea of a biological weapon that only he had the antidote for. The power of playing God was like an elixir to him. He liked the idea of holding the antidote that could save a nation and having the world leaders beg for his help. Especially the president of the United States. *"I will hold the fate of their criminal nation in my hands,"* he had been heard to crow repeatedly. Then they would be forced to listen to his every word. It made Elizabeth's skin crawl.

Out of the corner of her eye, she saw the object of her thoughts. Jimon Bumani came to stand beside her, putting his hand on her shoulder. "How are the plans coming along?"

he asked, his gaze fastened on the doctor.

"It seems like it's taking a long time," Elizabeth commented, mentally willing herself not to jerk her shoulder out from under his hand.

At that moment, the doctor was leaning over a worker, then suddenly stepped back, his face showing his excitement. He motioned for Bumani to come over. "I'll be right back," Bumani said absently to Elizabeth as he walked quickly toward the doctor.

Elizabeth watched the men confer, her feeling of dread growing with each passing second. When Bumani joined her again, she knew by the look on his face what he was going to say.

"We've done it!" he said. "The weapon is ready." He took her arm and helped her stand beside him. "Dr. Bruder engineered the Tracin virus, but we couldn't get it small enough to attach to the lungs. Today, we did it!"

Elizabeth forced a smile. "That's wonderful, Jimon." She touched his arm as best she could with the heavy rubber gloves on. "So what's next?"

"We will make an antidote, then we will need a human trial," he said. ""I want to see how fast this will work on a human." He leaned closer to Elizabeth. "As soon as we have tried it, and documented how it affected the host person, then we will manufacture enough to infect a city, which shouldn't take long at all with all the manpower I have at my disposal."

"You're only going to infect one city?" Elizabeth asked, furrowing her brow.

He was silent for a moment, his eyes boring into hers, as if he was trying to gauge her comprehension. "Human nature makes us social animals, Elizabeth. We crave contact with others. Because of that I only need enough to infect one city." He broke the eye contact and took Elizabeth's hand to lead her toward the door. "Research shows that the average person comes in contact with about twenty people per day. If they don't know they're infected, they will infect at least twenty others, and the virus will spread like wildfire, through towns, cities, then entire countries. And great will be the day when the leaders of the world will come crawling to me, begging me to help them."

He stopped in front of the door, the excitement plainly showing on his face. "But first things first, my dear. We need a human trial to see how fast the virus will contaminate the host and infect others. Then we will begin a pandemic, starting with the United States of America. Didn't we have a reporter that was bothering us, snooping around? I want to use him. Lizige said he may have known more than we thought."

Elizabeth's stomach lurched when she thought of Dylan infected with this virus, submitted to the horror and torture at the hands of Bumani. "He left this morning for his home country I believe," she said, keeping her voice level. "We'll have to find someone else."

Bumani watched her carefully, then nodded. He stood and walked over to talk to Lizige. *Please let Dylan be gone*, she thought. *Let him be on a plane to Canada right now.*

Chapter Six

When Dylan landed in Lusaka, Zambia, he gathered his luggage and quickly made it to the bus station. He got a two day visa and boarded an old 1982 model bus, brown with white stripes and an ugly green roof with several large holes in it. The cushions were split with the springs popping out, and the glass windows were cracked in many places. In all his travels he hadn't been in much worse. The bus was crowded with people of all shapes and sizes as well as some small animals and the smell was overpowering. He sat near a window and tried to breathe out of the small crack that let in fresh air.

The constant bouncing finally lulled him to sleep, clutching his bag on his lap. When he awoke it was dark and everyone around him was sleeping. He took out the package of food Nabulungi had sent with him, swallowing a few small bites. He laid awake for a while, but then was lulled back to sleep.

A few hours later, in the dim morning light, he was awakened by a crying baby and then wasn't able to fall back asleep. As he rode on the rickety, old bus, he watched the bush and trees surrounding small sugar cane farms, and tried to recite scriptures in his mind to feel the peace and maybe a whisper of the answers he was seeking. The landscape was very flat, matching his mood. He saw abandoned huts of the nomadic Masai tribes, and several different species of birds. As several people on the bus awoke, he tried to smile and greet them, but they did not seem very friendly, and looked away.

Perhaps it was because he was a stranger or maybe it was due to the fact that they spoke Nyanja, their native language, and Dylan only spoke a smattering of Lugandan.

He turned back to his own window and wondered what his family was doing. Had Melissa had her baby, finally making him an uncle? How were Avaeri's wedding plans going? It was still hard to believe that Nathan had asked her to marry him. She still seemed too young and he imagined he would always think of her as his "little" sister. His mother and Avaeri had been feverishly making her dress when he'd left. He hoped his grandfather was recovering from a close call with a heart attack and knew his parents would be taking good care of him. During Dylan's recuperation from the gunshot wound, his grandfather had spent a considerable amount of time at his bedside reading to him and reminiscing about his childhood. Dylan cherished those times. His family was everything to him and had always been supportive of everything he'd done. He only wished they would have taken the missionary discussions with him and joined the Church. He planned to take care of that as soon as he got home.

As Dylan traveled through the country it became less and less inhabited. The dusty road cleared occasionally to reveal overgrown crops with small thatched outbuildings to protect anyone watching the animals. It was a lonely stretch of road, the bus bouncing and chugging forward, its cargo the only apparent human beings for miles. There was land and not much else, as far as the eye could see and Dylan thought he would be glad when he was back from the edge of civilization again.

About a half-day's travel from their destination the bus began to sputter and rolled to a stop. The bus driver looked bewildered and got out of the bus, staring at it as if it would magically start up again. The passengers filed off the bus and Dylan followed suit. A light drizzle of rain began and he wondered what they would do next. He sat down by the side of a muddy road with the rest of the passengers.

After several hours, the bus driver still could not figure out what was wrong, and the passengers were soaking wet. One of the passengers on the bus had crammed his motorcycle on the roof, and he took it down, offering to take the bus driver to the next town. The driver took his head out from under the hood of the bus and agreed. The rest of the passengers were expected to wait until he returned. Dylan thought about getting back on the bus for some shelter, but with the holes in the roof it would likely be as wet, where at least outside he was away from the overpowering musty smell and could breathe fresh air. He began to move around and stretch his legs.

Most of the passengers gathered near the bus, setting up a makeshift village. Some were trying to gather rain water while others were struggling to deal with their animals, who were anxious to get out of their cages. Dylan decided to make camp on a hill slightly above the roadside, hoping for a little more shelter under a small tree. He was frustrated at having to wait, as he was anxious to report to his contact and get home, not to mention that the rain was beginning to come down hard. With his back against the bark and his body curled as close to him as possible, he settled down for the night. Hour after hour the heavens poured out water upon them, until morning finally came and found everyone wet, cold and miserable.

When the bus driver returned, he told the passengers that he had to wait for the part and that's where he had been. With all the misery, everyone was happy to finally be on their way again, their joy showing in their "hurrahs" as the bus roared to life. Within the hour, the rain had stopped and it looked like their luck had turned. The bus meandered slowly through the countryside, puffs of smoke belching from the tailpipe, making everyone wonder if they would ever reach the border, but not dampening their happy mood. After traveling most of the day, they finally reached the border of Zimbabwe and Zambia.

The band of travelers were so happy to have finally arrived

at the border, most were chattering excitedly as they were stopped at the Chirundu checkpoint, the main entry through which all goods and services pass. Dylan got out his papers for the officer to check, frustrated by all the delays and wondering if his contact was still here or if he'd already left. Glancing around, he didn't see anyone except the border officer and another guard. Dylan would just have to go on to Johannesburg and make contact there. He sighed and rolled his eyes as the officer boarded the bus and began meticulously checking each paper line by line.

After half an hour, the officer finally reached him. He took Dylan's passport and visa papers, looking them over carefully, glancing at Dylan several times. He was a small squinty man whose beady eyes kept darting back and forth as though watching a tennis match.

"Your visa expired yesterday," he said, his tone clipped.

Dylan sat up straighter. "Yes, the bus broke down and we had to wait for the part," he explained. "But we came straight here as soon as it was repaired."

The officer nodded, then looked through the passport. "Why are you here?" he asked.

"I'm a photojournalist," Dylan said, pointing to his camera bag. "I'm on my way home to Canada."

"You came here to make money off my people and leave," he sneered.

Dylan furrowed his brow. "No, I came here to take pictures to show the beauty of Africa to the Canadian people." His deeper instincts cultivated over the years were almost screaming that something wasn't right and his adrenaline started pumping. The man's demeanor wasn't normal. It was as if he had expected Dylan and rehearsed what he was going to say.

"You'll have to go back to Lusaka and renew your visa," the officer said finally.

Dylan shook his head. "No, I can't do that. Just let me pass.

I'm going home to Canada."

"No, you will go to Lusaka." The officer motioned for Dylan to get off the bus and come inside his small office. Dylan had no choice but to comply, so he got up and followed the small man. Inside the tiny checkpoint building, Dylan was told to wait behind the counter. The officer went back on the bus and finished checking the rest of the papers. Dylan set down his bag, pulling a small vial of film from the camera and putting it into a pocket of his cargo pants, and stuffing his gun into the belt of his pants. Then he sat down at one of the brown tables in the office to wait.

When the bus started its engine again, Dylan picked up his bag and went outside. The officer held up his hand.

"You will go back to Lusaka this very night," he said firmly.

"Everything is closed now, I won't be let in," Dylan responded back. "Let me go, please." He was still trying to be polite, hoping this wouldn't get ugly. He shifted his weight, assuring himself that his gun was still there. The guard in front of him had a rifle, and as Dylan looked around, it looked like his partner did, too. Their eyes were on Dylan, as if they were expecting him to make a move. Dylan knew he probably couldn't take them both without getting shot himself. Feeling desperate, but not wanting to show it, he stood firm. "I need you to let me be on my way." The officer smiled and shook his head, obviously enjoying the position he was in. He pointed his gun toward Dylan, then motioned for the bus driver to move along. When the bus was allowed to go, Dylan was not on it.

"Get in the back of the police truck," he said to Dylan, pointing his gun directly at Dylan's chest now. "You will go back to Lusaka." His partner came up behind him and Dylan was cornered. The first guard patted him down and as he came to the pants, his eyes widened and he confiscated Dylan's gun. "You were right, Yusef," he commented. "He was armed."

Putting the gun into his own pocket, he motioned for Dylan to get into the back of the truck. His eyes were bright as if he were drunk with power and Dylan knew the situation could spin out of control at any moment. He decided to cooperate and hopefully an escape plan would come to him.

Dylan climbed on board the old truck and sat on the floor. His eyes watched the retreating bus. His stomach was in knots, not knowing what he should do. *Stay calm*, he told himself. *That's the first rule.* The border officer climbed in beside him and tapped on the window leading to the driver's seat. The truck lurched forward.

Dylan sat there in the truck, bouncing over the roads, the air heavy with tension. He knew something was terribly wrong. Had his cover been blown? Had David Kanu reported him? Was this just a random thing? He had no answers. They traveled the bumpy road for approximately 130 kilometers, but which seemed like an eternity, and finally arrived around midnight to the outskirts of the capital city of Lusaka. By the time they stopped Dylan knew by the ache of his muscles that he had felt every single pothole on the entire journey.

When Dylan emerged from the truck, he could see the lights of Lusaka twinkling not far away. He stood in front of a large building, larger than any building Dylan had ever seen in Africa. He was hustled inside and they approached a desk with a man behind it.

They confiscated all his belongings, taking his camera out of his bag and destroying it before his eyes, smashing it flat with a bat. Parts flew in every direction. When the camera was nothing but a small pile of metal and plastic, they turned back to him.

"Take off your shoes, belt and shirt," the man behind the desk said gruffly as they patted him down one more time. Dylan held his breath, but apparently they didn't feel the small film canister and it remained in his cargo pants pocket.

Dylan took off his shoes and belt, but refused to take off

his shirt, wanting to maintain his dignity and as much of his clothing as possible. The man behind the desk stood and came around to stand in front of Dylan. He slapped him hard and before Dylan could react, the border guard and another guard who had joined them held his hands as his shirt was forcibly taken. He stood there in only his pants, shaking with rage. Remain calm, he said to himself over and over. The men put a paper in front of him and commanded him to sign it—to plead guilty to his crimes. Dylan stood rigid, his silence indicating his refusal. "I have done nothing wrong," he repeated several times.

The man from behind the desk slapped him again and shoved the paper in front of his face. Dylan saw that it was written in an African language. When he shook his head at the offered pen, the men conversed in a language Dylan didn't understand, then the border guard turned back to him.

"Wait here until morning, then you will be taken back to the police offices where your visa may be renewed if the judge so orders it," he said. He shoved Dylan toward a small door and out into a courtyard, his gun jabbing Dylan's bare skin on his back.

He was escorted to a large wooden gate, bigger than any gate he had ever seen before. As they approached, five uniformed men came out of a small building and started to unlock and pull on the gate. It looked to Dylan that the very jaws of hell were opening to receive him.

When they had passed through, the hinges began creaking and groaning as the men did their best to close it as quickly as possible. Dylan was pushed before another door and the guard knocked his signal. "We have a new prisoner, a foreigner under arrest," he said, grinning at Dylan. Dylan looked back at the large wooden door and the small office beside it. He squinted. There was a woman there, and in the flickering light, she looked like Elizabeth, the white shirt similar to one that she usually wore, but her hair was short and very dark. *I must*

be hallucinating, he thought. *It can't be Elizabeth.* He didn't
have much time to mull it over as they walked him down a
long concrete hall to a room about the size of his parent's
living room, where it looked like about fifty men were inside.
The guard threw Dylan in among them and left.

Dylan surveyed the room and could hardly believe what
he saw. The room was so small that men were not sleeping
lying down, but were back to back, squatting on a cold, hard
floor. He was quickly introduced to the captain of the room.
He stood over Dylan, wearing only a long white shirt, looking
down at him, his body and breath rank.

"Take off your pants and give them to me," he demanded.
"Only the captain should be dressed so fine."

Dylan stood as tall as he could, but was not as tall as the
captain. "No," he said simply, protecting his dignity as well as
the film in the pocket that he'd hidden there earlier.

The captain of the room raised his arm and punched Dylan
so hard in the head that he made a sickening thud when he
hit the floor. The pain was intense and the captain continued
hitting him, even taking off his boot to hit Dylan on the head
with it. Dylan fought back, knowing he was fighting for his
life, and was able to get in a few good punches of his own. The
other prisoners sat where they were, watching the fight, talking
excitedly and motioning toward Dylan, but not joining in. His
nose and lip bloodied, a cut in his scalp bleeding profusely, he
stood before the captain again, ready to defend himself. The
captain looked him over from head to toe, breathing hard,
as if he was weighing something over in his mind. All of a
sudden he laughed and slapped Dylan on the back, wiping at
the blood on his own face. "Okay, foreigner, that's enough. You
sleep over there." He pointed to a small space near the toilet
and the other men parted like the Red Sea to make a path for
him to follow.

The toilet was hardly more than a hole in the floor with a
wooden seat that smelled foul and looked like it was leaking,

but Dylan did as he was told. The other men seemed to settle down quickly and fall asleep, each resting against the back of another prisoner. Dylan had a choice to rest against the leaking toilet or just sit up straight. He chose to sit up straight and didn't sleep at all. If he didn't miss his soft bed at home in Canada before, he certainly did now. His head throbbed, he was cold, hungry and didn't know how he was going to get out of this.

Chapter Seven

Elizabeth stood with her arms folded across her chest, trying desperately to control her frustration. She looked at the two prison officials discussing whether she should be allowed into the prison and sighed inwardly. It had been a crazy forty-eight hours. With the doctor successfully altering the Tracin virus to suitably infect humans, which could be easily dispersed over a city, Bumani was ecstatic and hadn't stopped looking for Dylan to be his first "human trial." Lizige had convinced him that Dylan knew more than it seemed and that he was a loose end that needed to be tied up. Not needing any further encouragement Bumani became intent on finding Dylan.

With Lizige's help and at his urging, Bumani had made elaborate plans to capture Dylan, making sure he ended up in the Zambian prison where he could be used as a trial for Tracin and have all the privacy Bumani wanted. David had secretly passed Bumani's plans on to Elizabeth and she'd hopped the first plane she could when she found out what was going on, telling both David and Bumani she'd meet them at the rendezvous in Greece.

Bumani had come to trust her, thinking she was sympathetic to his cause and had traveled to Africa to help the people any way she could. Of course his way was the only way he knew. He had asked that she set up a warehouse on the Greek island of Lesvos to hold the weapon until it was ready for shipment to London. Her excuse for leaving early was accepted, Bumani congratulating her for thinking ahead and proud of her for wanting to get the warehouse ready for delivery of the weapon. *You are as organized and prepared as I am,* he'd complimented her.

Elizabeth had only smiled and nodded, wanting to get out of there as soon as possible. It was unbelievable that Bumani had sent Dylan to this prison, but she understood it. He wouldn't be disturbed here at the prison. He could subject Dylan to the toxin and no one would care. If other prisoners became infected, no one would care. It was ideal. But even if he was never infected he wouldn't last long here. She'd heard about Zambian jails and none of it was good. Tuberculosis and AIDS ran rampant, not to mention the overcrowding of the jail and the state of the prisoners. She needed to get him out.

Her interpreter turned to her. "They say you may start in two weeks."

Elizabeth shook her head immediately. "I must start tomorrow. I am with the International Committee for Humane Treatment of Prisoners in Africa. My orders say I am to examine the prisoners immediately," she pointed to the manufactured paper she held in her hand. "I must be allowed to examine the prisoners," she repeated.

Her interpreter turned back to the officials. *Stay calm,* Elizabeth told herself. *Getting emotional will get you nowhere.* Finally the three men turned to look at her. "It has been decided that you will be allowed in tomorrow," her interpreter announced. "You will be escorted to the infirmary and shown your post."

Elizabeth nodded, smoothed her white shirt and followed the prison officials out. She hoped Dylan could hang on until she got to him. She simply had to find him—not only for her job, but for her own peace of mind. She looked at her watch. Time for a check-in with Sam. It was getting extremely tiresome the amount of times Sam was requiring Elizabeth to report in and it could very well endanger her cover. She'd make it short tonight and didn't plan on mentioning Dylan's predicament at all. Sam's concern was Bumani and that's the report Elizabeth would make.

➤ ↔ —O— ↔ ⬅

When morning came the small slit in the top of the door let some sunshine in and Dylan lifted his eyes toward it, grateful for even the smallest amount of light. He said a short prayer asking for Heavenly Father's help in getting out of this predicament, and the strength to get through what the day would hold. Eventually the door to the little room was opened and the prisoners were allowed out. Dylan filed past the guards with the rest of the men, and was led to a small courtyard. Prison guards with guns were strategically placed throughout the yard. One man motioned for Dylan to get in a short line where he was given a long white shirt with the number eight on it. The only difference between him and the other men, besides his skin color, was the fact that he still had pants to wear under the long white shirt.

The next line was to hand out work assignments and in broken English the guard informed him that he was now in the Kamwala remand prison and was to work twelve hours of manual labor a day. Since he was new, his first assignment was to clean the prison toilets. Judging by where he had slept last night, Dylan knew this would not be an easy job. He hauled water in an old bucket to all the outside toilet holes to wash the waste away.

With no hat or sunscreen, and working in the unrelenting sun, by noon day he was burnt and in pain. His face and neck felt like they were on fire and carrying the water buckets across his shoulders was almost unbearable, especially with no shoes and the burning ground scorching the soles of his feet. Coupled with the sickening stench of both the water and the waste, it was all he could do not to retch until he had nothing left. He shook his head to clear his mind, trying to think of any scripture that could get him through this nightmare. The only one that came to him was, "For behold, the day cometh that shall burn as an oven . . ." It didn't help, but a rueful grin came over his face.

He worked until late afternoon, limping as best he could to get the job done. The guards took every opportunity they had to trip or push him, spilling his water and forcing him to go back for more. Their laughter tested Dylan's self-control to the extreme because he knew they were just waiting for him to strike back so they could beat or possibly shoot him. He only bowed low and went back to his duties, but the heat on his body was nothing compared to the heat raging in his soul at what he was being forced to endure.

His senses still on overload, he tried desperately to think of *any* scripture that could bring him comfort, strengthen his will and keep him sane. It was then that the account in Helaman 5 came clearly to his mind. Nephi and Lehi had been thrown into prison and when they were about to be killed, they were encircled by fire. "They were standing in the midst of fire, but were not burned . . . their hearts did take courage." Dylan definitely felt like he was standing in the midst of fire and he needed more courage to get him through this ordeal. He decided to exercise his faith in the Lord. If anyone could help Dylan, the Lord could, and somehow Dylan knew the Lord was aware of him and what was happening in his life.

Dylan was given a short reprieve at the afternoon meal where he stood in a long line to receive a small bowl with water and a little bit of cabbage. At that point, Dylan didn't care, his body needed nourishment. He sat quietly to the side of the other men, savoring the rest and taking in his surroundings. It was mostly old cement buildings loosely grouped together into a prison. With so much of it in disrepair there was a chance he could escape. It was well-guarded, however, so it wouldn't be easy, especially without shoes.

After the meal, Dylan returned to work, aware that several prisoners were watching and talking about him. He smiled, but it was not returned. His thoughts focused on trying to stay calm and formulate a plan for his escape. When the day was over, he was taken back to his cell, where a group of men, led by the captain, again demanded his tan cargo pants. Dylan wiped his hands on his now dirty white prison issue shirt and got into his fighting stance.

The captain came at him, but Dylan was ready. He knocked him to the ground, but the captain stood up quickly and nodded to someone behind him. Two men grabbed Dylan's hands and held them fast against his struggling. As the captain came toward him, Dylan kicked and landed his foot squarely in the captain's chest. With a roar he came back at Dylan swinging, punching him mercilessly in the face. Bloodied and bruised, Dylan stood as straight as possible, willing himself not to pass out. After several minutes, the captain nodded again. "Okay, foreigner, that's enough. You sleep over there." When Dylan was finally able to sit down to sleep near the leaking toilet, he raised his face to the rusted and cracked ceiling, silently begging his Heavenly Father to help him.

His thoughts turned to the scriptures, trying desperately through the pain to remember any of his memorized verses. His soul cried out from his memory, *"God, where art thou? And where is the pavilion that covereth thy hiding place?"* With astonishing clarity, the answer that had come in response to Joseph Smith's pleading from prison came to Dylan's mind. *"My son, peace be unto thy soul, thine adversity and thine afflictions shall be but a small moment; Thy friends do stand by thee, and they shall hail thee again with warm hearts and friendly hands."* A feeling of comfort overcame him and he fell into an exhausted sleep.

The next day started the same as before, with the prisoners being led to the courtyard to begin the day's work. Dylan's body ached from the work, the burns and the beatings, and he felt faint. By the noon meal, he knew he was dehydrated and suffering from sunstroke. He filled the bucket with water, splashing some on his own face, no longer caring that it was infested with all kinds of insects and who knew what else. It didn't help. He just felt dizzy and hot. He staggered toward the toilet, but didn't make it, spilling the bucket of water as he fell to the ground unconscious.

When Dylan awoke he had a cool cloth on his head and was lying on a mattress. "Oh, good, you're awake," said a soft, familiar voice to his right.

Elizabeth?" he said groggily, trying to get his bearings. *Was this a dream?*

"Yes, it's me." She came to stand next to him, coming into his view. "Just lie still."

"How did you get here? What's going on?" Dylan struggled to rise, but she pushed him back, adjusting the cloth on his head and smoothing back his hair. "Where's your glasses, and what did you do to your hair?" he muttered. It was now short and black instead of the beautiful long brown hair he'd grown to love. His thoughts were muddled and he was having a hard time focusing. *It must just be a dream,* he assured himself.

"Shh," she said. "You need to rest."

Dylan closed his eyes. He didn't need any further encouragement. His body and mind felt like a huge weight was crushing it. "Stay with me, okay?" he murmured and drifted back into an exhausted sleep.

Elizabeth combed back a curl that had fallen onto his forehead. If he'd been awake he would have seen how her heart ached to see the blood and bruises, and how desperately she wanted to get him out of here before he was killed.

><+>+O+<+><

Dylan awoke, groggy and disoriented. His face and shoulders hurt from the burns and bruises, but he felt better somehow. He closed his eyes for a moment, trying to clear his thoughts, remembering that he'd dreamed Elizabeth was here taking care of him.

"How are you feeling?" Elizabeth asked as she pulled back the small privacy curtain that didn't really give much privacy.

Dylan didn't smile, but swallowed hard and tried to find his voice. "It wasn't a dream. You really are here." All his red flags were going up. The only way she could have known where he had been taken was for her to have had something to do with it. "How did you get here?"

"That doesn't matter," she whispered, leaning closer and taking his hand. "The important thing is we get you out of here."

He held her hand to his chest, wishing he wasn't thinking what he was thinking. "What are you doing here?"

"I came for you," she answered. She pulled the picture of the Savior that he'd bought for her from her pocket. "I brought this for good luck," her voice cracked with emotion. "Looks like we could both use some luck right about now."

Dylan looked at her tenderly, pushing the thoughts of who she worked for to the back of his mind. He brushed back the long bangs away from her face, tucking them behind her ear. "I wanted to talk to you the day I left Kampala and invite you to come with me. I thought you were in danger. Looks like I was wrong," he grimaced.

"Maybe if I'd come with you this wouldn't have happened," she said, holding his hand to her cheek.

He sat up, leaning heavily on his elbow, and wincing from the pain. "I couldn't bear it if something had happened to you." He put his hand gently around the back of her neck and pulled her closer, gently touching his lips to hers. "Thank you for taking care of me," he murmured. "Sorry I haven't shaved yet."

Elizabeth smiled briefly, then looked down as if she didn't want to meet his eyes. "Dylan, there's something I have to tell you." She paused, watching him closely as if to gauge his reaction. "I'm not an aid worker."

Dylan drew back and laid back down. "I know. But tell me you're not working for Bumani and that you're not the reason I'm in here," he said, his smile fading.

"Of course I didn't have anything to do with you being put in here." Elizabeth took a deep breath, and briefly closed her eyes, as if she was steeling herself to do something she didn't want to do. When she finally looked at him her eyes were obviously troubled. "Dylan, I'm so sorry. I'm not who you think I am." Her finger lightly traced the bruise over his eye. "We need to get you out of here and I need you to trust me."

"All I want to know is who you work for," Dylan asked, the frustration at her evasiveness starting to override all other emotions.

Elizabeth looked away and shook her head. "I wanted to tell you so many times, but . . ."

Dylan licked his dry lips and put his hand over his eyes. Why hadn't he connected it before? *Maybe I didn't want to,* he thought. *I enjoyed her company so much I didn't want her to be in the line of work that subconsciously I must have known she was in.* He flashed back to all the times she had been uncomfortable talking about herself and what had brought her to Africa. Her connection to David Kanu. It all made sense now.

Elizabeth tried to hold his hand, but he pulled away. "Dylan, please . . ." she pleaded, but stopped and looked up as a prison guard approached. "Can I help you?" She stood as he reached for Dylan. "No, no, he's not ready."

The prison guard did not reply, just forced Dylan to his feet. He staggered against the guard and Elizabeth caught him.

"I'm trying to get you out of here," she whispered in his ear. "Be patient and trust me."

"I can't trust myself anymore," he replied grimly. "How can I trust you?" He didn't look back as he was led to another area of the prison which looked like solitary confinement to Dylan.

Each cell only had one man in it, with a small cot in the corner. Dylan didn't care. When the guard threw him in a cold cell, he made his way to the metal cot and curled up. He couldn't seem to think clearly. Elizabeth was here, she said she was trying to get him out. Who did she work for? Was it her who had him taken prisoner? His heart whispered that he could trust her, but his head wasn't so sure. He lay there for what seemed like hours until he finally fell into a restless sleep.

When he awoke it was dark outside. He stood and went to the metal bars that imprisoned him. Another prisoner sat near him in his cell, his legs curled under him and his fingers running aimlessly over the floor. When he looked at Dylan the whites of his eyes were almost glowing in the darkness, his long hair falling over his face.

"Hello," Dylan said. "I'm Dylan, what's your name?" He hoped to find someone who spoke English in here.

The other man was silent for a moment. "I'm Ojore," he said simply.

"Nice to meet you, Ojore," Dylan sat down, surprised and grateful that someone here spoke his native language. "What are you in here for?"

Ojore sighed and turned his head. "Does it matter?"

Dylan shrugged. "Not really. I just thought it was nice to finally have someone who speaks English to talk to."

Ojore smiled. "Ah, yes, you wouldn't find very many prisoners who speak English here." He moved closer to Dylan's cell. "What are you in here for?"

"I apparently have an expired bus pass."

"Ha, that is like me," Ojore laughed softly. "I spoke my mind one too many times and here I am." He stopped and came as close as he could to Dylan's cell. "I opposed Idi Amin's presidency and his tyrannical rule of my country. They threw me in here and left me to die."

Dylan shook his head. It was hard to imagine being in prison for having an opinion, something that was taken for granted in Canada. "How long have you been here?"

"I think about thirty years," he said. He drew his knees to his chest. "I was stupid to let my political views come before my family. I lost everything for my principles. My wife and sons have all suffered."

"Do they come and visit you?"

"No, they don't even know I'm alive. Besides, no visitors are allowed here."

"How many children do you have?"

"Two boys. Wonderful boys, with lots of energy."

Dylan smiled, remembering Serapio and his energy. "What was your wife's name?"

He covered his mouth for a moment as if reliving a wonderful memory. "Her name was Nabulungi. It means 'beautiful one' and she is very beautiful."

Dylan jolted and looked at his companion. It couldn't be! He was careful, not wanting to get the man's hopes up. "Did she live in a small village outside of Kampala? Near Barh Bira?"

Ojore gripped the bars. "Yes. How did you know?"

"Do you remember anything about the village?"

"A man lived there named Munyiga who always wanted something for nothing. We were a farming village, our home was just to the north of the village center."

Dylan smiled, remembering Akiki's complaint of Munyiga not paying for his use of the telephone. "That's incredible! I stayed in Nabulungi's home just last week. She talked of you and how you were taken from her."

Ojore sat back. "She still talks of me? She hasn't remarried?"

"No, she is raising your nephew Serapio. Your boys have grown and gone with families of their own."

Ojore was silent and Dylan crept closer to the bars. A small tear was coursing down Ojore's cheek.

"Tell me, tell me everything."

Chapter Eight

Elizabeth's heart was heavy as she watched Dylan being led away leaning on the guard. He'd looked so disappointed in her and she longed for the light in his eyes to return. Would he ever trust her again? She hoped that since he was an agent, too, he would understand that they were both just trying to do a job.

She finger combed her hair, never having been able to get used to the feel of wigs. Letting herself become attached to Dylan had probably been a mistake. How was she supposed to finish this blasted mission with Dylan as a distraction? But he was never far from her mind. She couldn't help herself. He had been someone to laugh with and talk to in a strange country, doing an impossible job. Besides, she felt responsible for him even being in here and planned on remedying that by helping him escape.

She straightened up the infirmary, then went to find Mulogo. Maybe he could help her figure out where they'd taken Dylan. He was still in need of medical attention, not to mention that she wanted to explain herself to him. She couldn't bear it if he turned away from her again. He was an agent, he'd understand. He had to.

She walked down the drab concrete hall and motioned to the guard to buzz her through the large metal door. He looked her over and gave her a lascivious grin. She ignored him and went to the offices down the hall, knocking on the last door.

"Mulogo, it's . . ." she paused, trying to quickly remember

her alias. "It's Christine, are you in there?"

The door swung wide and Mulogo greeted her with a big smile. "Christine, hello. What can I do for you?"

"I need to examine a prisoner who was suffering from sunstroke and dehydration and a guard just came and took him. I want to know where he was taken."

"Ahh," Mulogo said, his smile disappearing. "That might be difficult."

"Why?"

"The warden does not like your presence here. He has told everyone not to help you."

Elizabeth entered the room and closed the door. "Mulogo, I must see this man. He needs medical attention."

"Which man is it?"

"A white man, brown hair, beard, a new prisoner."

Mulogo folded his arms. He closed his eyes for a moment, then opened them and looked hard at Elizabeth. When she met his eyes and returned his gaze, he nodded his head as if he'd made a decision and went to the phone. He dialed a number, then spoke quickly into the receiver. After nodding his head several times, he hung up. "He is in the west wing, in what you call, solitary confinement. He is scheduled for release within the hour." His eyes were wide. "A very important man is with the warden now, paying for the white man's release."

Elizabeth breathed a sigh of relief at the news that Dylan was in solitary confinement. At least he wouldn't be beaten there or forced to work. But hearing that Bumani was probably here made her blood run chill. She had to get Dylan out of here immediately. "Can I see him?"

"He is allowed no visitors."

"Mulogo, I must see him. He needs my help."

Mulogo spread his arms wide. "I will see what I can do, but I make no guarantees. You have enemies here, Christine. I suggest you leave soon."

Elizabeth nodded her head. No one needed to tell her that

twice. As soon as she could get to Dylan, they'd both be out of here. "Did they say the name of the important man who came to pick him up?"

"They did not tell me, only that he is a powerful man who has bought the prisoner for his own purposes. His new owner wants him healthy and in the far wing of the prison as soon as the transaction is complete, then total privacy afterward. He came himself to make sure his orders were followed."

Elizabeth schooled her face so Mulogo would not see her fear, but that could mean only one thing. Her small window of time had run out and if she didn't do something now, Dylan would die.

>-+-<>-•-O-•-<>-+-<

Dylan's throat was parched and he would have given anything for a drink. He'd been talking to Ojore for the last three hours, giving every detail he could remember about Nabulungi and Serapio. Ojore was like a man seeing the ocean for the first time and not believing his eyes, wanted to see, feel and imagine even the tiniest details.

"She was a wonderful cook, wasn't she," Ojore reminisced. "I have missed her cooking."

Dylan smiled. "She is a wonderful woman, Ojore. You are a lucky man."

Ojore snorted. "Lucky? I am in prison wasting away. That is not lucky."

"Have you thought about getting out? Escaping?"

Ojore looked around as if someone may be listening. "Don't talk crazy."

"You've thought about it then?"

Walking to the small window in his cell that overlooked the courtyard, Ojore sighed. "I have thought about escaping many times. But I haven't had any chances. I am only let out for an hour each week and I am heavily guarded. Even if I got past the guards, beyond the fence is only a rocky wasteland and I would be an easy target."

Dylan slumped down in his cell. Was he destined to spend his next thirty years here, wasting away like Ojore? *Elizabeth said she was getting me out*, a small voice in his head reminded him. *Be patient.* Dylan shook his head. She must be working for Bumani if she had known where to find him. And if that was the case he would need to find a way out himself. *I can't trust anyone*, he thought. But what would Elizabeth be doing here if he couldn't trust her? Why would she want him out of prison if she worked for Bumani? It didn't make sense unless she really *was* trying to help him.

"Tell me what Nabulungi was doing when you left her," Ojore asked, bringing Dylan out of his thoughts.

"The last night I was there, she sat with me on the porch and we talked about a book that some American missionaries from the Church of Jesus Christ of Latter-day Saints had given her."

"What kind of book?"

"A book about Jesus Christ. Scriptures like the Bible that tell about the people who lived on the American continent before Christ came," Dylan sat up, his voice sincere.

"How do you know so much about this book?"

Dylan avoided his question, thinking for a moment, then throwing caution to the wind. Knowing they could both die in this prison he decided to just speak from his heart. "It's another witness of Jesus Christ's mission on earth, Ojore." He leaned forward, straining to see Ojore's face in the darkness. "His coming was foretold and anxiously waited for by people on the American continent. He even visited those ancient people and blessed them. It is a powerful book of scripture, and I hope Nabulungi reads it and feels that witness, too. I know it has brought me much happiness," Dylan said, looking directly at Ojore, hoping he could see and feel his sincerity.

"Happiness," he snorted. "I have had to find my own

happiness here in this prison." Ojore watched him for a moment and nodded. "I hope she finds the Lord if she hasn't already. Many times when I have been here with no one to talk to, I have prayed in my heart. I did not know if there was a God or if anyone heard me but these walls, but one night when I was feeling low and wondering if it would be better to be dead, I prayed in my heart to know what to do and I heard a voice say clearly to me, "You are not alone." From then on, I knew God knew who I was and where I was. I wasn't afraid anymore."

Dylan nodded. "God loves us, I know it. He's going to help us."

Ojore stood up. "I believe you, Dylan. I think he *will* help us, and I am ready."

➤—◇—⟦

Elizabeth walked down the hall toward Dylan's cell, carrying a small bag of supplies in her hand. Mulogo walked slightly ahead of her, and the guard was ahead of him, the keys jingling from his pocket, making an odd parade-type line. They passed several cells with men in them either sleeping or sitting on the floor staring. Dylan stood slowly when they came near, backing up as they opened his cell door.

"What are you doing here?" he asked, looking directly at Elizabeth.

"I'm here to finish treating your injuries," she said, motioning him toward the cot.

He folded his arms across his chest. "I'm fine. You can go."

Mulogo stood beside Elizabeth. "Do as she says, please."

Dylan stood defiant for a moment, then did as he was told. "I don't need any help," he muttered.

"Quit being such a baby," Elizabeth said as she took out some bandages from the bag. She leaned over his face as if she was going to bandage the cut on his head. "This is going to hurt. Just lie still and trust me."

"What do you . . ." was all Dylan got out before she stuck a needle in his arm. Within seconds he felt slightly nauseated, his heart was pounding and was beginning to sweat profusely. "What did you do to me?" he moaned.

Elizabeth continued to bandage his wounds, watching him closely. When it was clearly apparent he was in distress, she turned to the guard and Mulogo. "I think he's having a heart attack," she said, her voice both anxious and authoritative. She put her ear to his chest. "His heart rate is rapid, he's sweating. Dylan can you hear me? Where does it hurt?"

He moaned again and generally pointed to his heart.

"We've got to get him to the hospital in Lusaka," Elizabeth directed as she stood. "Mulogo can you and the guard carry him? We can take the medical truck into the city."

Mulogo backed up. "I can't carry anyone. I have a back injury."

Elizabeth sized up the guard. "You'll have to do it then. Maybe we could get that other prisoner next to this man to help."

"No," the guard said, looking around. "He is to stay here. He's been bought and paid for."

It was all Elizabeth could do not to show her disgust. "We don't have time for that," she said impatiently. "Look at him. You're supposed to deliver him healthy. We have to go to the hospital for that. We'll bring him right back." The guard still looked unsure. "How would you like to explain to your boss that you watched him die instead?" Elizabeth pressed. "Maybe he'll ask you to reimburse the money that was paid for this man out of your own pocket." At that statement, the guard's eyes widened. Knowing she had his attention, she put her hands on her hips. "We have to go now if you want to be back in time. Get this man treated and you'll be the hero for making sure his new owner got a healthy specimen."

The guard was silent for a moment, then spun on his heel

and began to unlock Ojore's cell. "Come on, help me get the prisoner to the medical truck."

Ojore stood, drawing up to his full height, just barely taller than the guard and nodded. He flipped his long black hair to the side, away from his face and stepped in front of the guard to Dylan's cell.

"If you try to escape I will shoot you," the guard warned Ojore, poking his gun into his back, leaving a small impression in Ojore's white prison shirt.

"He's not a dangerous criminal, is he?" Elizabeth asked as the two men came toward Dylan.

"No, he is a political prisoner," the guard sneered derisively at Ojore.

Elizabeth was already trying to help Dylan sit up. He was breathing hard. "We have to hurry," she said.

Ojore and the guard got on either side of him and helped him stand. They slowly made their way down the hall and to some stairs, practically carrying Dylan at the end. Mulogo insisted he needed to go back to his office and finish some paperwork, so Elizabeth, Ojore, and the guard were left to get Dylan to the medical truck, where Elizabeth's driver still waited. They were almost to the last guard outpost when a door opened behind them and Elizabeth glimpsed David with Lizige and Bumani close behind him. David spotted her and the look on his face spoke volumes. He turned abruptly to the left, trying to lead the party away from her, but Elizabeth could feel Bumani's eyes on her.

She quickly turned her head and practically pulled Dylan and the two men helping him the last ten feet of the hall. After the guard that was accompanying them showed his badge, they were buzzed through to the courtyard and Elizabeth jumped into the back of the truck. Glancing behind them she could see Bumani's unmistakable form quickly entering the outpost. He was pointing to someone behind him. "Hurry," she prompted, trying not to call any more attention to herself.

When Dylan was in the truck she motioned for Ojore to get in as well. "I'll need him to help the orderly at the hospital," she explained in a rush. She could see out of the corner of her eye that Bumani was speaking to the guard that had buzzed them through. She ducked behind the canvas flap of the truck, just as the guard in the office picked up the phone. As she got Dylan settled, she watched through a small slit in the canvas as David joined Bumani. He said something, his hands gesturing back toward where they had come, and with lightning force Bumani struck David across the face, then pulled a gun out and was pointing it at the guard in the room with them. Elizabeth bit her lip to keep herself from crying out David's name. She couldn't help him and risk being recognized. "Let him be okay," she murmured softly.

She turned back to the prison guard that had helped Dylan to the truck. "We need to hurry," she emphasized. "Just let the prisoner go with us and help get him into the hospital." She jabbed her finger in Dylan's direction, careful to stay behind the cover of the canvas.

The prison guard immediately shook his head at her request for Ojore to accompany them. "I'll have to get clearance for anyone to leave the compound and two prisoners would require at least two guards. Wait here," he commanded. He walked back toward the small central office where the guards congregated, pulling his walkie-talkie out and speaking into it. When he got no response, he pulled his gun and began to run, yelling what Elizabeth assumed was the other guard's name.

She stuck her head out for a moment to close the canvas flap, and saw that the only person now visible in the small office was Bumani and he stood calmly with his arms folded, his eyes never leaving the truck. She moved the hair of her wig around her face and ducked back inside. Elizabeth's heart was pounding and the hairs on the back of her neck prickled. Had he recognized her? Why hadn't he walked out to the truck? Was it luck or was there something else going on? If they were caught now they would all be dead. Dylan moaned and she knew this was their one and only chance for escape. She wished David were with them and that she could see for herself if he was safe, but it was impossible. Getting Dylan out of here without compromising herself had to be her priority.

><+>-0-<+><

Jimon Bumani looked down at David Kanu who was on the floor rubbing the side of his face where he'd been struck. He started to step over David and move toward the door, but David put his hand on Bumani's leg. "What have I done, sir?"

As David stopped him, they could hear the medical truck roar to life. David gave a silent sigh of relief, hoping Elizabeth had escaped, but knowing that it wasn't over for him. Bumani stood over him barely containing his rage. "I thought I just saw Elizabeth getting into that truck with the reporter, helping him escape." His voice was tight and controlled. "I hope for your sake that I am mistaken."

"I don't know Mr. Bumani," David said quickly. "I was only trying to go to the cell block where the warden directed us. I didn't see anything." He stood slowly before Bumani, his stance humble, his head bowed. "Why would Elizabeth be here? She's in Greece making the warehouse ready. You must be mistaken."

Bumani's eyes narrowed to small slits. He grabbed David by the arm. "You're quick to defend her, but since you have been the one working with her, you know her best." His fingers bit into David's flesh as they walked toward the door, stepping over the unconscious guard that Bumani had pistol-whipped. Several guards were shouting and running toward the outpost as they left. "I did not get to where I am by trusting people, but I gave my trust to you. Apparently you did not deserve it." He spun David around to face him. "I think you and Elizabeth are traitors," he hissed, his face mottled in his rage. "And before the day is out, you will tell me everything I need to know." He motioned to Lizige. "Take Mr. Kanu to the room where Dr. Bruder is waiting."

Lizige nodded. "Yes, sir."

"Mr. Bumani, I don't know anything about what you saw. I didn't see anything," David protested. "I have been loyal to you and done everything you asked. I am not a traitor." His eyes darted between Lizige and Bumani. "If I had anything to tell I would."

Bumani leaned down to the smaller man, so close David could smell the mint that he chewed on his breath. "You will tell me everything before you beg me to kill you," he promised, his eyes glittering. "And if that *was* Elizabeth, she will suffer for her betrayal, much more so than even you can imagine." He stepped away and David fell back onto Lizige. He was in trouble and he knew it. If only he hadn't told Elizabeth that Dylan was going to die. If only Elizabeth hadn't given in to her feelings for the Canadian. If only, if only. None of that was going to help him now. Lizige pulled him along the corridor toward the room where Dr. Bruder was waiting. His fate was sealed now for better or for worse. He hoped it wasn't the latter, but a part of him knew that it would be.

>⊢⦁⟩⊸○⊶⦁⊣⦂

Elizabeth crawled to the front and banged on the cab of the truck which lurched forward. "We can't wait!" she shouted back to the guard. He stopped mid-stride in reaching the office and did a quick U-turn, running after the truck and shouting for them to stop, firing haphazard shots with his gun. He began shouting to the guards to close the gates. Since the gates were so large, they didn't close in time and the jeep barely made it through, scraping the sides of the vehicle with the wood of the gate.

Bending over Dylan, Elizabeth said, "Hang in there. It's

almost over." She took another syringe out of her pocket and injected it into Dylan's thigh. "Just a few more minutes and you'll feel better."

Dylan was obviously too weak to move, just barely nodding his head. Elizabeth smoothed back his hair. "I'm sorry we had to do it this way, but it was all I could think of to get you out of there quickly."

Dylan turned away. "What did you do to me?"

"I gave you a cardio toxin to simulate a heart attack. Then I injected you with the antidote as soon as we got into the truck." She watched him for a reaction, but he just closed his eyes. Nodding to Ojore, she asked, "What were you in for again?"

"Political reasons," he said, trying to find a hand hold as the truck bounced over the roads.

"Can you make your way home from Lusaka?" she asked, also trying to balance herself and not fall over onto Dylan.

Ojore's eyes went wide. "You would let me go?"

"Yes," Elizabeth nodded, smiling. "Political reasons are hardly a just reward for rotting in a prison cell. Don't you agree, Dylan?"

Dylan nodded and opened his eyes to look at his new friend. "You need to get back home to your family, Ojore."

Ojore leaned over Dylan and looked him in the eye, obviously worried. "Will you be okay, my friend?"

"Don't worry about me," Dylan reassured him, taking his hand and coming to a sitting position. "I'll be fine." He turned to face him, wincing at the bouncing his bottom was experiencing on the hard metal of the truck bed. "It's more than coincidence we found each other in that prison, Ojore. This is a second chance for you."

"Do you know this woman?" Ojore nodded toward Elizabeth.

Dylan glanced at her as she clutched a piece of the canvas to help keep her balance. "Not really."

Elizabeth winced. "More than you think."

The truck bounced to a stop at a small airport. The driver got out and came around back. "We're here, Beth. You better hurry. The plane is waiting, but no doubt the guards have alerted the authorities."

Elizabeth reached out her hand to help Dylan out of the truck, but he pretended not to see it. She shrugged and jumped down herself. Emptying her pockets she handed Ojore several bills and coins. "This should help you get home," she said, thrusting the money into his hand.

"Thank you," Ojore said, shaking her hand warmly. "Thank you."

Dylan finally climbed down slowly and carefully. Ojore hugged him. "Good journey, my friend."

The truck driver took Ojore and started orienting him to his location, pointing him in the direction he should go first. Elizabeth walked toward the plane, then turned back to Dylan. "Aren't you coming?"

Dylan grimaced. "My legs feel like rubber."

"It's because your heart was in an arrhythmia, but you'll feel normal in a couple of hours." She walked back, again offering him her hand. "If you'd put away your pride and let me help you, you'll feel better faster."

Dylan stubbornly refused, walking alone toward the plane. Elizabeth shook her head. "I compromised my position, risked my life to get you out of that prison, and that's the thanks I get?" she said mildly.

"No one asked you to," Dylan ground out. "Who do you work for? Is Elizabeth your real name?"

"I could ask *you* the same question," she retorted.

They reached the stairs to the plane and Elizabeth stepped to the top and reached back for Dylan. "But to answer your question, I work for Jimon Bumani and I'm taking you to Greece where I'm supposed to meet him in two days."

Chapter Nine

Dylan stepped away from her and started to walk back toward the truck. The driver waved him away and tried to turn around, the wail of sirens sounding in the distance. "Wait," he said. "I need to talk to you." His suspicions had been correct and Elizabeth worked for Bumani. The disappointment was crushing.

"Hey," Elizabeth called after him. "Let me explain."

Dylan turned to face her. "What is there to explain? You work for an international terrorist and you're going to turn me over to him."

"After what we've shared, how can you think that? Get on the plane you arrogant . . . oh, you make me so mad!" Elizabeth marched toward him, her brown eyes spitting fire, her mouth a grim line. "If I wanted to turn you over to him I would have left you in that prison to die!" She grabbed his arm, her strength startling Dylan as she escorted him to the plane. "The guards could be here any minute. Get on that plane and I'll explain everything."

Dylan bit his lower lip to keep from laughing at her display of temper. He complied with her request, more than relieved that he'd obviously misjudged her.

After some wrangling they were finally seated on the small plane in chairs that were facing each other. After an equipment check they were in the air. Dylan sat with his arms folded staring at Elizabeth. "Start talking."

Elizabeth took a deep breath. "I'm an American operative

with the CIA. I went to Uganda six months ago to infiltrate Bumani's organization and get the same information you were looking for. Did he have a weapon and what was he planning on doing with it? Everyone knew that Bumani's brother ran a private hospital in Kampala, so I recruited David Kanu to help me, got a job at the hospital, and went from there. One of the hospital administrators took me into his confidence, told me that a powerful man was going to help the hospital with supplies in exchange for holding an experiment of a new virus at the hospital. I knew it was Bumani and asked to help."

"Why would Bumani trust you, especially since you're American and his hatred seems pointed at Americans?"

Elizabeth smiled grimly. "Apparently he feels that I'm sympathetic to his cause, having renounced my country to come and help the people of Africa."

Dylan shook his head. "Okay." He took a deep breath. "I'm just trying to figure this out. You have the trust of one of the United States' most wanted terrorists?"

"It does put me in a unique situation." She shifted in her seat, the vinyl squeaking loudly as she did so.

Dylan grimaced. "And you put that position in jeopardy by coming to break me out of prison?"

"Yes," Elizabeth said.

"Thank you," he said sincerely, leaning forward to look in her eyes. She nodded almost imperceptibly, then looked down, her eyelashes brushing her cheeks. Dylan continued to watch her almost with fascination. It had been so long since he'd felt this close to someone, that he could trust them to watch his back. He sat back, but his eyes never left her face. "I don't even know if Elizabeth is your real name."

"It's my given name. All my friends call me Beth." She seemed self-conscious as she tucked a piece of hair behind her ears and crossed her legs. "I could say the same thing about you. Is Dylan your real name?" He nodded and she seemed relieved. "Anyway, Bumani had the weapon and some radiation equipment delivered to the hospital the night I called you to come and take pictures. I didn't know David knew you or I wouldn't have asked you to come. It almost ruined everything." She had changed the subject from anything personal and Dylan wondered if that was deliberate.

"What do you mean?"

"Bumani was in the process of proving David's loyalties so he put Lizige on him as a watchdog. When David saw you he almost jumped out of his skin and was sure you would recognize him from South Africa."

"I thought he might have known me, but I didn't recognize him until you mentioned South Africa the next day at lunch," Dylan explained. The turbulence was starting to get to him and he was feeling nauseated, not to mention the giant headache he had. "Is there a bathroom on this plane? I'd hate to lose it in front of you."

Elizabeth was immediately concerned. "What's wrong?"

"I feel sick, that's all, and I have a whopping headache."

"Put your head between your knees," she counseled. "Here's a paper bag in case you lose it." She unbuckled her seat belt and came back a few minutes later with some aspirin. "This should help your headache." She offered him a bottle of water with the pills.

He took them and gulped the pills and water in almost one breath. "Thanks," he said, wiping the water from his mouth. "I've been dying of thirst."

"I'm sorry I wasn't even thinking," she said. "Let me get you another bottle."

When she came back he had leaned the chair back and appeared to be sleeping. She set the bottle of water down in the empty seat beside her with the pillow she'd brought for him and pulled the sweater she'd put on closer around her body.

He opened his eyes. "Is that pillow for me?"

"Yes," Elizabeth nodded and handed it to him. "You get some sleep."

"I will," Dylan agreed. "After I hear the rest of the story."

Elizabeth sighed. "It's a long story."

"I've got the time."

"Okay, so David recognized you and Lizige was suspicious and put a call in to Jimon. David had to admit that he thought he knew you and that you could be a liability. When the biological weapon was ready, Bumani needed a human trial. He chose you, but you were leaving the country. Jimon used Akiki to get your itinerary and made sure that you were taken into custody at the Chirundu border and taken to Kamwala prison. He was there at the prison tonight to start the experiment."

"Did he see you?" Dylan asked.

"I don't think so," Elizabeth said. "I did see him in the guard's office with David though and it didn't look good." Her face shadowed. "I hope he's okay."

Dylan's hand covered hers. "I'm sure he's fine. He seems like the sort of man that knows how to get out of a tight spot."

Elizabeth nodded and drew her hand away. Dylan blew out a breath. "How did he use Akiki?"

She seemed relieved to change the subject. "Akiki spied on you when you were using his phone line and got your itinerary."

"What do you mean spied on me?" he asked, wearily rubbing his eyes, the news going from bad to worse.

Elizabeth's face was serious. "Jimon Bumani is an incredibly smart and capable terrorist. Nothing stands in his way." She paused. "Akiki had boasted to several village leaders that he knew you worked for the Canadian government. One of Bumani's men got him talking and he admitted that he had seen your itinerary with a little mirror he had near the window. As soon as he told the information he knew, he was killed."

Dylan closed his eyes. He'd really liked Akiki. "So what does Bumani want with me now?'

"He thinks you'd be the perfect candidate to field test his new biological weapon on and since you might know too much, this is the perfect way to eliminate you."

Dylan sat forward. The information hadn't connected before. "Biological weapon. Of course! When I broke into the basement I saw radiation cards and protective gear. Did he manufacture it himself?"

"No, he brought in a renowned doctor, a genius really, Dr. Lowden Bruder."

"Isn't he the guy that made a new virus and then disappeared?"

Elizabeth nodded. "Jimon bought the virus and the doctor." She looked down and picked a small piece of lint off of her sweater. "They call it the Tracin virus because it's practically untraceable. Jimon gave the doctor whatever he needed as long as the doctor made the virus fit for a biological weapon. Two days ago, the doctor finally succeeded in making the virus small enough to attach to a human lung and spread within the body." Her voice sounded frustrated. "Bumani now has a powerful new weapon to unleash on unsuspecting people. He needs a human test, though, and you were going to be it. When I found out what he was going to do, I knew I had to get you out." She shrugged. "So I did."

"Does Bumani suspect you? What excuse did you give him for your absence?"

"I'm meeting him in Athens in two days. We're making arrangements for shipment to London. From there, I'm not sure where he's going to send it, but it's somewhere in the U.S.," Elizabeth took a drink from her own bottle of water, delicately swiping at a small droplet that had escaped down her chin. "I have a safe house for you to go to so you can recover while I meet with Bumani. I can't screw up this investigation because if he's gets away with this weapon . . ." She left her words hanging but her meaning was clear.

Dylan nodded. "I understand. Maybe I could help you by notifying the Canadian government, I'm sure they'd want to be in on it. If you could just hook me up with a computer or a phone I could let my superiors know."

"There's a lot to do when we land, we'll have to see," Elizabeth said. She stood. "Let me go see how much longer we'll be in the air. I need to check in with my supervisor as well. She's one of those 'by the book' kind of people that demand on time check-ins."

After spending so much time with Elizabeth he thought he could read her pretty well and he knew she was holding something back from him. *I probably would too, if I were in her shoes*, Dylan thought. But he didn't understand why Elizabeth didn't want to notify the Canadian authorities. He would think the more help the U.S. had in stopping the attack the better. It just made more sense to have back up.

He watched her leave the cabin, and pull back the curtains to go and talk to the pilots. He waited a few moments, then followed her. She was just outside the cockpit door talking to someone on the phone. *Probably her superior*, he thought. If he could use a phone, he could let Andrew know where he was at least. Everyone would be worried since he didn't meet his contact in Zambia and hadn't checked in. Elizabeth saw him and motioned for Dylan to go back to his seat. He smiled and complied. At least the truth was out and he could be honest with her. The thought gave him hope for the future, the first he'd had in a long time.

Chapter Ten

Elizabeth walked toward Dylan who was sleeping soundly. She hated to wake him up because she knew that rest would do him the most good. She set down the small package she held in her arms in the chair next to Dylan's. Watching his chest rise and fall, she felt relief wash over her that he was safe. His hair was tousled, and combined with the bruises on his face, his masculine air was touched with vulnerability. She gently shook his arm, trying to find the cleanest spot she could on his tattered prison shirt, and felt the tautness of his muscle beneath the cloth. He didn't stir. Kneeling beside him, she placed her hand underneath his cheek, and tried again. "Dylan, it's Elizabeth, you need to wake up now, we're about to land."

Dylan slowly opened his eyes. The Elizabeth he remembered leaned over him. "Your beautiful long hair is back," he murmured, reaching out to run his fingers through it.

Elizabeth shivered and drew back. "We'll be landing in about twenty minutes. I brought you a change of clothes and a razor, the bathroom is through there," she pointed to a curtain behind her. "I thought you might want to clean up. Oh, I almost forgot. Here's an ointment for your burn. It should take the sting away."

Dylan stood and helped her up from her kneeling position. They stood close together for a moment, their eyes saying what their voices could not. After a moment, he reached over and grabbed the package from the chair. He straightened and looked as if he was going to say something to her, but changed his mind. "Thank you," he finally murmured before slipping behind the curtain.

Elizabeth sat down, watching him leave. She knew he'd been through a lot and she hoped he'd trust her again, enough to confide in her what he was thinking. Her feelings for him were growing and she needed him to trust her, to understand that she was torn. She wanted to tell him everything, but the truth was, she was an undercover agent for the United States government and the national security of her country depended on her performance. As soon as they landed in Athens she had to concentrate on that. There was no other choice. She straightened her shoulders and strengthened her resolve to use her training and compartmentalize her feelings on this mission. It was more difficult than she'd imagined, especially since this was the first time she'd ever had a blur between her personal life and her job. There was something about Dylan that drew her to him. He didn't seem like any other agent she had ever known. It was overwhelming that they'd found each other under these circumstances.

Fifteen minutes later he emerged from behind the curtain looking like a completely different man. The khaki Dockers contrasted with the blue short-sleeved shirt, a big difference from the dirty prison wear and tattered cargo pants. But the biggest difference was his clean-shaven face revealing a strong jaw, the cleft in his chin as pronounced as she'd thought it would be. The absence of a beard showcased the bruises he'd received in prison, but also brought out his deep green eyes, which were staring at her. He sat down across from her and buckled in for the landing. "What?"

Elizabeth averted her eyes. "Nothing. You look different is all."

"I'm assuming you took all the precautions with your cover and disguise at the prison so no one would describe you to

Bumani and he wouldn't know it was you who broke me out," he said.

"Yes," Elizabeth nodded slightly. "I was very careful, but when he showed up so unexpectedly . . ." her voice trailed off. "There's obviously a small chance that he recognized me and he'll figure it out, but I'm always careful. My name was on an earlier flight's passenger manifest and I'm checked in at a downtown hotel. With any luck, Bumani won't suspect a thing."

Dylan shook his head. "You shouldn't be meeting with Bumani. It's too dangerous. Why don't we just notify the Canadian and American governments of his plan and go home? We know the threat is high and both governments can go on high alert."

"I can't," she said softly. "We're so close to finding out the final phase of his plan, but we don't know it yet. If we let Bumani slip away, we won't know when or how he's coming after us. All we'll know is he has an extremely dangerous bio-toxin to release on innocent people."

The pilot's voice came on the intercom warning them that they were starting to land and should be buckled in. Elizabeth averted her eyes for the landing, choosing to look out the window instead of at Dylan. He never took his eyes off her and she could feel his stare. She wondered what he was thinking, and wished she could explain everything to him. She pointed out the window. "You're missing the view," she commented, briefly glancing at him. "The little houses dotting the neighborhoods and the skyline of Athens are pretty amazing, not to mention that you can see the Acropolis."

Dylan didn't reply just continued to look at her. His gaze was beginning to make her uncomfortable. "Do you have something to say to me?" Elizabeth asked.

The plane bumped to a stop and Elizabeth stood up. Dylan stood with her. As they exited the plane, Dylan held her arm. "Do you trust me?"

Elizabeth just looked at him, sadness in her eyes. "Let me do my job, then ask me that again, okay?"

Dylan released her with a sigh. "At least there aren't any more lies between us," he commented. "You can trust me Elizabeth. I hope you know that." His green eyes looked so sincere, but Elizabeth couldn't meet his gaze. She didn't want him to see that the tears were dangerously close to the surface so she busied herself with getting a carry-on bag from the overhead compartment.

They got off the tarmac and headed for the airport terminal. Dylan was surprised at how large and spacious the terminal was. "This must be new. When I was here ten years ago it was completely different."

Elizabeth nodded. "It is. They just finished it a few years back. I like it a lot better now."

They made it to the immigration lines and Elizabeth walked over to a guard sitting at a small desk. Dylan followed. She flashed him a badge and spoke with him for a moment, then he waved them through.

"Should we exchange some money over to drachma?" Dylan asked.

"No, they use the euro now," Elizabeth explained. "I've got enough euros, so don't worry." She walked quickly through the terminal, trying to get around the masses of people. She finally reached back for Dylan's hand. "We need to stay together. I don't want to lose you here."

Dylan raised his eyebrows, and she turned away. Since they had no luggage, only the lone bag that Elizabeth had retrieved, they could bypass the huge lines for the luggage carousel and go immediately to the curb. It was completely congested with cars, taxis, and buses all vying for a space closest to the building. They pushed their way down to the buses and crammed into one already brimming with passengers. There were no seats so they stood holding on to the metal bars descending from the ceiling of the bus. Dylan was trying to shield Elizabeth from the lurching of the bus and being flipped forward. She was grateful because every time she fell into someone they gave her a hard look. It was a very uncomfortable position trying to keep from falling on her face, and constantly being thrown against Dylan. She was sure her face was flaming red by now.

They careened around the highway, the driver seemingly unaware that he was driving a large bus and not a small car as he cut several people off and drove like a madman. When they finally entered the city Elizabeth breathed a sigh of relief. *Maybe the bus driver will slow down a little*, she thought. Suddenly the bus screeched to a halt in the middle of the road and the bus driver opened the doors, screaming in Greek at a retreating car. Elizabeth felt herself falling in slow motion, but before she crashed to the floor, Dylan caught her. "Are you okay?" he asked.

Elizabeth could hardly breathe, Dylan's face just inches from hers, his eyes holding hers captive. Her heart thudded in her chest and the blood roared in her ears. She blinked slowly. "I'm fine," she said, trying to catch her breath. "Sorry."

"It's the bus driver," he cursed softly under his breath. "He almost killed us just because somebody cut him off." He helped Elizabeth to her feet. "Turn this way and I'll stand right behind you and help you keep your balance."

Elizabeth did as she was told, leaning against his steady frame, his strong arms surrounding her. Those feelings of being safe and protected came back, and she closed her eyes for a moment relishing the feeling. He held her so close she could feel his breath on her face and his heartbeat against her back beating in time with her own. It was as if she belonged in his arms and she relaxed. No one had ever made her feel this way. She wanted to be with Dylan, to protect him, not to mention how her insides melted when he looked at her. *But she was on assignment* her head told her. It was impossible.

They stopped in front of several concrete-looking buildings and Elizabeth led the way off the bus and up the hill. Dylan took the bag from her and she smiled gratefully at his thoughtfulness. They zigzagged through a marketplace that was a cacophony of sound with several street musicians playing various instruments, food vendors hawking their wares, and outdoor clothing shops with shirts flapping in the breeze. The tantalizing smell of roasted chestnuts wafted to him and his stomach growled. He held Elizabeth's arm.

"Can we get some?" he asked pointing to the chestnuts. "There's nothing like Greek roasted chestnuts."

Elizabeth smiled and nodded. She got two bags for them and handed one to him. "So you've been to Greece before?"

"Yes," Dylan said between bites. "I was here with my family about ten years ago."

"Tell me about them."

All of Dylan's training came crashing back to him. No personal information was the first rule. *But this was Elizabeth,* he reasoned. *Even with all we've been through, we're on the same side and I feel like I can trust her.*

"I have two sisters," he continued, the internal argument settled. "I think the thing they liked best about Athens was the food. My one sister couldn't stop eating the baklava, and the other loved the souvlaki." He smiled at the memory. "I loved all the history, the archaeological finds. It's just so amazing that so many people lived and died here."

"Yeah," Elizabeth agreed. "It's always made me wonder if there were civilizations like that on this part of the world, couldn't there be something like that in North America and we just haven't found it yet?"

"I read a book that said there was a civilization on the American continent that was swept away," Dylan said cautiously, wondering how much he should really say.

"Oh? What book was that?"

"The Book of Mormon," he said nonchalantly. "Ever heard of it?"

Elizabeth wrinkled her nose. "Are you talking about

Mormons? The ones who have a bunch of wives?"

"Yeah, I'm talking about the Mormons," Dylan said, laughing. "But they don't have a bunch of wives. They're just regular people, like us."

Elizabeth took his arm. "So this book they have tells of an ancient civilization?" She looked at her watch, as if she was in a hurry and only politely listening.

Dylan knew this wasn't the time to talk of sacred things. "Yes, it does. You should read it sometime," was all he said. "Where are we going exactly?"

"We're actually late, so we better get a move on." She quickened her step as she headed toward the neighborhoods. As they walked, Dylan marveled at the small well-kept yards of each house. Elizabeth opened the gate of a little whitewashed home and climbed the small porch steps. The door swung wide and a large man immediately enveloped Elizabeth in a hug.

"Yassou, Beth," he said loudly. "You made it!"

She drew back. "Yassou, Antonis. How are you?"

"I'm fine now that you're here. I was worried." He ushered them both inside. "I'm Antonis Mukakis," he introduced himself, holding his hand out to Dylan.

"I'm Dylan Fields," he replied, feeling safer with his alias for now, until he figured out what was going on. He set the bag down near the door and Antonis ushered them into a small, sparsely furnished living room.

"Dylan's going to be staying with you for a few days," Elizabeth explained. "He just got out of a Zambian prison so be gentle with him."

Antonis crossed his arms in front of his chest. "A Zambian prison, eh?" He clucked his tongue. "Well, don't you worry. You can recover here."

Dylan immediately shook his head. "I'm fine. I have a few things I want to do myself."

Elizabeth motioned for Dylan to sit down on the flowered

camelback sofa. "I need to talk to Antonis for a moment," she said. "You should probably sit down. I'll get you some water."

Doing as he was told, Dylan acted like he was sitting down quietly. But as soon as Elizabeth and Antonis left the room he followed discreetly behind, trying to hear what they were saying.

Elizabeth was speaking in Greek and from his limited understanding she was telling Antonis to keep him busy and away from phones and computers. *Why would she do that?* Dylan wondered. *What's really going on?* He heard the refrigerator opening and went to sit down.

"Okay," Elizabeth said, entering the room. "You are in very capable hands with Antonis. I will be back here in three days after things are squared away with my assignment and we can get you home." She handed him a bottle of water. "Do you need anything else?"

He stood, looking down into her brown eyes which almost seemed to be glowing, his hands on her shoulders. "Don't go. Stay here with me. I don't want you anywhere near Bumani. He's a dangerous man and there's no telling if your cover has been blown or not."

"Don't worry about me," Elizabeth reassured him, touched at his concern. "I'm always careful. You need to worry about yourself and getting well." She flipped her hair over her shoulder. "Besides I've been working closely with Bumani for the last three months. He trusts me."

Dylan snorted. "Bumani doesn't trust anyone, you should know that." She gently touched his sunburned face and was going to say something, but he shrugged off her concern. "I'm fine, a little sunburn never hurt anyone."

"It's more than sunburn and you know it," she said sternly. "Not only did you endure that prison, but you also had a cardio toxin injected into you. It'll take a few days to get over that."

Dylan hugged her, then drew back and rubbed her arms. The warmth of his hands made her shiver. "At least let me help you. Don't leave me here wondering if you're alive or dead. I need to know you're okay."

Elizabeth glanced at Antonis. "I'll make contact as soon as I can, but that's all I can promise." She leaned up and kissed him quickly on the lips. "I'll be fine, don't worry."

"I am worried, especially when I hear you tell someone to keep me away from computers and phones," he said.

Elizabeth's face registered surprise, then broke out into a grin. "I should have known you wouldn't sit down, and I didn't realize you spoke any Greek."

"Not much, but enough to know what you said," he replied. "Tell me what's really going on."

"Nothing, really, it's for your own good," she said, glancing at Antonis. "You need to rest and I was leaving instructions because I knew you wouldn't."

Dylan wanted to believe her and the earnestness of her tone made him think she was telling the truth.

"Don't worry," she reassured him. "Everything will be fine. I'll come back for you in a few days." She turned and gave Antonis a hug, then walked through the door and down the sidewalk they had come up together. Dylan watched her go out the large living room window. He had a feeling in the pit of his stomach that she was walking into a trap.

"She will be fine," Antonis said. "Come, you must be hungry. There is a wonderful Greek tavern not far away with good food you will like. Come."

Dylan did not answer, his eyes were on the woman who was fading farther away down the block. Antonis joined him at the window. "She is a strong woman. Do not worry." Dylan was silent.

Elizabeth could feel his eyes on her and wanted to turn around and run into his arms. But it was a matter of national security and she wouldn't let her country down. All of her personal feelings had to be put aside until her mission was finished.

Chapter Eleven

Dylan followed Antonis past the marketplace and near a small souvlaki shop until a small flight of steps came into view. Antonis led the way down the stairs and it took Dylan's eyes a moment to adjust to the darkness of the basement tavern. Several men sat at a bar, calling for more *ouzo*, a popular Greek beer. Others were gathered around tables. Dylan mopped his brow as it seemed especially hot inside the tavern. Antonis led the way to a table. "Do we need to ask for a menu?" Dylan asked.

"There's no menu here," Antonis replied. "Just look around at what everyone else is eating and tell me what looks good to you, I'll order it for you." He sat down heavily. "It's sort of like a private men's club," he explained. "But the grilled fish here is incredible." He motioned to a large, dark-haired man behind the bar who started toward them. "The owner's name is Spiro, he owns the souvlaki shop next door, which is definitely the best in Athens."

Spiro stopped at their table. "Antonis," he greeted. "Kalispera, how are you?"

"Fine, fine," Antonis said. "We're here for some of your grilled fish and bread." He tilted his head toward Dylan. "Is that what you would like?"

Dylan nodded. "Sure, although I hear you make the best souvlaki in Athens."

Spiro beamed. "Yes, that's true. You must come back again and try some of that."

At that moment two men in the corner started to play on their bouzoukia. Dylan thought the instrument looked like a cross between a banjo and a ukelele, but it's sound was beautiful and haunting. "It's an old Rembetika song," Antonis breathed and slapped the table to the beat. Soon he broke into song with several other patrons. After a few moments the whole tavern was singing. Dylan leaned over. "I'm going to find the bathroom," he said, but doubted Antonis heard him. He slipped away as Antonis walked closer to the bouzoukia players. He found Spiro in the back.

"Hi, I don't speak much Greek. Do you have a telephone here?" he asked.

Spiro nodded, his bushy brows peeking over the rims of his glasses. "We have a public cardphone booth in the back," he jabbed his finger toward the kitchen.

"Efkharisto, thank you," Dylan said, heading for it. He didn't know how much time he had, so he wanted to hurry. He made it to the small kiosk and began dialing in the codes for a secure line. After two rings Andrew Blythe answered. "Andrew what are you doing answering the phone?" Dylan asked.

"Dylan," Andrew sounded relieved. "Where are you? We've been trying to track you for days after you missed your contact at Chirundu. Some even thought . . . well, you know."

"No, I'm not dead. I'm in Athens, Greece. Bumani is here making arrangements to send his new biological weapon to London."

"How did you find that out?"

"I'm here with an American operative."

"Dylan, you be careful. There's a big scandal going on in the intelligence community right now and word is there's a mole. Some big operations have been blown wide open. They haven't caught anyone yet and Bumani is the biggest operation around right now. Can you trust this guy?"

"I don't know, I think so. She seems trustworthy." Dylan looked around. He could still hear the music so Antonis was probably still singing.

"It's a woman!" Andrew exclaimed. "Be extra careful then. Make sure she doesn't pull the honey trap on you."

"Do you think I became an agent yesterday? The honey trap is the oldest one in the book. I could spot that a mile away." Dylan laughed. The honey trap was the name the agents used when a female agent lured information out of someone with her feminine charms. Elizabeth was definitely not like that, but he knew he still had to be careful to not let his personal feelings cloud his judgment.

"Now I'm really worried about you my friend. You should get to the safehouse near Piraeus until we figure this out. I'll make sure there's some money and papers there for you. Until they catch this mole, the whole intelligence community is at risk. Watch yourself."

"I will," Dylan reassured him. "See you at home." He disconnected the call and turned around, almost bumping into Antonis.

"What are you doing?" Antonis said, his voice low.

"Just checking in with my boss," Dylan said, easing around him. "Has our food come yet?"

"Yes, I came to find you." He put his arm around Dylan. "You shouldn't leave my side. Athens can be a very dangerous place." His voice sounded menacing.

"I can take care of myself, Antonis," Dylan shot back evenly. "You shouldn't ever worry about that."

They went back to their table and ate in silence. Antonis had been right about one thing. The grilled fish was incredible. When he was taking his last bite, Dylan noticed a small man come in and lean over the bar to Spiro. He nodded and looked over at Antonis and Dylan, reaching for something under the bar. It made Dylan nervous. "I think it's time to go, Antonis."

Antonis had been watching the door as well. "I agree." They both stood up and headed to the door and up the stairs. As they stepped to the sidewalk, the eerie silence of the previously bustling marketplace met them. It was as if everyone had disappeared and the streetlights had suddenly gone out. The small amount of light left illuminated the sidewalk, and they started walking quickly away from the tavern. When they reached a stand of what looked to Dylan were trees laden with ripe oranges, a man wearing dark clothing, with a hat pulled low over his face moved in front on them. "Yassou," he said. "We need to talk." He tapped a fancy walking stick in his hand and Dylan could see a blade glinting out of the top.

"What would you want to talk about with a weapon like that?" Dylan asked calmly.

Several other men suddenly appeared out of the trees, silently joining them to stand behind the man with the walking stick. "You must know what this is about," the first man said, his words punctuated by the tapping of the walking stick. He moved steadily toward Dylan. Dylan felt Antonis shrinking behind him, moving backward, away from both men.

"Why don't you spell it out for me," Dylan replied, trying to watch Antonis out of the corner of his eye. What was he doing? Had he known this attack was lying in wait?

"Okay," the man with the knife said as he quickly took a swing at Dylan's face with his stick, the blade coming within centimeters of Dylan's cheek. He lunged backward just in time, his attacker smiling as he moved in closer still. "You must be taken care of so the weapon can be safely delivered." He swung again, but Dylan ducked and came up fast, punching the man in the face before he could raise his arm again.

"What weapon?" Dylan said, his breath coming hard, looking down at the man who was still on his back. He leaned down to confiscate the blade, but his attacker quickly jumped to his feet. Dylan backed up calling out for Antonis. "I could use some help here!" The other men had surrounded the two fighters and Dylan knew Antonis was gone.

Dylan successfully avoided two more swings with the walking stick, but not the third. It grazed his shoulder, cutting the fabric through to his skin. Dylan held the wound as he came around with his feet, landing a hard kick to the face. His opponent fell backward, but regained his footing. He nodded to his companions and the other men grabbed Dylan and held him fast. The blade from the walking stick was held to his throat, the man coming close to his face. Dylan squinted in the darkness, trying to make out his features in the shadows. "Who are you?" Dylan asked. "At least let me know who I'm up against."

At Dylan's words his opponent backed away, seemingly melting into the safety and darkness provided by the trees. "You are no match for us," he hissed. He tilted his head to the man on his right who proceeded to take his revenge on Dylan's ribs.

The punches were punctuated by the tapping of the walking stick in the owner's hand. "When the government of the United States is begging for mercy, their puppet governments around the world will bow to us," the man said between punches. He reached down and picked up his hat, dusting it off and returning it to his head.

Dylan watched him through the haze of pain, trying to notice any identifying marks or movements, but couldn't place him. Struggling to free himself, he tried to shake off the blows, but Dylan was still weak from his prison experience. Just when he thought he would pass out he heard a gunshot.

"That's enough," Spiro shouted, holding a gun high over his head. "I have called the police, they will be here any moment." The men turned back to the leader, watching for his reaction. He nodded and the men started to disappear.

The leader leveled a finger at Dylan. "This isn't over yet," he said, before he also disappeared.

Dylan sank to the concrete holding his ribs. They felt like they were on fire and he could hardly breathe. He could feel that at least one rib was broken, maybe more. Spiro stood over him. "You should leave, now."

Closing his eyes, Dylan nodded his head. "I plan to, as soon as I can catch my breath."

Both men heard the sirens approaching. "Hurry," Spiro said simply, shoving some money into Dylan's hand before going back in the direction of the tavern.

"Thank you," Dylan called as he staggered to his feet and walked quickly away toward the metro station he'd seen earlier. Hopefully he could catch a train to Piraeus and get to the safehouse. He could get the money and papers Andrew had left for him, and go find Elizabeth. His stomach wrenched with fear as he realized they had obviously been betrayed by Antonis. If those were Bumani's men and they had found Dylan, chances were they knew of Elizabeth's rescue of him and she would be in danger. His gut was telling him he needed to get her out of there.

Chapter Twelve

Elizabeth sat across the dinner table from Jimon Bumani. *He really is an attractive man,* she thought to herself. His dark skin contrasted with the light green shirt he was wearing open at the neck. His black hair was tightly curled and matched his eyes, like two coals burning into her eyes whenever he looked at her. He was definitely an intense person. But his exterior was marred by the fact that she knew his heart was evil. She shifted her thoughts and tried to concentrate on the task at hand.

"The warehouse is ready for the shipment and everything you asked for is in place," she said, taking a bite of salad. The slightly sour taste of spices, oil, and vinegar in a Greek salad was like nothing else in the world. Her taste buds savored the incredible flavor and she resisted the urge to run her tongue over her teeth to get the last taste. No one could make salads like the Greeks. The flavor and color were inviting from the first bite to the last.

Bumani waved his hand. "I do not want to talk business tonight, Elizabeth. I want to talk about you." He leaned over the table and took her hand. "You look beautiful tonight. That dress suits you perfectly."

Elizabeth looked down at her gown. She'd been surprised when Bumani had told her to meet him on the Mytilini ferry and to bring an evening dress. It had seemed an odd request at the time. She'd hastily found a deep sapphire blue gown that scooped at the neckline, and was fitted to the waist but flared out at the legs. She had accessorized with a gold-colored scarf around her neck. The satin feel of it, combined with her freshly washed hair and a light touch of makeup, had given her confidence for the meeting tonight.

"I'm glad you like it," she replied, demurely. "But we can't talk about me all night. I'm curious about your project. Is everything in place? When does it arrive in Athens?"

"So many questions," he said as he bent to kiss her hand. His eyes bored through hers. "Why do you want to know?"

Elizabeth backed off. She didn't want to blow her cover now. "Just a woman's curiosity," she said casually, taking another bite. "We can talk about something else if you'd like."

"I'd like to know more about you Elizabeth Spencer," he said, leaning back in his seat and taking a small bite of salad.

"There's not much to tell. I'm a small town girl, just wanting to make a difference in the world. That's why I became an aid worker," she said smoothly, her rehearsed cover slipping easily out of her mouth.

Bumani said nothing, watching her. She was beginning to feel as if she was a mouse in a maze that had just been cornered and was being watched by a cat. "What about you, Jimon? What motivates a man like you?"

He captured her eyes and held them. Elizabeth squelched a repulsive shiver at being under his gaze. "My parents were killed when I was four and I was sent to live with my grandparents. I was recruited to the rebel cause at thirteen when men came to my village and rounded up all the men and boys. The elderly, women, and girls were shot before our eyes, including my grandparents and we were taken to a training facility in the desert."

Jimon casually took a bite as if he was telling Elizabeth what the weather forecast was going to be. "I have fought against tyranny my whole life, waiting for my chance to rule, to show my capabilities. I had to fight my way up the ladder in the army until I was the leader in a kill-or-be-killed world.

Now that I am established I fight for the rights of others who were oppressed like me, against the world that either does not care or takes advantage of them." He spread his arms wide. "My empire is vast, my army is strong. The world and the United States," he spat, "everyone that exercises tyrannical rule over the freedoms of those who fight for the cause—my less fortunate brothers-in-arms—will listen now."

Elizabeth resisted the urge to ask how exactly he was going to carry out his plan. She could feel his suspicion of her growing. She smiled. "I'm sure everyone will listen, Jimon."

The waiter came into the room and set down several different seafood dishes, including squid and octopus. Elizabeth closed her eyes briefly. The squid's legs were arranged so that those at the table could cut a piece off. It did not look appetizing to her, but Jimon was already cutting himself a piece. He motioned to her. "Cut yourself a piece and I will tell you how I will make the world listen to me."

She smiled weakly and began to cut. Taking a small bite, she kept saying to herself, "It tastes like chicken, it tastes like chicken," as the rubbery squid slipped down her throat. *I'm sacrificing so I can hear his plan*, she thought. Taking a drink, she washed the rest of it down. "I'd love to hear what you're going to do, Jimon. And know how I can help," she added.

"I knew you were sympathetic to my cause," he said, wiping his mouth with a napkin as he stood and moved around the table to be next to her. "You have enjoyed your time in Africa, have you not?"

Elizabeth nodded, wondering where this was going.

"And you want to help me liberate my countrymen from the starvation and oppression they have suffered preventing them from taking their rightful place on the world's stage?"

Elizabeth nodded again as he took her arm to help her up. "Let's take a walk on the deck under the stars. I want to see your face in the moonlight," he said. "Join me, please." He opened his dinner jacket and showed her a document sticking out from the inside pocket. "I have the plans with me tonight, but I want time to know you better before we discuss the final phases. We will spend the evening together, enjoying one another's company."

Elizabeth knew she didn't have a choice. It was not a request. There was something different about Jimon tonight and she could feel that something was wrong. She couldn't pinpoint it, so she pasted a smile on and nodded her head. She had to be prepared for anything.

>—◦—◦—◦—◦—◦—<

Dylan opened the door to the safe house and almost collapsed on the small couch just inside the door. His chest felt as though it were on fire. He lay there for a moment, then staggered into the bathroom. He turned on the light and caught a glimpse of himself in the mirror. Fading bruises, and healing cuts dotted his face. He ran his hand through his hair that was so much longer than normal. It just wasn't him, the person that he wanted to be, that was staring at him in the mirror. But he didn't have time to think about that now. He had to get to Elizabeth. If Antonis had betrayed them, then Bumani probably knew the plan and Elizabeth was in extreme danger. No matter where their personal relationship was, or perhaps because of their personal relationship, he couldn't stand by and watch her be hurt. He said a small prayer in his heart, asking Heavenly Father to keep her safe, to keep his instincts sharp, and the Spirit close to him.

He turned on the shower, the water pressure hardly more than a trickle, shedding his clothes and climbing in to wash off some of the grime of the last few days. It was difficult as he could barely raise his arms above his head without experiencing excruciating pain. The bruising around his ribs was already purple and angry-looking. He finished as quickly as he could, going into the bedroom and rummaging through the dresser drawers looking for a shirt and pants his size. When he found a gray button-down shirt and some jeans, he returned to the bathroom. Opening the bathroom cabinet he found bandages and medical tape. He bandaged the cut on his arm, and then taped his rib cage as best he could, alleviating the pain somewhat. He dressed carefully, easing the shirt over his ribs without too much movement on his part. When he was finished he went to the refrigerator and took out the money and papers that were wrapped in the freezer.

Turning off the lights, he heard a knock at the door and froze. He opened the top drawer in the kitchen where firearms were kept and drew out a gun. Making the weapon ready, he crept forward to the door. After a few moments a knock came again, this time the agent's code of one knock, pause, then four more knocks, pause, then two final knocks. Dylan looked through the window before opening the door. "What are you doing here?" he asked.

Andrew Blythe stood before him, his pepper-gray hair pasted to his head from sweat as if he'd been running. He came inside, his breathing heavy, proving Dylan's assumption correct. "After I talked to you on the phone, I figured you could use some help so I hopped the first plane here." He moved into the kitchen and got himself a bottle of water out of the fridge, which he drank in one gulp. "I was close by in Spain so it wasn't too much trouble."

"I've got it under control, Andrew. Were you running?"

"I'm sure you're in control." He nodded to Dylan as he moved back into the living room and sat down on the small couch where Dylan had laid not too long before. "I had to jog the last few blocks here and got turned around. I was worried about you, especially when I heard there was a woman involved so I came to make sure . . ."

"I can handle myself," Dylan said, chuckling. "I've been doing this a long time." He sat down on a chair opposite Andrew. "What's the real reason?"

Andrew's face clouded. "Something big is going down, Dylan. It's all over the network. We have all sorts of informants coming out of the woodwork to warn us of a big attack, and instead of concentrating on that, we're worrying about the investigation into the intelligence community for a mole."

"Do they have an idea who it could be?"

"Not that I know of," Andrew said rubbing his hands together. "Is it cold in here to you?"

"No, but I'm hardly ever cold," Dylan said. "Are you working with the Americans on this?"

"Everyone's pointing fingers at everyone else, it's a mess." Andrew sighed. "But Bumani is the biggest operation right now and I have this gut feeling that the mole is tied to Bumani somehow. He's a very dangerous man." Andrew looked intently at Dylan. "Could this agent you've been working with be the mole? Is there any possibility at all?"

Dylan thought of Elizabeth, his heart saying no, but his head considering it. After quickly analyzing what he knew of her he didn't think so. He thought of her with Bumani, especially if her cover had been blown and his stomach tightened. *If he hurt her . . .* He couldn't think that way. He had to stay focused. "No, no way. Elizabeth is not the mole, but she's in danger. I've got to make a plan." He drew a small canister from his pocket, fingering it as if reluctant to let it go. "Here's the evidence I collected in Uganda." He rolled it around in his hand. "I took a few beatings for this, so keep it safe will you?"

Andrew took the film from him and clenched it. "I will. I guess we can safely say the threat assessment is completed and should be considered high risk?"

Dylan nodded. "The pictures show the crates that the biological weapon came in as well as the radioactive gear they were using."

Andrew fingered the canister, then gave a grim sigh. "The director of National Defense is aware of the situation, and is waiting on our next briefing. I downloaded the latest information on Bumani before I left. We tracked him to a ferry and we're going to join him there and see what we can find out." He stood. "We've got to hurry though. The ship leaves within the hour."

Dylan was already ahead of him, out the door. "Let's go."

They made it to the main port in about ten minutes. All that was standing between them and the ship was a busy road which took another ten minutes to cross. "We're lucky we weren't killed," Andrew huffed. "That light said walk just long enough for us to get into the middle of the street. I thought for sure that bus was going to hit us."

"You should have seen the look on your face," Dylan chuckled. "Traffic here is definitely not like Canada. And with no crosswalks, pedestrians have no rights in Greece." He looked down toward the docks. "That's probably why they have that little traffic island for all the people who didn't quite make it across."

Andrew caught up with Dylan's long strides as they started toward the boats. "Bumani is on the Mytilini, so we'll have to go around," he said between breaths. "These boats are going to the Saronic gulf islands." They passed several small harbor shops and Andrew stopped in front of one window, shaking his head. "Look at this."

Dylan stood with him looking at the uzis and assault weapons on display along with some other heavy weaponry. "It still stuns me that you can just buy that on the street," he said sadly. "Do you think we are fighting a losing battle? All this is accessible to terrorists or anyone else that has a grudge."

"If we don't fight against it, who will?" Andrew shrugged. "Someone has to take a stand."

"It's so frustrating." Dylan started walking again. "I don't think I can do this anymore."

Andrew fell into step beside him. "What do you mean?"

"I think I'm ready to get out of the service and have a normal life," Dylan stated flatly. "I hope you understand what

I'm saying. I don't feel I'm supposed to do this for the rest of my life."

Andrew shoved his hands into his pockets. "What else would you do?"

"Get married, have a family, maybe teach, I don't know. I'm ready to explore my options."

"Yeah, I sort of had a feeling that's where you might be headed. Especially after you were shot. You've been different these last few months."

"My life is changing," Dylan admitted. "I found something incredible that changed my life, and I want to pursue it." They had walked by several shipping company offices and now were passing some strip clubs. Dylan looked away, embarrassed by even the advertisements of what was inside.

"What did you find?"

Dylan paused, wondering how he should tell his friend, his mentor, hoping he would take it well. "I joined the Church of Jesus Christ of Latter-day Saints," he blurted out quickly.

Andrew didn't miss a beat. "When? Why didn't you tell me?"

"I don't know, it never seemed like the right time. You were out of the country." He felt silly about telling Andrew now. They'd reached the end of Akti Miaouli, the street bordering the harbor. "It was because of you, though. I liked how you talked about Emma joining and how the church hadn't changed her, but rather added to what was already inside her. That's what I wanted. Something that would make better what I'd already been trying to do as a person."

Andrew looked thoughtful. "Emma got married in the Mormon temple last year and seems really happy. They're expecting a baby in a few months."

"Congratulations," Dylan slapped him on the back, remembering the pictures Andrew had shown him of his family. "I'm so happy things worked out for Emma. How's Julia taking it?" Julia was Emma's daughter from her first marriage.

"So far, so good. You know I don't get to talk to them all that much."

"That's what I'm talking about. I want to have a normal job that I come home from every night. I just need a new direction in my life." He started down the hill that led to the boats. "After this mission, I'm getting out."

"And I'll support you in it," Andrew said adamantly. "You should know I'd support you in anything you do. You've been like a son to me."

Dylan smiled back. "I know. I'm grateful to you Andrew. I guess I didn't want you to ever be disappointed in me or think that I was weak for leaving the service."

"Couldn't happen," Andrew said gruffly, slapping Dylan's back. "I just want you to be happy." He stared up at the ferry before them. "Here's the Mytilini." They quickly went into the ferry office and bought tickets, boarding the ship shortly before it launched.

Dylan was surprised at how modern the ferry was inside. The carpet looked new, it was air-conditioned and had several lounges, restaurants and even an arcade. His stomach growled at the buffet laid out in the restaurant. From where he was standing he could see several plates with gyros, souvlaki, falafel, salads and bread. But they didn't have time to eat. "Where are we going?" he asked.

"Lesvos," Andrew replied. "We should get there around eight o'clock tomorrow morning. I got us a cabin with a window and a television, but I don't think we'll be spending much time in it." He fished some notes out of his pocket. "Bumani has a private suite at the other end of the ferry, but I'm not sure exactly where so we'll need to find him right away."

A crew member stopped them and asked if they needed help. Andrew shook his head and the young man made sure they knew they could ask him for anything. "I've heard about this crew," Andrew commented. "They're mostly from Lesvos where the ferry is based and are known for being extra friendly and helpful. We might be able to use that in locating Bumani."

Dylan had stopped listening. Looking across the room into the lounge, he stared right into the eyes of David Kanu.

Chapter Thirteen

Dylan grabbed Andrew's arm. "There's one of Bumani's men. I know him from the hospital. Let me go talk to him, and you run back up."

Andrew nodded and circled around the lounge.

Dylan crossed the large foyer and went into the lounge, making note of the three exits and four people sitting at various tables. Agency training made doing so a habit that he hardly thought about anymore. He sat down next to David and ordered a club soda from the bartender. "Hello, David. Where's Elizabeth?"

David glanced at him sideways. Sweat dotted his forehead and he looked very pale. "She's with Bumani. I tried to get to her, but they're heavily guarded." He took his napkin and blotted the sweat from his upper lip.

"What's wrong? Are you sick?"

"I'm infected with Tracin," David said, his voice devoid of emotion.

Dylan steeled himself not to back away from him. "When? How did this happen?"

David took a long drink. "Bumani thought he recognized Elizabeth at the prison helping you escape. He knew if it was her that I had somehow helped you. He used me as his guinea pig in your place." David looked at Dylan, then silently held out his hands, which were deeply bruised. "The rest of my body looks the same," he said. "Bumani only stopped torturing me when I broke." His voice started to tremble. "I admitted that

117

it was Elizabeth who had helped you escape." He bowed his head, obviously ashamed. "He was so angry when he realized Elizabeth had betrayed him. I need to warn her that he knows." He closed his eyes. "I never should have let her go to you."

Dylan's mind was racing. His suspicions were correct—Bumani had Elizabeth and knew she had betrayed him, He had to get her out of there immediately before she was killed. "How are you planning to warn Elizabeth?" he asked urgently.

"We have a pre-arranged check in time which is in half an hour," David murmured. "We have earpiece communication." He slowly opened his wounded hand to show Dylan the small earpiece.

"Are you contagious?" Dylan asked. "Shouldn't we try to get you off this ship?"

"Apparently I become contagious 24 hours after infection unless I die first. Then I can't infect anyone," David explained. "Once the virus is introduced to a host it matures in 24 hours and then is able to be passed to others. Death to the carrier is certain soon after it becomes contagious. I've got an hour left. After I warn Elizabeth, then I can take matters into my own hands so innocent people won't get hurt." He swirled the ice cubes around in his drink. "The feelings Elizabeth has for you put us all in danger and may get her killed. If you just could have left her alone to do her job . . ."

Dylan leaned over the bar. "I'm going to get her out of this. I need you to trust me."

"You don't even know what you're really dealing with," David almost sneered. He leaned close to Dylan. "Bumani is going to deliver Tracin to the United States and plans to infect an entire city. When they become contagious it will spread across the United States like wildfire. Then he will be the person holding all the cards, since he is the only one who has the antidote."

"Elizabeth said the shipment was going to London. How will it be delivered to the States after it leaves London?"

David shook his head. "Not London, England. London, Ontario, Canada." As soon as he finished speaking, Dylan heard a pop, and David looked wide-eyed as if he was completely surprised, then slumped forward onto Dylan's shoulder.

He pushed him upright. "David?" A small bloodstain was forming on the front of David's shirt. He'd been shot! Dylan laid him gently on the bar and the earpiece fell out of his hand. Dylan picked it up and signaled to the bartender. "We need a doctor here. Something's wrong." He saw Andrew struggling with someone near the back of the room and was at his side in moments.

"Let's get out of here," Andrew hissed in his ear, trying to subdue the woman he held in front of him as the bartender shouted for help and motioned toward them.

Dylan helped him hold the writhing woman between them and followed Andrew to their room as the lounge erupted with activity. "Is she the shooter?" Dylan asked as they walked briskly down the hall, holding her arms.

"Yes." He stopped and pulled off the dark wig as the woman stood calmly before them. "Dylan, I'd like to you meet Sam Fowler. She's old agency like me. Been on the force a long time. And she has some explaining to do."

The woman turned toward Dylan, standing almost as tall as he was. Her hair was pulled back into a tight bun because of the wig, but in the light it looked to be a bright red color. High color in her cheeks marred her normally fair skin. She stood mute between them, her face impassive. "Well at least she stopped struggling," Dylan commented.

They got to their room without incident and sat at the small table. Andrew sat across from Sam and Dylan flanked her. "What's going on, Sam? What are we up against here?'

She stared back at him, saying nothing. Andrew slapped the table. "There's a terrorist on this boat making plans to kill thousands of people. Start talking!"

"It's not a boat, it's a ferry," she said, her voice low.

Andrew rubbed his neck. "Very funny. You know me, Sam. I thought I knew you. What's going on here?"

"I'm on a deep cover assignment just like you. I had to prove my loyalty to Bumani so I did. He needs a pilot for his plane and I fit the bill. This was the final test." She took a deep breath. "It killed me to have to do that, but David was going to die a horrible death anyway," she said softly. "It's a small price to pay to find out what Bumani's really up to," she said. "He plans to kill a lot of people. I need to find out how."

"We already know he's going to deliver Tracin to the United States through Canada. How is he going to do it?" Dylan asked.

"I don't know," she said angrily. "I haven't seen any of the flight plans. You've got to let me go so I can get back to Jimon. He'll suspect something and then everything I've worked for will be ruined."

Dylan looked at his watch. "I've got to go," he said to Andrew. "We've only got a small window of time here. Are you okay here or are we all three going?" He noticed Andrew watching Sam and wondered what he was thinking. *How well did they know each other?* he wondered.

"Yeah, I'm okay here. I know Sam, and if she says she's undercover, then I believe her. Are you going to try to warn Elizabeth?" Andrew asked. "Bumani will take the first chance he gets and take care of all his loose ends." He took Dylan aside and led him to the front of the room. He pulled out a plastic bag. "You need to get ready. You can't go out like that now." He shoved the bag into Dylan's hands. "That guy told you the weapon is going through Canada to the United States?"

"Yeah," Dylan nodded. "He said the Tracin shipment is going to London, Ontario, and Bumani plans to get it across the border to infect a city and eventually all of the United States when people become contagious. Then he'll blackmail the government with the antidote. He was trying to warn Elizabeth that Bumani knows about her."

Andrew looked over at Sam, who was looking sullenly at them. "Do you think we can trust her?"

Dylan followed his gaze and shrugged. "You're asking me? Wasn't it you who taught me never to trust anyone?" He started to take a few things out of the bag. "There's no way we can check her story right now. If your gut says you can trust her, then go with it. If you have even a hint of doubt, don't let her out of your sight."

"Yeah," Andrew replied, his eyes tired and suddenly sad. "I've never seen you so anxious to help out another agent. She must be pretty special." He paused, looking hard at Dylan. "Go get Elizabeth out of there, but be careful. Don't let your heart rule your head. I don't want to waste years of agency training." Andrew clapped his shoulder and went back to sit by Sam.

When Dylan emerged from the bathroom, his hair was buzzed short, he had blue contact lenses, and a moustache. "How do I look?"

"Like you won't be recognized." Andrew traded him places. "Good luck. What's the game plan?"

Dylan showed him the earpiece. "Elizabeth has a check in within a few minutes. I can warn her then and get her out of there. Maybe she'll know more about Bumani's plans."

"We'll talk more when you get back." Andrew looked at Sam and lowered his voice. "I want to believe her, you know. She was one of the best agents out there in her day. It's inconceivable that she would change sides."

"Be careful, my friend," Dylan warned, opening the door. "Don't let your heart rule your head," he said, giving Andrew back his own advice. Andrew nodded to him and closed the door softly.

He walked up onto the deck and spotted Elizabeth and Bumani strolling near the railings. Her scarf was blowing in the breeze, her hair clipped to the back of her head, and Bumani held her arm. "There they are," he whispered to himself. He tried to calm his surging adrenaline and assess the situation. At least she appeared to be okay and he was there to watch her back. There were four guards total, two in front and two in the back of them. He kept her within his line of sight, noticing how Bumani couldn't keep his eyes off of her. Dylan watched intently, partly wishing he could be closer to hear the conversation and partly wishing he wasn't there at all to see them being cozy.

>─<◆>─◦─<◆>─<

Bumani brought her hand up to his lips and kissed it gently, while Elizabeth smiled coyly at him, trying as bravely as she could to keep her repulsion in check. She turned to the railing, watching the last rays of sunshine bounce off the magnificent blue of the Mediterranean Sea. She'd never seen such a brilliant blue in an ocean before. The wind whipped her scarf and the small tendrils of hair around her face, and she tasted a faint salt spray on her lips. The air was crisp, and playful gulls were in the waves near the shore calling to one another. It was exhilarating. But still she had a sense of foreboding and her heart began to pound in her ears. She had to be on guard, her danger antennae in full gear.

"Beautiful isn't it?" Jimon commented softly as he moved behind her and enveloped her in his arms. He took the wildly flying scarf and slowly unraveled it, the silky feel of it brushing across her throat. When it was free, he put it in front of her face and slid it backwards around her neck, using it as leverage to turn her in his arms. It didn't hurt her, but it did feel a little scary having a terrorist with a scarf tight around her throat.

Elizabeth willed herself to be calm. "There's nothing like it in the world." She turned in his embrace as he obviously wanted her to do, and he pressed his body close to hers. "Jimon," she breathed. "I need to go freshen up."

He bent to kiss her. "You look fine to me."

She pushed him gently away. "I'll be back in a moment and we can pick up where we left off."

He reluctantly let her go. "I'll wait here for you. Hurry

back," he said as he brushed a tendril of hair away from her face. "I'm looking forward to dancing on the deck with you tonight," he said quietly as he turned her face toward him, and kissed her.

Elizabeth closed her eyes, trying to think of Dylan kissing her, not Jimon Bumani. Dylan had awakened so many feelings in her that she had long since buried. She was having a hard time concentrating, but knew if she didn't get hold of her emotions she would get herself killed. Feelings in this business were an unwanted commodity. Yet it was so easy to compare Dylan's sensitive, sweet kisses to Jimon's forceful ones as if he was to possess her simply with his kiss. *The point is, you shouldn't be thinking of Dylan at all*, she reminded herself. "I'll be right back," she promised, planning to splash her face with cold water and get this job done as quickly as possible.

"Lizige will accompany you," Jimon ordered. "We wouldn't want you getting lost on this big ship."

Elizabeth nodded, but her stomach sank. She'd wanted to be alone for a few moments and gather her thoughts before checking in with David. At least Lizige couldn't accompany her into the ladies' room. She couldn't wait to talk to David and reassure herself that he was all right.

As soon as she got to the bathroom, she ran the water in the sink, took the earpiece out of her bag and put it in. "David, are you there?"

After a moment's hesitation, Dylan spoke. "Elizabeth, it's me, Dylan. David's dead and Bumani knows who you are. You need to get out of there now."

Elizabeth closed her eyes. She'd felt like something was wrong all night. "David's really dead?" she croaked. "How? Did he make it out of that prison?"

"Yes," Dylan said softly. "I'm sorry. He was here on the ferry trying to tell you that you were recognized at the prison and his cover was blown, but he couldn't get through Bumani's guards. He was waiting for your regular check in when I found him in the lounge. He was able to tell me Bumani infected him with Tracin in my place, and then he was shot and killed."

"Did he suffer?" she managed, her emotions raw. "Was he tortured?" It was her fault David's cover had been blown. The guilt washed over her. David had been a friend to her and she keenly felt his loss.

"Let's get you out of there and talk about this later. I'll meet you downstairs," Dylan said, his voice urgent.

"Okay, but this isn't going to be easy. Bumani has guards escorting me everywhere. Obviously he's not willing to chance that I'll escape." She turned off the water. "I think I can still get the final plan out of him. Bumani's been hinting around at telling me all night, practically taunting me with it. He's carrying the final flight plans with him, maybe I could steal them or at least get a glimpse of them. As soon as I have that I could go back to my cabin." Her voice gained strength. "Without that information David died in vain and all our work is for nothing." She turned off the water and adjusted her gown. "I have to go. As soon as I can get away I will. What room are you in?"

"I'm here with my boss, Andrew Blythe. We're in Room 818," he said quickly. "Bumani's not going to tell you anything Elizabeth. He knows you're agency. Let me come and get you right now."

"No, I can do this. I can convince him I'm still loyal to the cause, and if I can't, I'll just steal those plans," Elizabeth countered. "Don't worry, I can take care of myself." She could hear his frustrated sigh, but was still determined that she could do this.

"I'll watch your back," Dylan promised. "Be careful, Elizabeth."

"I will," she said softly. She opened the door and Lizige was there.

"Is everything all right?" he asked, his eyes traveling down her frame.

"Fine," she answered and brushed by him. Jimon was waiting for her precisely where she'd left him. The hairs on her neck stood on end as she approached him, knowing he knew her true identity and probably had plans to kill her.

"Would you give me the pleasure and dance with me?" he asked.

"I'd be delighted," Elizabeth lied, looking into his eyes and seeing only hardness there.

He gently guided her to the middle of the deck and as if by magic, three bouzouki players emerged and began playing.

Dylan watched intently as Bumani held her, his hand on her waist, her hand in his, as he swirled her expertly around the deck. Elizabeth played her part well, not giving away that she knew she was in danger. Dylan had to admit she was a good agent. Foolhardy maybe, but good. She was smiling and laughing at what he assumed or hoped was polite chatter. How well did they know each other? And how far would she go to steal those plans?

As soon as the thought crossed his mind, he urged it to leave. He had to stay focused on the mission at hand and keeping her safe. But this whole ordeal was starting to feel like a nightmare that was continuing in slow motion. Here was Elizabeth, someone he had begun to care deeply about, looking more alluring in that gown than he ever remembered her in her cargo pants and white shirt at the hospital, dancing with a dangerous terrorist who was bent on killing as many people as possible, and probably had his own torturous plans for her. To make matters worse, he was having to watch, wishing it was him holding her close and dancing under the stars in the Mediterranean sea.

Finally he willed himself to move closer as they stopped dancing and sat on a small bench near the railing. What was she doing? Was she okay?

Elizabeth knew Dylan was watching her, and it comforted her and made her nervous at the same time. Bumani sat next to her with his arm ever so comfortably resting across her shoulder. She wondered what he had planned for her demise. He was gently caressing the exposed skin on her neck and trailing his fingers ever so slightly down her shoulders. Elizabeth was concentrating on her breathing. This could truly have been a romantic moment if she were here with Dylan. She turned in Jimon's arms, knowing she only had a short amount of time to find out his plan before her life would be forfeited.

"Is there anything else we can do to prepare for the airplane, Jimon? I know you told me we're flying out of Lesvos tomorrow morning. Maybe you should show me the flight plans so I can prepare everything for you."

His eyes narrowed. "It's much too warm out here, my dear Elizabeth. Let's go back inside. Perhaps you would care for a drink?" Jimon suggested. "Then we can talk more about the future and my plans."

Elizabeth stood and turned to head for the door, but as she did he reached down and captured her face in his warm hands. He kissed her hard, with enough intensity that she knew he wanted more.

"I'd really like that drink now," Elizabeth said, as she broke off the kiss none too soon for herself, yet way too soon for Bumani.

His lips twisted into a smile, almost sneering at her obvious discomfort, as he led her back inside the lounge area, stopping to whisper to Lizige and shake hands with the bouzouki players. They finally made it to the bar, and Bumani ordered her a drink. "What's wrong Elizabeth? You seem tense."

Elizabeth smiled, knowing it was a game of words now. "I'm nervous, Jimon." She wasn't lying. "You're a powerful man."

His chest puffed up at her words. "You should fear me, Elizabeth. I am a powerful man." He leaned closer to her. "I would like nothing more than to spend the entire evening with you alone. To get to know you better."

"Jimon, you know all there is to know about me. I want to

know about you," she said as sweetly as she could muster, her hand at her neck.

Dylan watched from the corner of the room as Bumani led her to the bar. He noticed that Bumani had pulled Elizabeth in closer to him, and watched as his hand caressed her back and he placed soft kisses in her hair as they sat down. He wondered what they were talking about and why it was taking her so long to get away from this man. He watched the wandering hands on Elizabeth's back and he clenched his fists, feeling his face redden with anger. He wanted nothing more than to deck this man—to rush in and save the woman he cared about. But he stayed where he was, watching and waiting.

With Jimon's hand wandering over her exposed flesh at her back, Elizabeth's feeling of foreboding grew stronger. She knew now she wasn't going to get anywhere with Bumani, that he was only playing with her and in this game she would lose. "I think I need to cut the evening short and get some sleep, Jimon," Elizabeth said softly, wishing she'd taken Dylan's advice and gotten away when she'd had that small window of opportunity.

He nuzzled her neck. "The night is still young my dear. We have plenty of time for sleeping. I thought you wanted to discuss my future plans."

"But we're getting up early to transfer the toxin to the plane. I want to be ready." She pulled away gently. "We wouldn't want anything to go wrong now."

Bumani straightened. "You're right. You will see my future plans soon and there is no need to rush. I will see you bright and early in the morning." He snapped his fingers and Lizige appeared at his side. "Lizige, Elizabeth is tired and wants to return to her cabin. Please escort her there." He uttered a Lugandan phrase and Elizabeth thought that it meant, "You know what to do." He flicked his hand and turned toward the bar as if he was finished with her.

Lizige nodded, a small smile on his lips. He looked at her

and Elizabeth's blood ran chill. That was the order. He was being told to kill her, she just knew it. Her entire body tensed. His eyes were hard as flint, watching her, knowing what he had to do. "Jimon, I don't need anyone to escort me. I know my way around the ship. Just let me go, please?" she asked, tilting her head to look at him, desperately hoping she was wrong, but knowing that she wasn't.

He barely looked at her. "I wanted to spend more time with you. But as you said, Elizabeth, we need to be ready for tomorrow and we don't want *anything* to go wrong. Lizige will escort you," he said with finality. "I'll see you tomorrow." He turned back to his drink and Lizige held out his arm to her. She had no choice but to take it.

They walked slowly down the hall, the door to her cabin looming closer and closer. Lizige seemed to quicken his step and Elizabeth steeled herself. She would not go easily.

Chapter Fourteen

Dylan followed carefully behind, wondering if they were calling it a night and Lizige was escorting her to her room since they were going below deck. He was a little relieved it wasn't Bumani taking Elizabeth to her cabin, but Lizige looked like he was up to no good. They had quickened their step, Lizige gripping Elizabeth's arm. Dylan was almost running to keep up with them, worried now. He turned down the hall, cursing himself for not asking Elizabeth what room she was in. As he turned the corner, the hall was empty and he had no idea which room they could be in. He started down the hall, listening carefully. He didn't have to wait long. He heard Elizabeth scream and within seconds Lizige was in the hall crouching over as if in pain. For a moment, Dylan wondered if Lizige had been shot or something.

"Hey!" Dylan shouted, and then ducked as Lizige straightened and pulled a gun to shoot in his direction.

Dylan popped back up quickly, but Lizige was disappearing around a corner and had opened the heavy, creaking door to the stairway. Dylan made the decision to let him go, and ran toward Elizabeth's room.

"Elizabeth!"

"I'm here," she called.

He found her in the bathroom, the water running into the small sink, and she was trying to splash water in her eyes. "I'm trying to flush out the spray," she explained, then jumped when she saw him. "Dylan?"

129

Dylan remembered his disguise. "Don't worry, it's me. What happened?"

She grabbed a towel and began dabbing at her eyes. Dylan led her to a chair, his arm supporting her. "I was expecting a physical attack and was priming myself for it, but he sort of maced me instead." She tried to open her eyes which were red and puffy. "I got in one well-placed kick that probably really hurt with the heels I'm wearing," she smiled faintly, but it faded. "It was more than likely Tracin that he sprayed me with," she said quietly.

Dylan felt like slamming his fist into the counter, but held her close instead, stroking her hair. "If only I could have been sooner," he cursed softly under his breath. "What do you know about Tracin? What's the antidote?"

"Bumani carries the only antidote on his person at all times," Elizabeth groaned. "How could I have been so stupid? Of course he would want to eliminate me since I know so much."

Dylan clicked on his watch, activating the stopwatch to read twenty-four hours and the countdown began. Passengers coming down the hall were looking through the open door at them and Dylan helped Elizabeth to her feet. "Let's get out of here in case he decides to come back."

She looked up into Dylan's eyes through her own puffy ones. "I'm sorry I didn't listen to you and get out of there when I had the chance."

He pulled her into the hall. "You were doing what you thought was right. Did you get the final plans?"

"No, he didn't want to talk, if you know what I mean. It was painfully obvious I wasn't going to get anything out of him. I'd had this weird feeling all night that something wasn't right, but I thought I could handle it and get those plans so David didn't die in vain."

Dylan reached for her hand as they walked quickly down the small hallway. "We've got to get you somewhere safe." He pulled her into the stairwell, checking above and below them for anyone on the stairs. It was empty. "Bumani is a dangerous man. David knew he was going to hurt you and had been trying desperately to reach you. He was worried about you."

Elizabeth turned to face him. "David is a hero to me," she said softly. "You said he was infected with Tracin."

Dylan closed his eyes momentarily. "Yes, in my place."

"You can't feel guilty about this, Dylan. It's not your fault." She reached her hand up to touch his face. "None of it is your fault," she said. "If anything it's my fault for not being more careful at the prison. I just couldn't bear the thought of you getting hurt. So I saved you and killed David."

Dylan crooked his finger under her chin and tilted it toward him. He looked her in the eye. "You did not kill anyone. Jimon Bumani is the bad guy here. And we will not let him win."

Her eyes pooled with moisture, but she nodded. "I hardly recognized you with short hair and the moustache."

He looked down into her face, her eyes red and tired, her hair coming down in places. He reached up and undid the pins until it fell free around her shoulders. He ran his fingers through it carefully and she watched him, her brown eyes shining, not breaking the gaze between them. He bent as if to kiss her when an elderly couple opened their cabin door behind them and came into the hallway, arguing loudly in Greek. Dylan let out a breath and Elizabeth laughed.

"Let's get out of here," she said, taking his arm. "We've got to find Bumani's final plans. Maybe there's a copy in his state rooms."

As they walked, Elizabeth highlighted the layout of Bumani's private apartments on the ferry. "I could maybe get by the guards since they've seen me with Bumani already." She led him toward the state rooms, taking a shortcut out onto the deck toward the starboard side and Dylan saw her shiver with cold. He stopped and put his jacket around her shoulders. "I don't want you anywhere near Bumani again. There's got to be another way to see those plans." He looked around them to make sure they weren't being followed then led her to the railing. "Are you okay?"

Elizabeth leaned over the railing, her hair hiding her face as she stared at the churning water below them. She was going to die. She had not expected to face this.

Dylan lifted her face. "What are you thinking?"

"That I don't want to die," she said before her voice cracked and the emotions overcame her. Dylan held her close as she cried, lightly resting his chin on her head.

"We're going to get through this," he reassured her as well as himself. "You're not going to die." He lifted her face to his. "I will do everything in my power to make sure that doesn't happen, okay?"

Her eyes shining with tears, Elizabeth only nodded. She trusted him and knew he would keep his word.

"I think the first thing we should do is tell Andrew what's going on. Maybe he'll have some ideas that don't include you being anywhere near Jimon Bumani." She took his arm and they hurried back inside. Dylan kept a close eye on anyone who looked like they may be following them, and made several twists and turns on his way to the cabin. He probably wasn't readily recognizable to anyone with his changed looks, but Elizabeth had been seen all over the ship with Bumani and he was worried about her safety. Yet, for the moment, Elizabeth seemed lost in her thoughts and content to let him lead the way and no one gave them a second glance. They made it to Dylan's cabin and he went in to get Andrew. "They're gone," he reported, coming back into the hallway.

"Who's they? I thought you were only here with one guy." She had leaned down and taken off her shoes while she was waiting for Dylan, dangling the heel straps with one finger. She flexed her feet, then froze at Dylan's next words.

"An American agent, Sam Fowler showed up."

Elizabeth's face registered her surprise and she gasped.

"Sam Fowler is my supervisor on this mission." She reached down and put her shoes back on, then started toward the foyer, her step determined.

He grabbed her arm and stopped her. "She's the one who shot David. When Andrew and I questioned her she said she was in deep cover and had to prove her loyalty to Jimon before he'd let her pilot his plane." Loosening his grip on her, he continued. "There's more. Andrew said there's a mole in the intelligence community and he thinks the mole is involved in the Bumani operation."

"Who does he think it is?" Elizabeth asked, drawing her eyebrows together in thought. "There's not many people with access to this mission. David, myself, Antonis, Sam, the director above her, that's about it. It's classified a high priority mission. What about you?"

"Same here. Only a few people have access to any information regarding this mission. Andrew and myself are the two main ones."

Elizabeth pursed her lips and furrowed her brow. "Well, apparently Sam thought I wasn't doing a good enough job and she's come to personally oversee operations." She sighed. "She did threaten to take over this mission for me, demanding extremely detailed reports and reporting more than normal. Maybe she planned to take over all the time."

"Do you trust her? Andrew didn't seem so sure." He jabbed a finger toward the empty room. "And now they are both gone. That either tells me Andrew had to move her or Sam got away. Neither are very good scenarios, especially since now we don't have any back up. We better be on our guard and think of something."

Elizabeth set her jaw and turned her back on Dylan, starting back toward the door. "Come on. I've got an idea."

He followed her as she led the way to the foyer. She stopped near the bar. "Jimon and Lizige are still there," she breathed. "How do you like that? Infect her with Tracin and come back for a drink." She turned to Dylan. "We've got to find Dr. Bruder. Maybe he can help us with the antidote."

She swayed slightly and Dylan caught her. "Maybe you should sit down. I can find Dr. Bruder."

"No, I can do this," she shook her head adamantly. She delicately held her skirt above her feet and started to climb the staircase. "We're in this together as partners. Besides I have a plan."

Dylan smiled at her retreating back. "Okay then. Partners."

⊱┈◈┈○┈◈┈⊰

Dylan had watched in amazement as Dr. Bruder did everything Elizabeth had predicted he would. She had knocked on the door and while talking to him had pretended to faint. She only had to ask if they could get some air while they talked and he had hurried away with her. Dylan's job was to search his cabin for papers and anything to do with the antidote. It was a luxury cabin so there were two rooms to search. The sitting room had yielded nothing, and he was in the bedroom trying to pick the lock on his briefcase. He looked at his watch, frustrated that time was slipping by so quickly. He bent again to his task. Just as the locks flipped up, allowing him access inside, he heard the cabin door open and Elizabeth's voice. "You've been wonderful, Dr. Bruder, thank you."

"You are welcome," Dr. Bruder's deep baritone responded. "I wish I could have been more help."

"How did your research with the new virus go? I know you perfected it, but did you finish making the antidote for it?"

"Yes, I did," he said abruptly. "Of course that's highly sensitive information."

Dylan rolled his eyes as he looked through the briefcase papers as quietly as possible. There wasn't much there and none of it had to do with the antidote. He closed it and crept to the bedroom door. It was quiet in the sitting room and he wondered if Elizabeth had left. Since the door was slightly ajar, he peeked through the crack and what he saw made his blood run cold. Jimon Bumani stood in the doorway, a gun glinting from the light of the chandelier and pointing directly at Elizabeth.

Chapter Fifteen

Elizabeth stood perfectly still, facing Jimon head on. "Why infect me with Tracin if you were just going to shoot me?"

Jimon grimaced and let his hand drop. "I don't want to shoot you Elizabeth. I wanted to get to know you better, to trust you and have you trust me. I thought you understood what your destiny was—to stand beside me." He shook his head angrily. "But you betrayed me and now you will become a martyr for the cause."

Dr. Bruder drew out a handkerchief and wiped his face. He was sweating profusely. As he moved to stand next to Jimon, he found a gun pointing at him. "Jimon, I am loyal to you," he protested, his cultured, accented voice cracking.

Jimon motioned with the gun for the doctor and Elizabeth to stand against the wall. "I researched you, Elizabeth," he said, an edge to his voice. "I know you have two parents who still live in your childhood home in Oregon, one brother, Mark, who is an excellent cross-country runner and is about to graduate high school. He's been offered several scholarships and is looking at three top marine biology programs across the country. You, yourself were an excellent student, scoring in the top five percent for your college entrance exams. You went into the medical field, aspiring to become a doctor, although you had many choices. You speak four languages fluently and that is probably why you were recruited to be a field agent for your government."

He tapped the gun on the desk, watching her, his eyes

squinting slightly, as if trying to read her very thoughts.

"Through the entire background check, though, there was no mention of any boyfriend, or significant other at all. Why is that Elizabeth?" He walked over and slid his arm around her waist, drawing her to him. "Why have you not given your heart to anyone?"

Elizabeth tilted her chin defiantly, but stood mutely by, pushing her hands against his chest to distance herself, to no avail. He was strong and had her in a vise-like grip, the gun in his other hand.

"I knew you would come to the doctor as soon as you were infected. You are a predictable American trying to solve your own problems, not seeing the big picture." He whirled on the doctor. "What did you tell her?"

"I told her nothing, sir," Dr. Bruder stammered.

Just then the announcement came over the system that they were docking in Mytilene on the island of Lesvos and the announcer outlined the disembarking procedures.

Bumani leveled the gun at the doctor. "You will never tell anyone anything," he said and pulled the trigger.

Elizabeth turned her face away, twisting against Bumani's arm. The report from the gun was deafening and her ears were ringing. She wondered what Dylan was doing and why he hadn't shown himself. Had he left before they came in?

Bumani tilted her chin toward him. "I'm sorry you had to see that," he said, "but the good doctor had served his purpose as have you." He bent for a kiss but Elizabeth turned her face away. "Ah, my dear, what we could have had together. Unfortunately you will die now, too."

He let go of her and she stood before him.

She wasn't afraid to die, but meeting Bumani's eyes, and remembering his synopsis of her life, she realized she hadn't reached the goals she had set as a young girl, wanting to help people, wanting to find love, and to have a family. She felt like she'd been on the brink of something special with Dylan, but now . . . She raised up her chin a notch and ruthlessly blinked away the tears that had come unbidden. At least she would have her dignity.

Bumani did not raise the gun, just stood looking at her. After what seemed like several minutes, Lizige appeared at the door. "We must go. Everything is ready."

Turning, Bumani nodded at Elizabeth, as if acknowledging her courage and left. When Elizabeth heard the metal door clanging at the end of the hallway signaling their departure, she sank into the nearest chair.

Dylan emerged from the bedroom and she felt relief that he was there with her. He knelt in front of her. "Are you all right?"

"I'm fine. Where were you? Why didn't you do something?"

He stood and made his way over to the doctor. "What was I supposed to do? He had a gun on you or else you were pasted to his side the whole time. I figured he probably wouldn't shoot you since you're infected with the virus." He turned the doctor over and he groaned. "Dr. Bruder, can you hear me?"

Doctor Bruder nodded.

"We need to know how to make the antidote. Can you help us?" He shook the doctor slightly.

"Bumani has one and I have one," he whispered slowly.

"Where is the one that you have?" he asked urgently. "Where is it?"

"Bumani carries his with him at all times," he rasped. Dylan's face fell, and Elizabeth's heart sank. She wasn't ready to die. "But I hid mine," the doctor continued. His head fell backward and Elizabeth wondered if he had fainted.

Dylan shook him again. "Where did you hide it? Dr. Bruder, where did you hide it?"

The doctor opened his eyes. "I knew Bumani might betray me. I was greedy and couldn't see past all the money he offered me until it was too late. He is an evil man, using my research for an evil purpose. I told my brother to take the antidote to the palace of Knossos in Crete, and hide it at the bull leaping wall so I'd have some insurance against Jimon. It looks like I won't be needing it now." He smiled briefly. "I always wanted to be as daring as the bull leapers," he whispered, then closed his eyes for the last time.

Dylan laid his head gently on the floor. "Come on, we've got to get out of here," he said to Elizabeth. She seemed reluctant to leave the doctor. Dylan slid his arm around her shoulders. "Everyone is disembarking, and he'll be discovered soon," he said gently. They went to the small staircase that would lead them upstairs, but Elizabeth was short of breath.

"Wait," she breathed. "I need to rest for a moment."

They went slowly up the stairs, then stopped on the next floor and Dylan found a small corner that had a chair for her. "What are the symptoms of the virus?" he asked. "Are you starting to show them?"

Elizabeth nodded. "Every person will react differently. Muscle weakness and shortness of breath is one of the first symptoms. That is followed by extreme tiredness, double vision or blurred vision, drooping eyelids and difficulty swallowing. Sweating and slurred speech can also occur right before the subject becomes contagious."

He patted her hand and looked at his watch. "You've still got several hours to get the antidote into you. We'll just go to Crete and get it."

"You can't, Dylan," Elizabeth said softly. "You have to go to the plane at the Mytilene airport and stop Bumani. The plane carrying the Tracin is due to take off and it will hurt so many more people than just me. There isn't enough time to do both."

He gently pulled Elizabeth up to stand next to him. "I'll make the time. I'm not going to lose you." He ran the back of his hand down her cheek and bent to kiss her.

She turned her head. "Don't. We don't know how the virus

is passed exactly. I could infect you if we . . ." A blush crept up her face. "I don't want you to get hurt."

He ran his thumb over her bottom lip. "Elizabeth, I care about you, and if we're going to be partners, we're going to go through this together. All of it," he emphasized. "Besides, we know you're not contagious for twenty-four hours." Dylan replaced his thumb with his lips, and kissed her. This time she didn't protest. "I want more time with you," he whispered into her hair.

She snuggled deeper into his arms, feeling the comfort he was offering. If she was going to die, she wanted to spend as much time as possible with Dylan. They stopped at her cabin for a moment so she could change out of her evening gown and into more comfortable shoes. When she joined Dylan in the hall, she was dressed in jeans and a plain sky blue T-shirt, with running shoes. "This feels much better," she said.

"Okay, we're going to have to separate to disembark, just in case anyone's watching." Dylan looked around, then pulled out the earpiece they'd used earlier. "I've kept pretty close watch and so far it looks like we're clear, but we can't take any chances. We'll use the earpiece to communicate."

She squeezed his hand and nodded, glad he was thinking clearly. "I'll see you on land."

She walked to the main lobby and went down the gangplank, adjusting the earpiece so it wasn't as noticeable. "Can you hear me?" she asked, her voice low.

"Loud and clear," Dylan responded in her ear. She smiled.

As she descended, Elizabeth spotted a small crowd disembarking that had Lizige in the center of it. "There's Lizige, do you see him? Bumani can't be far behind."

"I see him," Dylan responded. "Let's follow him, but be discreet." Lizige led the crowd through the harbor and ended up getting into a small red car that was waiting by a side street.

Elizabeth quickly hailed a cab. "Dylan, he's in a car. We've got to go now or we'll lose him. I'm in a taxi and we're ready to go."

Within moments, Dylan appeared and got in beside her, Lizige's car pulling away at the same moment.

Elizabeth tapped the driver on the shoulder and gave him instructions to follow the red car. He nodded and pressed the gas pedal, pulling into the light traffic, Lizige's car easily in sight.

"We need to find Andrew and Sam. I think Sam knows more than she was letting on, and we could use some back up before this goes too far," Dylan said. Elizabeth nodded, but didn't reply, her focus on the red car in front of them.

They followed Lizige at a safe distance, as he took several twists and turns, but not surprisingly, they ended up at the airport. Lizige went through a security gate and disappeared into a small hangar. Dylan paid the taxi driver and stood with Elizabeth on a small sidewalk in between two buildings. "We've got to get in there." He circled around, seeing several men working on different small planes in various states of repair. With the guards and the workmen, they'd have to find a different way. "Come on," he said, taking Elizabeth's hand.

They went into the main building of the airport and Dylan went up to the first desk he saw and asked the woman behind it if he could speak to the person in charge. Within a few moments a thin, Greek man came toward them, his small eyes magnified by his very large glasses.

"Can I help you?" he asked, his English perfect, the accent hardly noticeable.

Dylan flipped open the identification that Andrew had brought for him. "I am a Canadian Intelligence agent. You have a terrorist's plane in the far left field of your airport. I need you to notify the authorities immediately and hold that plane until they get here." He glanced at Elizabeth standing next to him, who was beginning to look very pale. "I also need a plane to the island of Crete."

The airport manager swallowed hard, his olive skin turning pale. He took two steps to speak to the woman behind the desk. She made a phone call, then began typing on her computer. When she looked up, she nodded to him.

"We have a flight ready that can take you to Crete," the manager told Dylan. "Greek authorities are on their way to collect the terrorists and search the plane you suspect. These people will be dealt with, don't worry." He leaned closer to Dylan. "I served in the Greek Air Force and want to assure you that we will assist you in any way we can. I've arranged a car and driver in Heraklion to take you anywhere you need to go. The driver's name is Michaelis and he knows that island of Crete like the back of his hand. He will be able to help you."

The airport manager's immediate compliance with Dylan's request put him at ease. He had done everything Dylan had asked him to do and was former military, too. Well, most Greek men were since they were required to serve at age twenty, but the airport manager seemed eager to assist him. With the authorities on their way to stop the plane, Dylan could concentrate on finding that antidote to save Elizabeth. He put his identification back into his pocket, the relief evident on his face as he glanced at her. "Thank you," he said to the manager. "I will be back to explain everything after I've collected some evidence from Crete. Which way should we go to board the plane?"

When they were directed to the correct boarding strip and on the plane, Dylan's immediate concern was Elizabeth. She was pasty white, and seemed very tired. He looked at his watch. They still had over seventeen hours before it became contagious, but he wondered if that was just a guideline and it affected people differently. He got her a pillow and blanket, helping her get settled into her seat. *Maybe I should leave her here*, he mused, before discarding the thought. At least if she was with him, he knew she was safe. And if the unthinkable happened, they'd be together.

Chapter Sixteen

It was a short flight and before long they were landing at the Heraklion airport in Crete. It was a busy airport, but Dylan waded through the crowd as best he could, clearing the way for Elizabeth. Most people took one look at the cuts and bruises on his face and steered clear of him. He grimaced, knowing he probably looked terrible, but there was nothing he could do about it now. His ribs were also starting to ache again, but he shoved the pain to the back of his mind and concentrated on Elizabeth and getting that antidote into her as soon as possible.

The couple finally reached the curb and a small sedan was there, with a driver leaning against the car holding a sign with Dylan's name on it. He was wearing sunglasses, his long hair glossy black and pulled back. It wasn't Dylan's nature to get into strange cars, with people he didn't know, but the airport manager had been eager to help and Dylan's focus was on Elizabeth and her deteriorating condition. It would be short trip since the Knossos palace was only a five-kilometer ride from the airport, they'd be in and out, and Elizabeth would be made well once they had that antidote. He had to believe that. Sizing up the driver, he said with an authoritative voice, "Are you Michaelis?"

The man nodded. "I'm told you need the best driver in Crete and that is me. I will take you anywhere you need to go," he said, putting out his hand for a handshake. Instead, Dylan caught Elizabeth as she began to sway. Michaelis got on Elizabeth's other side and they helped her into the car. "We must hurry," Michaelis said. "She doesn't look well."

Elizabeth leaned heavily on Dylan. "Yeah, pick up the pace," she joked. He slid into the car next to her, Michaelis closed the door and went around to the driver's side. "You don't need to baby me," she protested. "I'm fine."

"I know, I just wanted to," he said, holding her close. Dylan instructed Michaelis to take them to the Knossos palace. The car took off and Dylan put his arm around Elizabeth to steady her. "The driver's in a big hurry," he murmured. She sank deeper into his arm and seemingly fell asleep. He noticed Michaelis watching them from the rearview mirror and something pricked in the back of his mind. Where had he seen this guy before? He couldn't place him, but he put himself on alert. Worrying about Elizabeth had definitely clouded his focus, and he tried to gather his thoughts, not wanting any trouble until Elizabeth was safe.

After twenty minutes of driving and several apologies for seemingly wrong turns, Dylan knew they weren't going in the right direction and it wasn't an accident. The best driver in Crete couldn't find the biggest tourist attraction on the island! He kicked himself for trusting the airport manager, who had so easily duped him. That didn't happen often, but Dylan had walked into that trap by breaking the cardinal rule of a field agent—trust no one.

Easing Elizabeth out of his arms, he reached for his gun. Without missing a beat, Michaelis caught Dylan's eye in the rearview mirror. "Please keep your hands where I can see them," he said. When Dylan didn't immediately comply, he reached over the seat with one hand and pointed a gun at Dylan. "Don't even think about it," he warned.

He quickly pulled the car over to the side of the road on the edge of a long, rocky beach surrounded by cliffs. He turned around, his gun deliberately in Dylan's face. "Why are you going to the Knossos palace?" he asked, his voice calm.

"What evidence are you after? We know you talked to Dr. Bruder before he died. What did he tell you?"

Dylan's mind was racing. "How do you know about Dr. Bruder? Who are you?" he countered, trying to buy some time. Elizabeth sat up slowly, taking stock of the situation.

"Answer me first!" Michaelis demanded, his voice raised. He motioned with the gun toward Elizabeth. "You better tell me, or the lady will be sorry."

Dylan held up his hands. "Okay, okay. There's a vial of antidote hidden at the palace. We're going to look for it." Elizabeth's arm was slightly behind his back and he could feel her trying to reach for his gun.

"Antidote to Tracin?" the driver asked, his tone skeptical. "Mr. Bumani didn't say anything about that."

"That's because Dr. Bruder didn't tell him. It was an insurance policy," Dylan explained. He noticed that the more they talked, the more the driver seemed to lower his guard and the gun. At the same moment he realized Elizabeth wasn't going to be able to get the gun. It was at the wrong angle for her to get it out of his holster without being seen. She slid her hands in front of her and shrugged slightly, signaling to Dylan that she wasn't able to get it. He focused back on the driver.

"Where is it hidden in the palace?"

"Let's go there together and look for it," Dylan suggested. "Then we can sell it and split the profits."

Michaelis laughed. "I won't be splitting anything with you. Get out of the car."

Dylan had no choice but to comply. He opened the door and eased Elizabeth out with him. The driver stood over them, the gun pointed directly at Dylan. "Give me your gun," he demanded. Dylan took it out of his holster and threw it on the ground in front of him. The driver kicked it away. He watched carefully as Elizabeth leaned heavily on Dylan. "What's wrong with her?"

"She was infected with Tracin," Dylan replied. "Why do

you think we want the antidote?"

The sarcasm was lost on the driver as he backed up slightly. "Then I would be merciful to kill her."

Dylan pulled Elizabeth tightly against him. "Let's go to Knossos together. Let me help you," Dylan repeated, trying to take the focus away from Elizabeth.

"You won't be going anywhere." He kept the gun pointed at them as he motioned for the couple to walk toward the beach. After going down a steep slope that was riddled with dark, razor-like rocks, he pointed them in the direction of a cliff that rose sharply to their left. When they were standing in front of it, Dylan saw the opening to what appeared to be a cave. He felt the gun in his back urging him on.

He reached for Elizabeth's hand and they went inside. It smelled musty and wet, the rock walls slick with water. They stumbled several times, the way lighted only by the small pen light that Michaelis carried behind them. After walking about twenty feet in, the ceiling kept getting lower and lower as they went, making walking upright difficult. "Stop here," Michaelis commanded. He told them to sit down with their backs to each other. Elizabeth looked at Dylan with her eyebrow raised as if to ask him what he thought was going on. Dylan just shrugged.

When they were seated, Michaelis pulled two pairs of handcuffs from his pocket. When Dylan and Elizabeth were back to back, he handcuffed their hands together. "Tell me exactly where the vial is hidden," he demanded, standing over them to admire his handiwork, shining the small penlight in Dylan's face.

"Why would I tell you anything?" Dylan asked. He struggled to lift his arm without hurting Elizabeth, looking like he was trying to see his watch face in the darkness. "Did we mention that she becomes contagious pretty soon?"

The driver backed up, his eyes wide, then narrowing as if he was wondering whether to believe Dylan or not. He decided not to take any chances. "Never mind. I don't need you. I have enough men to search the palace," he boasted, backing away from them. "And you will die in here together. No one will find your remains." He laughed. "I don't have to waste a bullet. You'll either die of exposure or Tracin," he predicted. "It doesn't matter to me." He turned and started to walk out of the cave, his light dancing crazily on the walls as he scrambled over the rocks. Dylan and Elizabeth sat alone in the darkness and cold of the cave.

"Well, I've been in some pretty tight spots, but I think this one is definitely in the top ten," Dylan said wryly. "Do you think we have to worry about the tides coming in?" Elizabeth shrugged her shoulders. He pulled on the handcuffs, testing their strength. "Feels pretty tight, how about you?"

"Yep," she agreed. "You didn't happen to have a spare handcuff key around did you?"

"No," he replied. "How are you feeling?" he asked, trying to look over his shoulder at her. He couldn't see anything in the pitch blackness. He again felt her shrug her shoulders against his back.

"Just tired. Like I've been awake for too long and my body is exhausted." She rubbed his back with her own. "Do you have a bullet-proof vest on or something?"

He realized she was feeling the tape on his ribs through his shirt. "No, I think I broke some ribs when I was attacked outside the tavern where Antonis took me to eat." He leaned forward slightly. "He left me to die, you know. He's probably working with Bumani somehow."

Elizabeth shook her head. "No way. Antonis would never betray me."

"Well, he did betray me," he said. "Maybe he's been the mole all along."

"You're jumping to conclusions," Elizabeth replied, her voice tight. She stopped speaking, took a deep breath as if clearing her mind and started to scoot forward. "Could we just sort of lean against each other and stand up? At least we could get near the opening of the cave for some light."

Dylan agreed. "Okay, on the count of three, lean against me. One, two, three." They both pushed against each other, struggling to stand on the sharp rocks that made up the floor of the cave. He tried not to push too hard against her smaller frame, but the truth was the effort made the pain in his ribs knife through him, his breaths coming short and shallow. After an eternity, they made it to a standing position and started forward, but hadn't gone far when the opening became too narrow for two people to get through.

"Let's sit down and think this through," Elizabeth suggested. "Besides, I think I need a little rest." She leaned against him as though her muscles were crying out at the exertion.

Dylan nodded and sat down carefully, trying to ease Elizabeth down onto the rocks. Both were silent

"So what's the tightest spot you've ever been in?" Elizabeth asked, her voice echoing off the walls.

Dylan thought for a moment. "Probably that Zambian prison you broke me out of," he said. "I didn't think I was going to get out of that one." He thought of the scar that he now carried near his heart. "I had a mission go bad not too long ago and I was shot," he said softly. He felt her turn as if she wanted to look at him.

"Where were you shot at?" she asked.

"Near my heart," he told her. "Just a few centimeters either way and it would have severed the artery. The doctors said I was really lucky." He tilted his head forward. "Getting shot changed my perspective on a lot of things. I definitely don't take anything for granted anymore."

Elizabeth was quiet for a moment. "I've never met anyone like you," she said, her voice low. "But I'm glad I met you when I did." Her voice sounded thick like she was holding back tears. "I've never been shot," she said, clearing her throat. "I don't really like guns, but I have used them of course." She tilted her head back. "My nose is itchy," she announced, changing the subject to something less serious.

Dylan couldn't help laughing. "Sorry I can't itch it for you." She maneuvered her shoulder as best she could to rub her nose on it.

"We've got to get out of here." She wiggled closer to the opening. "If only I had a lock pick I could get us out of these cuffs in no time." She pulled on them in frustration. "A toothpick would do at this point, anything!"

At her words, Dylan had an idea. "Wait a second." He pulled their hands around and began to undo his belt. "Do you think a belt buckle would do? You could use the prong."

Elizabeth nodded. "Definitely. Can you get it off?"

He stretched their handcuffed hands and managed to get the belt off. He handed it to her gladly, hating the tremor in his hand. The darkness was starting to get to him and he was feeling claustrophobic. "How long do you think it will take you?"

"It depends. I don't think I've ever used a belt buckle before and it's pretty dark in here." He felt her working with her left hand first, muttering to herself something about tumblers and levers. In a few moments his right hand was free.

"Wow, you did it," he said rubbing his wrist.

"Don't sound so surprised," she shot back, chuckling. "It's going to take a few minutes for the other one since I can't see what I'm doing exactly."

Dylan sat quiet while she worked, not wanting to distract her. It seemed like hours had gone by and the darkness was starting to make him feel disoriented. He couldn't wait to get outside. He was wet, cold and tired, but not complaining. They were alive and together which was a miracle. It brought the scripture in 1 Nephi 21:9 to his mind: "That thou mayest say to the prisoners: Go forth; to them that sit in darkness: Show yourselves." *Probably not quite what Isaiah meant, but appropriate for the situation,* Dylan thought.

The second pair of handcuffs took considerably longer and when they were finally free Elizabeth tilted her head, rubbed her neck and released a huge breath. "I never thought I'd get that one," she confessed. "Let's get out of here." She handed him back his belt. "Thanks for being so patient."

"I'm just glad you knew how to do that," he said as he stood and started for the opening of the cave. When they finally reached it, they both took a deep breath. "Okay, now we've got to get to that palace before Michaelis." He glanced at his watch. "You've only got twelve hours to work with."

They walked up the beach and made it to the road. With no other choices they started walking. Dylan knew they wouldn't be able to walk the whole way, but hoped that a car would come along. *Please Father, help us*, he pleaded. He took Elizabeth's hand. "Can you walk or should I carry you?"

She smiled. "I think I can walk. I hope someone comes along and gives us a ride."

"Me, too." He looked up at the scorching sun. "I think we're only an hour's walk from the palace, judging from how far he drove." He took her hand. "We can make it."

They walked along in silence for almost half an hour, listening to the crashing of the ocean in the background. Elizabeth watched the wandering goats who seemed to be watching them from their rocky perches, their bells tinkling occasionally, the warm breeze carrying the music to them. She felt like she was seeing the world through new eyes, wondering if she'd ever have a chance to see these details again. Impending death had changed her perspective as well, like Dylan said his had when he was shot. Why did it take almost dying to realize how good life was?

Dylan was looking at his watch, and she knew he was concerned about the time element. To tell the truth it was never far from her mind as well, constantly wondering when her time would be up. She put one foot in front of the other, her energy waning. Was the sky always so blue? Dylan squeezed her hand and she thought again how grateful she was to be spending this time with Dylan. He had turned out to be a great partner and ally. If they'd had more time to explore their feelings, she knew she would tell him that she was in love with him and hoped he felt the same way. But it wasn't fair to say it now, it would be sort of like a death bed confession and she didn't want that. Without a future, she would try to keep her feelings to herself.

Dylan kept a close watch on Elizabeth's progress, slowing down his walk to match hers. He was surprised that no vehicles had passed them. But as he registered that it was after lunch time, he realized that with the Greek tradition of shutting down in the afternoon, they probably wouldn't have anyone on the road for a while. He looked over at Elizabeth. "How are you doing?" he asked, the concern evident in his voice.

"I've been better," she said, her breath coming hard. "But I can do it." She squeezed his hand and gave him a small smile. "How much time do I have left before I become contagious?"

"Just over eleven hours," he said. "Plenty of time to get the antidote into you."

She smiled grimly. "If we find it first."

At that moment, they both heard the roaring of a car engine coming toward them, going very fast. Dylan stood in the middle of the road and flagged down the car. It was a blue taxi.

"Can I help you?" the kindly old man said. "Are you lost?"

"No, we're not lost. We need a ride to the Knossos palace," Dylan explained.

"Hop in," the taxi driver said. "I'm going near there and can drop you off." He reached his hand toward Dylan. "I'm George," he said.

Dylan and Elizabeth returned the introduction and barely made it in the car before he stomped on the gas pedal, watching his passengers in the rearview mirror. Elizabeth leaned against Dylan's shoulder, her breath almost gasps. "Thank goodness someone picked us up," she murmured. "I really don't know how much longer I could have walked."

"Well, we'll get the antidote in you and you'll feel a lot better," Dylan reassured her. Elizabeth only nodded.

They watched the scenery slip by as George chattered on about his daughter arriving in Heraklion and how excited he was to see her. "I would normally be napping at this time of day," he told them. "But something told me I needed to go early." He looked at them in the mirror. "Maybe it is fate that I picked you up. I am never early for anything," he chuckled. "My wife was astonished when I left."

Dylan said a silent prayer of thanks to his Father in Heaven for sending George to them. Within ten minutes they were going down the ancient road that led to Knossos. "Does everyone in Greece drive fast?" Dylan asked, laughing.

"It's a Greek tradition," George said, laughing with him. "Here we are."

Dylan looked at the gates rimming the ancient palace, and wiped the sweat from his brow. He was so thirsty and there was no water in sight. He could only imagine how Elizabeth felt. The sun was dropping in the sky, but the heat and humidity were still unbearable. Dylan got out of the car and reached back to help Elizabeth. He took out some money, thanking George profusely for picking them up. "No problem," George said. "I could wait here for you if you need me to wait." He tapped on the steering wheel. "I have the time since I am running ahead of schedule today." He looked at Elizabeth. "Would the lady like to stay here and rest for a moment?"

Dylan considered it, seeing how tired Elizabeth was, but with her adamant shake of the head, he decided it was better they stay together. "Don't worry about us, George," he replied. "We're just so grateful you came along and stopped for us. It was nice to meet you." George waved and they watched him speed down the road they had just come from.

"Well, he certainly got us here in a hurry," Elizabeth

commented. She started to walk toward the main gate, but stumbled to her knees. Dylan hurried to her side and helped her up.

"Are you okay?"

"You keep asking me that," she snapped. "I'm not okay." She blinked several times. "I'm starting to have really blurry vision." She held on to his arm, her breath coming fast. "I'm sorry, Dylan. I'm really not feeling well."

"I know. I wish there was something more I could do." He clenched his teeth in frustration, feeling so helpless. The only thing he could do was find that antidote as quickly as possible. He strode toward the main gate, hoping that no one had gotten there before them and taken it. Everything depended on finding that vial.

Chapter Seventeen

He led Elizabeth to the main gate and paid the admission price. Dylan grabbed a map, then started down the ancient stairs into the courtyard where once kings and queens had walked. It had been a long time since he'd been here and he couldn't quite recall exactly where the bull-leaping fresco was. The palace at Knossos was large and Dylan didn't have a lot of time. He looked around at the painted columns, most red with black bands at the top and bottom and wished he were here sightseeing with Elizabeth and not trying to save her life.

She leaned against a column, watching him, then swayed slightly as she looked up at the top of the columns to see where his gaze had gone. He put his arm around her to steady her. "It's beautiful, isn't it?" he gestured at the courtyard with the map still in his hand.

"It's wonderful," she said slowly, as she leaned heavily on him to climb the staircase, blinking her eyes rapidly as if to clear her vision. Her breath was coming in short gasps after going up the steps and Dylan tightened his arm around her. "How far do we have to go?" she asked.

Dylan stopped and flipped open the map with his free hand. He leaned closer trying to decipher the small lettering. "The palace has four wings arranged around a rectangular, central court, which is actually the nucleus of the whole complex," he read from the English translation of the pamphlet. "The east wing contains the residential quarters, the workshops and a shrine. The west wing is occupied by the storerooms with the large pithoi or storage jars, and the throne room. The north wing contains the so-called "Customs House" and the south Propylon is the most imposing building in the south wing." He pulled his arm from around Elizabeth's shoulders temporarily to re-fold the map. "It doesn't say where the bull-leapers fresco is."

"Can we ask someone?" Elizabeth said, wiping her face of the dust and grime.

"I wish I'd brought a hat." She looked around to see if anyone was close by. "It looks like there's a tour starting. Do you want to ask them?"

Dylan thought about it, but really didn't want to wait. Elizabeth was deteriorating fast and the sooner they got that antidote into her, the better. "Let's see if we can find it on our own. How hard can it be?"

Elizabeth nodded and took his hand. He led her past the tour guide who was explaining that the palace looks upon the distant Mount Jouctas and that mountain is the sacred place of the mother goddess, source of fertility and life. "If she's the goddess of life, we could certainly use her blessings," Dylan murmured, watching Elizabeth beside him, wishing he could do more for her.

They started at the south wing and didn't see much beyond guard towers and staircases. It was slow going as they went through several rooms and up and down crumbling stairs. Elizabeth wasn't complaining, but Dylan could see how hard it was for her. He resisted the urge to pick her up in his arms and carry her the rest of the way knowing how independent she was. Moving as quickly as possible through the south wing to the west wing, they found themselves in a sort of antechamber to the throne room. Elizabeth sank to one of the stone benches that lined the room.

"It's amazing how much light is in here and how they manipulated the windows," Elizabeth noticed, her breath coming hard.

Dylan sat down beside her, knowing she was trying to distract him from the situation at hand. "How are you feeling?"

"Tired," she replied. "Like I want to lie down and sleep, but I'm afraid if I close my eyes, I'll never open them again." She leaned against Dylan's shoulder and pressed her face into his shirt. "I am so glad you're here," she whispered.

He put his arm around her, feeling helpless. "Elizabeth, in my religion, we give people who are sick health blessings using the power of the priesthood and consecrated oil to heal them if it's our Father in Heaven's will." He paused, emotion beginning to well up in him. "I can't do that for you, since I'm not carrying any oil with me, but I would like to say a prayer if you don't mind. I think we could use all the help we can get."

Elizabeth looked up into his face, her eyes pools of moisture, and nodded. He didn't move from their position, just held her in his arms and offered a heartfelt prayer to his Father in Heaven that they would be guided to the antidote that would help Elizabeth and have the Spirit to be with them if it wasn't to be found. It was difficult for Dylan to finish the prayer, his throat was tight and his emotions difficult to control.

When he was done, Elizabeth interlaced her fingers with his and was silent for a moment, trying to gain her composure. "Thank you," she said finally, as evenly as she could, her voice cracking with all her emotion. "Thank you so much, Dylan. I've never felt so good when I really feel so bad if you know what I mean. I can't explain what I'm feeling right now."

He nodded and helped her to her feet, holding her close for a moment. The Spirit was strong and words were not needed. They walked into the next room which was apparently the throne room. Behind the small throne of King Minos there was a wall painting which showed griffins in a field of lilies. It was beautiful to look at. "The lilies are pretty," Elizabeth commented softly. "But I could do without the griffins." She walked slowly to the throne. "It makes you wonder what kind of men sat on such a throne. I sort of thought it would be bigger or more grand."

Dylan agreed. "I've always loved archeological stuff and wondering what it was like to live back then. What kind of people walked these same halls?"

They walked by, Elizabeth's gaze still fixed on the lilies. "It reminds me of the flowers at home. My mom spends hours in her garden, digging around in the flowerbeds. I didn't like to get dirty so I didn't help her." Tears began to fall. "I wish I had. I wish I could tell her how much I loved the flowers and our yard, and how much I love her."

Dylan stopped and gathered her in his arms, holding her close, stroking her hair. "Shh, you will. You'll be able to tell her."

She straightened and wiped her eyes. "I'm sorry I'm blubbering all over you. There's just so many things running through my head right now."

"Let me be there for you Elizabeth. I'd rather know what you were thinking than to have to guess." He held her away from him and looked into her eyes. She gave him a small smile, tucking her hair behind her ears. "Are you okay now?"

She nodded and he led her down to the bottom of the grand stairway. They found themselves in a hall of colonnades and to their left was a large suite of rooms.

"I remember this," Dylan exclaimed. "It's the queen's apartment." He looked up at the large painting of dolphins near the door. "If I remember right, we're getting close to the bull-leapers wall." He pulled her to a small room just off the main rooms. "This is the queen's bathroom and bathtub," he told her. "They adjusted a stream to run underneath the palace so they had plumbing almost as good as ours."

Elizabeth took a deep breath and smiled wanly. The shadows in the room made her look pale and gaunt. He knew this was not the time to sightsee. "It should be close now."

After negotiating through several corridors, they saw the

bull-leaping wall standing tall at the top of a staircase. "There
it is," Elizabeth said softly, almost in a sigh of relief.

It was magnificent. The fresco showed the figure of the
powerful and virile bull with an athlete leaping over the bull's
horns and about to flip over the bull's hind legs to the waiting
spectator. "Do you think they really did that for fun?" Dylan
asked.

Elizabeth shrugged. "Probably. Was there much else to do
out here?"

Dylan chuckled and they started up the uneven staircase.
"Be careful," he warned. He took her arm and helped her to the
wall. "Where do you think Dr. Bruder's brother put it?"

"I have no idea, so let's start looking." Elizabeth kneeled
down and started going along the bottom of the wall. "Maybe
there's a loose stone or something."

"That's what I was thinking." He started going along the
side at eye-level. After several minutes he gave up. "I'm not
seeing anything, how about you?"

Elizabeth leaned against the wall and wiped the beads of
sweat running down the side of her face. "Nothing, but I'm not
seeing too well right now anyway."

Dylan watched her, pulling his sweat-soaked shirt away
from his body. The sun was still beating upon them and they
were both hot and tired. He stood beside her. "Any other
ideas?"

"Nothing's really coming to mind."

He watched the tour group coming closer to them and
wished they could find the vial before they got here. He
squinted in the sunlight and noticed something strange about
the tour group. They were all men, and several of them were
staring straight at Dylan. One in particular who was leading
the group looked familiar to Dylan. It was Michaelis, the car
driver who'd left them for dead! He wasn't wearing sunglasses
anymore and he was carrying a walking stick. At that moment,
with the stick tapping in his hand, Dylan recognized him. He

was the ringleader of the gang who'd attacked him outside the tavern in Athens. "I can't believe it didn't register before," he murmured, but it had been dark and hard to see anything in that stand of orange trees.

He pulled Elizabeth to the side of the wall to shield her. "Come on, we've got to hurry." She looked up at him, almost groggy, blinking her eyes repeatedly. "What's the matter?"

"It's right here, I know it's right here," he was almost muttering, knowing how close they were and how desperately they needed to find that antidote. He took Elizabeth's arm and led her to the far side of the fresco, nearest the bull-leaper in the air. "The answer's got to be right in front of us."

He paced a little, careful not to get too close to the edge. "Dr. Bruder said he wanted to be daring like the bull-leaper," he said, thinking out loud. "He didn't see himself as one." He stepped back as far as he could on the ledge and looked at the fresco carefully. Something seemed wrong in the eye of the person standing next to the bull, watching the bull-leapers. It seemed larger than the others. He walked closer to it, staring at the eye. Something small glinted in the sunlight. He pried it out and a small vial slid out into his fingers.

"I found it," he said, letting out a breath. He went over to stand beside Elizabeth, holding it out to her. She gave him a wan smile, but didn't take it from him.

"I can't use it Dylan." She said it slowly, her eyes large, and tears were streaming down her cheeks.

"You are going to take it Elizabeth, we don't have much time." He kept his eye on the tour group that was getting closer, not seeing the car driver anymore.

"We have the antidote, Dylan. The ability to thwart everything Bumani is working for is right in your hand. Tracin would never hurt anyone again because we could duplicate the antidote."

Dylan shook his head, his mind racing. She was right, but how could he sacrifice her life? He couldn't. "We'll find another way, Elizabeth, I won't lose you," he said, his voice urgent. "We'll stop the plane, get Dr. Bruder's research, arrest Bumani, there's a hundred other ways to get the antidote duplicated." He tried to put the antidote in her hand. "I want more time with you. Please, take it, save your own life and give us a chance."

Elizabeth seemed mesmerized by the amber fluid floating in the small container. As she reached to take it from Dylan, they heard a pop next to them, the dust kicking up near their heads and Dylan's instincts forced them to the ground. Someone was shooting at them! He pulled Elizabeth's head down and kept her close as they made their way to the staircase. Both Elizabeth and Dylan slipped and slid down the uneven stone steps, Dylan doing his best to shield Elizabeth. His taped ribs protested the movements and his chest ached with the effort. Forgetting the pain, they ran for the central courtyard, heavy footsteps thudding in the gravel and dirt behind them, as they darted through several small hallways. Dylan pulled Elizabeth behind a wall. "Stay low, Elizabeth, hurry," he urged, his breath coming in gasps now. He tried to calm his beating heart and listen for the man chasing them.

"I can't Dylan," Elizabeth whimpered. "I can barely see. Leave me and save yourself." He tried to hand her the vial, but gun fire sprayed all around them. She sank down and crawled to a small crevice underneath the staircase.

"Elizabeth!" he shouted as he fell back among the columns.

"Give me the vial, I know you have it," the car driver's voice roared through the small corridor, the echo reaching every crevice. "That's all I want, just the vial."

Dylan slipped among the columns, trying to keep an eye Michaelis, but the shadows were everywhere. They were surrounded. He found a loose stone at the base of a column where he crouched. He quickly counted over to remind himself which one it was and then slipped the antidote inside.

He crawled in the direction Elizabeth had gone, hoping to find her before anyone else did, but it was too late. He looked up to see her standing before him, surrounded by men with guns.

"Get up," the ringleader sneered. "I knew you'd come for it, and sure enough, you found it for us. Give me the vial."

Dylan stood mute and the man standing beside him, smashed his gun into Dylan's face. He fell to the ground, bleeding and in pain.

"Dylan!" Elizabeth shouted. She knelt beside him and cradled his head in her arms.

"Search him," the leader ordered. Elizabeth was thrust aside and Dylan was thoroughly searched.

"There's nothing, boss," one of the men reported.

The leader kicked Dylan in the back. "Where is it?"

"We didn't find it," Dylan managed to get out between his clenched teeth, the searing pain making it difficult to breathe. "We're looking for it the same as you."

"I don't believe you. I saw you claw something out of the fresco." He turned to the group of men. "It's got to be here somewhere. Search everything." He pointed to the man on his left. "You stay here and watch them. If they so much as move you can shoot them." He gave a wide berth to Elizabeth as he walked around her. "She is infected with the Tracin so do not get near her," he advised. "She may or may not be contagious."

Elizabeth helped Dylan lean against a column. He wiped the blood from his forehead with the bottom of his shirt, the cut he suffered from the gun blow still bleeding. They huddled together for a few moments. "What are we going to do?" Elizabeth whispered.

Dylan watched the men searching the entire room. "Just sit back for now," he said, pulling her close to him.

She leaned against him. "How's your head?"

"I have an incredible headache. How's yours?"

"Same. My vision is pretty blurry and I'm feeling completely exhausted. How much time until I'm contagious?"

Dylan looked at his watch. "Eight hours."

She sagged against him. "I think I'll just close my eyes for a moment."

The man guarding them watched his group search every nook and cranny they could see. When nothing turned up, they began to get frustrated. The leader kicked at the dirt, then turned on Dylan, getting right in his face. "Where is it?" he yelled. "I have to have that vial!"

"Why?" Dylan asked calmly.

"Mr. Bumani doesn't like loose ends. If I don't have that vial I become a loose end," he shouted. He cocked his gun and pointed it at Dylan. "Where is it?"

"I told you, we didn't find it." Dylan readjusted his weight against the column. "Why don't we all go back to the fresco and look? Dr. Bruder said he'd had his brother hide it there, I swear, that's what he said."

The leader stroked his beard. "I will take my men back to look." He pointed to their guard. "You stay here." He snapped his fingers and all the men started back for the fresco. Their guard sat down, his gun still pointed at them.

Dylan held up his hands. "You don't have to worry, we're not going anywhere." The guard just looked at him and didn't reply.

For six hours, Elizabeth slept and Dylan held her. He watched as big lights were brought in to help the search through the darkness of the night and he could hear the men sifting over every inch of that fresco. Dylan took stock of their situation. From his dealings with the ringleader, he knew he didn't do his own killing. In Athens, he'd had someone else beat Dylan, and in the cave he'd only left them for dead, so Dylan didn't think he would kill them. Of course, he had the option of ordering someone else to do it. He looked over at their guard who was looking more and more sleepy as the night wore on. Dylan wondered if his inattention was their opportunity for escape. He took his arm from around Elizabeth and carefully stretched, then stood, mindful of his injured ribs. As his movement, the guard immediately snapped his head up and stood with him. "What are you doing?" he asked, his accent thick.

"My legs are asleep, man. Can I stretch them for a minute?" Dylan asked.

The guard nodded, but held his gun on Dylan. Dylan walked in a slow circle, stretching often. His head still throbbed, but the last hour had relieved some of the white hot pain he had been experiencing. *What I wouldn't give for a Tylenol right now*, he thought grimly. The guard followed him about in his lazy circle and after going around the room twice, Dylan made his move. He turned around quickly, slicing the guard's wrist with a karate move and knocking the gun out of his hand, then coming around with a jab to his windpipe. The guard fell to the ground almost immediately, holding his throat, gasping for air.

Dylan sprang into action. He went to the fourth pillar, scratching at the small stone that held the prize everyone was looking for. He retrieved the vial, but heard the click of the gun hammer near his ear. The guard was silent as he held the gun on Dylan, his hand reaching out for the vial. Dylan's shoulders slumped and he knew it was over. He'd failed. He stood slowly, his hands raised and he reached forward to give the vial to the guard. They stood facing one another when suddenly Elizabeth came out of nowhere, kicking the gun from the guard's hand. Before he could react he was on his back with his arm twisted behind him. "One move and I'll break it," she said softly.

Dylan looked at her with admiration and she smiled back. "Need some help?" he asked.

"I think I've got it," she replied. "But I think we better hurry before somebody comes to check on us."

Dylan retrieved the gun and held it on the guard before handing Elizabeth the antidote. "You've only got an hour and a half," he said. "Drink this now, Elizabeth."

Elizabeth stared at it for a moment, her indecision playing out on her face before she nodded and swallowed the entire contents of the vial. Dylan used the gun to deliver a well-placed hit on the guard's head which rendered him unconscious. Elizabeth stood near the entrance, looking a little disoriented. He grabbed her arm and almost dragged her as quickly as possible through the old palace, heading for the exit, praying they wouldn't be seen. They made it to a large painted column and stood behind it when a gunshot whistled over their heads. Dylan yelled, "I'm going to run for it!" He shook Elizabeth. "Can you run?" She shook her head so he slung her over his shoulder and ran as fast as he dared, knowing if they were caught they would be killed.

He ran through the central courtyard and felt Elizabeth struggling. He stopped and put her down. "I think I can make it now," she said, color returning to her cheeks.

He didn't have time to ask her if it was the antidote that was giving her the strength to move or the adrenaline as two more bullets whistled overhead, missing their mark. They zigzagged through several storage areas that held storage pots that were thousands of years old. They hid behind those for a moment, assessing the situation.

"Dylan, look," Elizabeth pointed. They were close to the front gate, where several trucks were parked and a small scooter was in front of them to the left of the gate. The driver had apparently left it running while he spoke with someone at the entrance. Its lone headlight was beaming toward Dylan and Elizabeth, calling them like a beacon. Dylan peeked around the large vat and saw Michaelis talking to several men, gesturing with his hands and shouting loudly in Greek. They pointed him in their direction.

"Let's go," he said, reaching for Elizabeth's hand.

They ran for the scooter, Dylan hopping on and Elizabeth grabbing him around the waist. Revving the motor, Dylan took off, both the owner and Michaelis chasing them. He heard one more shot, but didn't dare take his eyes off the road. They quickly passed several cars, Dylan knowing they had to get a head start because the small engine in the scooter was in no condition to outrun the larger engine in the car that was chasing them.

The mountainous roads were treacherous and Dylan slowed down to maneuver them. Elizabeth leaned her head against his back to shield herself from the wind. Dylan decided to head back to the airport and alert the authorities there. He pressed on the gas and the scooter made a whirring noise, the engine pressed as fast as it could go. Just before they reached the turn to the airport, a black sedan caught up to them. The driver swerved toward them, forcing Dylan into the gravel. With small rocks spraying behind them, he maneuvered the scooter safely back on the road, barely avoiding a long drop onto the cliffs below where the churning sea was anxious to claim them. "Hang on," he shouted to Elizabeth.

The sedan was in front of them now, slowing down so they would also have to slow down. Dylan braked as if he were complying, then sped around the car, narrowly missing a large truck in the other lane. But the sedan caught up once again and stayed right behind them. Dylan squinted through the rays of the rising sun, trying to keep his eye on the driver of the sedan. When he finally saw him, the driver was pointing his gun out his window and Dylan braced himself for the shot, zigzagging as best he could, praying that Elizabeth wouldn't be hit. But the shot never came. He looked back and was surprised to see another car was engaging the black sedan, forcing him to the side of the road. Horns were honking as the two cars pulled to the side and several men jumped out to surround the sedan. Dylan pulled over to the side. "Stay here," he told Elizabeth.

"No way," she responded. "I'm right behind you."

They approached the cars slowly, assessing the situation. Michaelis and two men had been pulled from the car and were being held on the hood with their hands behind their heads. Before Dylan could react, Elizabeth had started to run toward a large Greek who had his back turned to them.

"Antonis," she shouted, waving.

Antonis Mukakis turned to greet them. "Beth, I'm so glad you are safe. I didn't know if I was going to make it in time."

"How did you know what was happening?" Dylan asked, joining the pair. He turned Elizabeth toward him, his back facing Antonis for a modicum of privacy. "We can't trust him Elizabeth. He was part of this," he jabbed his finger toward Michaelis who was having his hands cuffed behind his back. "They were planning on killing me in Athens and you at Knossos," he accused, his eyes narrowing as he turned back toward Antonis. "Antonis was in on the whole thing."

"You're wrong," Elizabeth defended him. "There's an explanation, I know there is."

Antonis overhearing her remark hung his head. "I am sorry my friend. I was not part of this gang, but I recognized them that night in Athens as part of the terrorist group November 17. They are very dangerous people and if they were mixed up in this I knew I had a contact that could give me information, but I couldn't help you if they recognized me. I only today got word that there was an antidote that could ruin the whole project they were helping Bumani with. The plan was to let an agent find it for them and then kill him and the woman who was with him. I got here as soon as I could." He held Elizabeth's arms. "I am sorry I left your friend in Athens, but I knew Spiro would help. However, I let you down and did not take care of him like you asked."

Elizabeth hugged her old friend. "You saved our lives today, Antonis. All is forgiven."

Antonis reached out his hand to Dylan. "Do I also have your forgiveness?"

Dylan shook the proffered hand. "You did save our lives today," he admitted grudgingly. "Next time give me a heads up, though, before you leave me without any backup okay?"

Antonis nodded and laughed. "It's a deal." He turned to the men who had subdued the car driver. "Where were you headed?"

"To the airport. We've got a plane to catch, literally," Dylan quipped.

"There is a detachment of law enforcement there," Antonis said. "We'll take our friend there to question him."

One of Antonis' men was ordered to return the scooter to its owner as Dylan, Antonis, and Elizabeth all drove together in Antonis' car. Arriving wind-blown and out of breath to the airport, Antonis, Dylan, and Elizabeth all hurried inside.

"Where do you want to start?" Antonis asked Dylan, stopping to watch several of his men escort the prisoner who was in the midst of their security detail.

"I think I know who can tell us the answer to that question," Dylan said, looking at Andrew Blythe walking down the airport terminal coming straight toward them.

Chapter Eighteen

Elizabeth felt Dylan's hand tighten around hers as Andrew approached them. He was disheveled, his clothing rumpled and hair not combed. Not to mention he sported a blackened eye that was almost swollen shut. He quickened his pace when he saw Dylan and Elizabeth.

"What happened to you?" Dylan exclaimed.

"There's no time," he said quickly, looking around the airport. "We need to go where we can talk."

At that moment Michaelis stepped forward, accompanied by several guards. He was handcuffed, but Dylan instinctively moved in front of Elizabeth and she smiled at his protectiveness.

"Someone you know?" Andrew asked, walking toward the man scowling at them. Dylan and Elizabeth followed.

"He attacked me outside a tavern in Athens and followed us here," Dylan supplied, his face grim. "Not to mention we have a reliable witness who recognized him and his men as part of the November 17 terrorist group." Antonis stepped forward and Dylan motioned toward him. "Antonis Mukakis, this is Andrew Blythe a deputy director in the Canadian Security Intelligence Service." Dylan made the introductions quickly. "Antonis caught these guys right before they either shot us or ran us off the road."

Andrew sized up Antonis then nodded. "Let's all go somewhere we can talk," Andrew said, telling the guards in Greek to bring the prisoner along.

Dylan started forward, but Elizabeth held back. "I am starving," she said. "There's a little kiosk back there, and I'm going to get us some food."

Andrew turned as she spoke, and the small entourage stopped behind him. "We'll be in the far office, I'll tell the guards to expect you," he said, then he walked on, leading the small party to the opposite end of the terminal.

Dylan bent to kiss her. "Thanks, I'm really hungry. Are you feeling better then?"

Elizabeth nodded, her hand going to her throat. "It's amazing. I'm feeling a lot better, but now that the adrenaline has stopped pumping through my body, I'm realizing that I'm still very tired and very lucky."

"Maybe I should take you to the hospital and get you checked out," he offered.

"No way, not until this is over," Elizabeth shook her head. "We're partners, remember?"

"I remember," he said, smiling at her reminder. "See if they have any souvlaki, will you? I love that stuff."

He stopped as Elizabeth held out her hand. "I'm afraid I don't have any money with me," she said softly. Pulling out a billfold, he gave her several bills. "I'll pay you back," she promised.

"Don't worry about it," he said. "Besides, having you well and healthy is payment enough." He turned to go. "I'll meet you in the office," he called over his shoulder.

Elizabeth watched him walk away, marveling at how different he seemed from Africa. He was clean-shaven, his brown hair now very short, and his clear green eyes were always watching for opportunities to help her. He seemed happy, the light from within shining to all those around him. Elizabeth realized that she felt happy when she was around him, but also something more—something that was intangible, different and unexplainable.

She slowly turned to the kiosk, her mind working overtime.

A lot had happened in the last twenty-four hours. She'd had a lot of feelings when she thought she was going to die, wishing she could talk to her family one more time, and knowing that she wanted to spend her last moments with Dylan. But when they'd been in the darkened room, in an ancient palace in Greece, and Dylan had prayed to a God—a God he seemed to know personally—she'd felt something she'd never felt before. It was like the light was turned on inside her. Comfort had washed over her and she'd known everything would be okay. It was an amazing feeling that she wanted to experience again, but was both afraid and excited at the thought of it.

She ordered some souvlaki and two baklava, then went back toward the offices where she was supposed to meet Dylan. She maneuvered through a disembarking crowd, and passed several airport chairs, sitting down in one. Eating the baklava first, she could almost hear her mother say no dessert before dinner. It was strange how many childhood memories had flashed through her mind when she thought she was going to die. She knew when she got back to the States that she wanted to go back to Oregon and spend some time at home and do some re-evaluating of her life. This mission had changed her and she realized after Bumani's recitation of her life that she still had dreams she wanted to fulfill, and she had a lot of thinking to do.

Finishing her souvlaki, she got up slowly and walked to the appointed office. The guards let her by when she gave her name and she opened the door. Dylan and Andrew flanked the man who'd been chasing them, and Andrew was speaking to him in Greek. Apparently the driver wasn't cooperating since both of the men questioning him looked so frustrated. They all turned to look up at her when she entered.

Dylan stood. "Hey, that smells good. Looks like you found some souvlaki."

She nodded and held out the wrapped food to him. "I'm sorry, Andrew. I didn't ask if you wanted anything."

Andrew waved his hand. "I'm fine." He raked his hand through his already disheveled hair and gave her a small smile before coming to stand in front of her.

Andrew waited a moment until Dylan had taken the food, settling back in his chair to eat it. The prisoner's gaze was fixed on him, so he turned his back.

"How are things going?" Elizabeth asked. "Can I help? Where's Antonis?"

"Well, the guy's name checked out," Andrew said wearily. "And Antonis was able to give us some more information before he was called away. He told us to tell you he'd keep in touch," he said, his voice low. With that he turned back to the prisoner and spoke loudly. "Meet Michaelis Kamais, a member of the November 17 terrorist group, and proud supporter of Jimon Bumani's attempt to bring the free world to its knees."

Michaelis smiled at this introduction. "It is already happening." He pointed to the clock. "The package has already started its journey and the plan is set in motion."

"What do you mean?" Andrew asked leaning close to him over the table.

Michaelis was silent, staring at the ticking clock.

Andrew ran his hands through his hair again, but this time his motions were slow and calculated. Elizabeth wondered how much he was really hurting. "Why don't we take a break?" she suggested. "I want to talk to you about something."

She stood and Andrew straightened slowly. "What about him?" Dylan asked.

"Let the guards watch him. We'll be back," Andrew replied. "It will give you some time to think," he said to Michaelis.

They walked into the hallway. Andrew spoke briefly to the guards, then led the trio down another small hallway, into a security office. Several televisions were monitoring the airport and two guards were there manning the station. Andrew nodded to them, and walked into the glass room next to it. "We can talk in here."

Dylan held out a chair for Elizabeth, then sat down next to her. Andrew sat across the table from them. "What did you want to talk about?" Andrew asked.

"Well, for one, I think you needed a break and maybe to even see a doctor," Elizabeth started, ticking her suggestions off on her fingers.

Andrew immediately shook his head. "I'm fine."

Elizabeth accepted that and moved on. "Two, I think we have a lot of the information we're looking for, but we need to put our heads together and analyze it."

Rubbing his temples, Andrew stopped and stared at her. "Wait right here," Andrew instructed and hurried out of the room.

"Was it something I said?" Elizabeth asked mildly. Dylan shrugged. "What happened to him?"

"I don't know," Dylan said. "We got busy questioning that guy and Andrew didn't have time to fill me in."

Andrew came back into the room carrying his laptop computer. "I don't know why I didn't think of it," he commented. "It must have been the stress of the last few days."

"You look like you've been through a lot," Dylan said. "What happened? How did you get off the ferry?"

Andrew sat down and started plugging in his laptop and booting up the computer. He looked at Dylan, his good eye red-rimmed, bloodshot and weary. "After you left, Sam pulled a hidden gun on me. She kept talking about us ruining everything she'd worked for, and then she escorted me back to her suite and used me as an easy way to explain where she'd been."

"Do you think she was really just trying to solidify her cover with Bumani?" Dylan asked. "What if she's the mole they've been looking for? Elizabeth said she'd been acting strangely since the mission started, demanding reports and check-ins more often than normal."

"I can't believe she would do that, after following her career and working with her over the years, but I guess people can change." He lightly pounded his fist on the table and shook his head. "But she wouldn't betray her country, she loves it too much. I know that. I just can't believe she would be the mole."

"The way this mission went down is too perfect, though," Elizabeth chimed in. "She doesn't answer to anyone except the director himself, she had full control over the mission and everyone on it. She handpicked David and I. She certainly had opportunity, but what would be her motive? That doesn't make sense."

Andrew nodded at Elizabeth and turned to face Dylan. "I don't have any answers, I can only go with what my gut is telling me. If she was only trying to solidify her cover, she certainly did that. Bumani seemed almost giddy. She's obviously part of his inner circle now. That could be really good or really bad. If she's the mole, she's helping Bumani kill a lot of citizens in her own country. If she isn't the mole, she'll help us capture him. That's what it comes down to."

Dylan rubbed his neck. "So what happened after she took you to Bumani's suite?"

"They took me to the airport hangar, and Bumani's goons worked me over pretty good. When the airplane they were working on left, I was left behind," Andrew finished wearily. "In the commotion I was able to escape."

"What do you mean the airplane left?" Dylan asked, his eyes wide. "I told the airport manager to hold it until the authorities arrived."

Andrew snorted. "He was in on it all along. That was their heads up that they'd been discovered and they moved up the timetable. Where did you disappear to anyway?"

"Elizabeth was infected with Tracin. We went to the doctor to see if he could help us with an antidote, but Bumani shot him. Luckily, he was able to tell us about another vial before he died. We went after it."

"That's great!" Andrew clenched his fist. "If we've got the

antidote then Bumani's plan is ruined. Where is it?"

Elizabeth looked down, her feelings of guilt apparent on her face. "I drank it," she said softly. "To save my own life."

Andrew was speechless. "You did what?"

"I made her drink it, Andrew. I wasn't going to stand by and watch her die. We can get the antidote another way. Bumani has one on him, we can stop the plane, there are other options," Dylan said, rushing to Elizabeth's defense.

"We hope," Andrew muttered, expelling his breath in a frustrated sigh. "It really would have given us the upper hand if we had that antidote right now."

Elizabeth drew the bottle from her pocket. "I kept the bottle. There's some residue inside. Maybe we can duplicate it."

Andrew nodded. "I *am* glad you're all right," he said, looking her in the eye. "Don't make any mistake about that." He turned back to the computer. "Okay, let's see what we've got." He typed a few things into the computer, then looked at Dylan. "So what do we know for sure?"

Dylan ticked off the points on his fingers. "We know the Tracin is going to London, Ontario, Canada on a plane. We know the plane has already left and they're going to try to get across the border." He bent toward the computer. "What's the next major town across the U.S. border from London?"

"Detroit, Michigan," Andrew answered, looking at the map on his computer. "Are there any places in Detroit that are prime terrorist targets?"

"I think you need to look at this from a different angle," Elizabeth spoke up. "There's got to be some sort of connection between London, Ontario, and Detroit. I mean, think about it, why would he pick that border crossing? If he wanted a prime terrorist target he would pick New York or Washington D.C. or somewhere like that. What's so special about Detroit?"

Andrew stared at her, but his eyes looked through her. "And we know it's a special airplane. I heard them talking about how they'd acquired it and got a glimpse of it at the hangar. They bought a Black Ops Thrush crop-duster counterinsurgency aircraft on the black market." Andrew looked at Dylan's puzzled face. "Surely you've heard of that?"

Elizabeth nodded. "Isn't that the aircraft the U.S. uses in Colombia and Asia to spray and kill cocaine and heroine crops?"

"Yes it is. I wonder how much Bumani paid to get his hands on that." The muscle in his jaw was working, and his face showed how tired he was. "I heard the maintenance guys say it was fueled for twelve hours of flying time. So they'll have to refuel somewhere. That will help since they have a head start on us." Andrew typed slowly on his computer, using the hunt and peck method. "I don't have my glasses," he said apologetically. "And to tell you the truth I have a whopping headache."

Dylan came around the table and slid into the chair next to him. "Let me do it. What are we looking for?"

"Something that connects the two cities, or maybe someone. There's an itinerary of any high level officials that will be in that area in that file there," Andrew said, pointing to an icon on his desktop. He scraped his chair backwards, pinching the bridge of his nose with his thumb and forefinger as he tilted his head back. "Is anyone important going to be in those cities in the next forty-eight hours? Any big events at all?"

"Let me see," Dylan said, scrolling down. He was quiet for a few minutes as he sifted through several lists. He finally stopped, blinked his eyes at the screen as if he couldn't believe what he was seeing, and cleared his throat. "You're not going to believe this," he breathed. "Guess who's going to be in both London and Detroit this week?"

Chapter Nineteen

"Who?" Elizabeth asked expectantly.

Dylan waited a beat. "The father of the President of the United States, accompanied by the President's wife," he said finally. He scrolled further down the page. "They're appearing at an air show that is showcasing government aircraft. It makes a stop in London, Ontario, today, then moves to Detroit tomorrow." He read from the computer page. "His father will be demonstrating the P-38 Lightning which is a twin-engine, single seat Lockheed fighter-bomber that he flew for reconnaissance duties during World War II." He stopped reading. "That explains a lot."

Andrew put his head in his hands. "Yes it does. If he infects the President's father or wife with Tracin, he will be able to hold the president emotionally hostage and the fate of the nation will be in the hands of a man trying to save his family's life." He folded his arms and leaned on the table before he stood. "They've probably registered the crop-duster in the air show so no one will suspect that it's filled with a biological weapon." He snapped his laptop closed. "We don't have much time. I need to make some phone calls and see if we can track that plane and explain why we have to detain a United States war hero in Canada."

"Is there anything I can do?" Dylan asked.

Andrew shook his head. "We'll probably be flying out of here within the hour, so don't go too far. You might want to think about cleaning yourselves up. There's some shops in

Heraklion. You look terrible," he said, giving them a once-over, their dusty, sweaty appearance and no sleep readily apparent on their faces.

"Hey," Dylan protested, running his fingers through his hair, which did nothing more than make him look more disheveled. "Elizabeth still looks good."

Andrew smiled as he stepped out of the door and began speaking to the guards. They pointed toward several areas on the television screens they supervised. Andrew nodded and was gone.

Elizabeth stood next to Dylan. She looked down at her dirty T-shirt, suddenly feeling the overwhelming need for a shower and change of clothes. "I'm going to take his advice and see if there's a clothing shop nearby or something." She touched his sleeve. "Even though you don't think so, I do need to wash up and change my clothes."

Dylan looked at his own dirty, torn clothing. "I'll come with you."

They walked through the airport terminal and out onto the street. Dylan hailed a taxi and they went into town. As soon as he could, Dylan rolled down his window. The sun had risen and was dancing its rays across the ocean, the air filled with the song of gulls and the smell of the sea. He breathed deep. It had been a long, trying night. But Elizabeth was alive and they had a real chance of stopping Jimon Bumani. He put his arm around Elizabeth and she snuggled into him. He kissed the top of her head. "How are you feeling?"

"Tired," she said. "Like I'm ready to go home." She shifted her weight. "I'm so glad to be alive. I realized that there's a lot of things I want to do with my life still."

"Like what?"

"I don't know, spend more time with you," she said softly. "Maybe go back to medical school. I'd like to get married someday and have children. Go to soccer games and PTA meetings. Do something that I absolutely love."

"Me, too," Dylan agreed. He cuddled her closer, enjoying the feel of her in his arms. She belonged there.

All too soon the taxi stopped in downtown Heraklion. The central marketplace was crowded, but there were several, shops, taverns, and kiosks. Dylan paid the driver and held out his hand for Elizabeth. She took it, self-consciously looking down at her apparel. "Don't worry," he assured her, tucking her hair behind her ear. "You look beautiful." She smiled and followed him.

They walked to a row of clothing shops. Dylan had been shopping with his mother and sisters many times and didn't feel uncomfortable at all. Elizabeth looked at several outfits, fingering the material and holding different shirts and shorts up to herself. Dylan found a tourist souvenir T-shirt that proclaimed, "I Love Greece" on it and had the bull-leaping fresco underneath the lettering. "This would be a perfect souvenir for us," he said, holding it out to her.

Elizabeth agreed, taking the T-shirt in his outstretched hand and putting it with the khaki cargo shorts she held. "It is perfect," she laughed. "I'll take it."

They made their purchase, Dylan finding another T-shirt that was exactly the same as hers for himself. "I don't want to forget this trip," he told her.

"I couldn't ever forget this trip," she murmured, looking up at him, her eyes sparkling, mirroring his smile.

They found a public restroom where they could change. Elizabeth came out with her face freshly scrubbed, looking every bit like a tourist. Dylan had washed the blood from his face and also changed. They walked hand in hand past a garbage and Elizabeth stopped to throw her tattered T-shirt away. "I don't think I can salvage it,'" she explained. "And there's some bad memories that go along with that shirt."

"Some good ones, too," Dylan countered, taking her hand. The feelings between them crackled, but remained unspoken. They walked around the marketplace for a few moments, watching the people eating and laughing, obviously enjoying themselves. Dylan looked at his watch. "We'd better get back. I'm sure Andrew is wondering where we are."

Elizabeth nodded, not wanting their shopping trip to end. Dylan got another taxi and they headed back to the airport. Several Greek fighter jets were on the far runway and the airport seemed to be under tighter security. Dylan got out of the car and was stopped by two guards. He showed his identification and was ushered immediately into the back office where he had previously questioned Michaelis. "What's going on?" he asked the guard.

"Wait here," was all he said.

Within seconds Andrew walked into the room. "Where have you been?" he demanded. "We've got to leave. We're late as it is."

"What's going on?" Dylan asked again.

"Sam is piloting the plane with Bumani on board and it's on course for Ontario. We're detaining the president's wife and father and they're upset about it. We've got to get back and explain ourselves, not to mention close our borders before that plane can get over Canadian soil." He turned to Elizabeth. "The United States is scrambling to somehow contact Sam. They think she's the mole they've been looking for and have doubts as to her loyalty. They've raised the threat level and everyone is on high alert. They want you back in the country for debriefing and to hopefully stop any Tracin from entering the United States, even if they have to shoot down the plane with an American agent on it." He grimly delivered the last of the news. "I don't believe Sam has betrayed her country. She needs a chance to explain herself."

Elizabeth nodded. That made sense, but no one was anxious to have a plane loaded with biological weaponry in their airspace. "How am I going to get home?"

"Greek jets are waiting for us. You'll be escorted to Langley. We're headed back to Ottawa." He opened the door behind him. "The jets are waiting. We've got to go."

They walked to the tarmac under guard. Andrew motioned Dylan to the plane they were taking, but he held up his hand, asking for a moment to say goodbye to Elizabeth. Andrew assented and boarded the plane alone. Dylan held Elizabeth's arms. "I don't know if we'll see each other again," he shouted over the plane engines.

"I know," Elizabeth shouted back. She wrapped her arms around his neck. "I love you, Dylan," her voice was fervent. "I couldn't tell you before when I thought we might not have a future together."

He leaned back to look in her eyes, brushing her hair out of her face. "I'll find you," he promised. "When all this is over, I'll find you and we'll have that future."

"I'll pray for that." She reached up to touch his face. "I think you should pray that we get the plane down safely and no one gets hurt. I think God really listens to you." She leaned in closer. "I liked the feeling I had when you prayed for me. It was like a light turned on and someone was really there listening." When she spoke it was as if the drone of the plane engines faded away and her voice was the only sound.

Dylan could see Andrew motioning from the door of the plane, but he didn't want to leave Elizabeth. He held her close, speaking directly into her ear, her long hair swirling around them like a protective blanket. "I will pray, for both of us, but you can pray too, and have that feeling every day. You'll feel it in the LDS church, Elizabeth, that's where you'll find it." And with that, he closed his mouth over hers, the world and all its problems melting away in their kiss. She curled her fingers in his hair, pulling him closer, all their unspoken feelings communicated in the meeting of their lips, the mingling of their breath.

When they broke apart, Elizabeth looked radiant, the sun illuminating her face and the tears pooling in her eyes. She stepped back and waved, walking toward the waiting plane.

She looked back twice and Dylan waved his goodbye. When she was safely aboard, Dylan joined Andrew. The door shut with finality and Dylan took his seat, watching out the window as Elizabeth's jet taxied down the runway. He bit his lip, trying to gain control of his own emotions. It was as if part of him was flying away with her and he could hardly bear it.

"You okay?" Andrew asked, putting his hand on Dylan's shoulder.

Dylan didn't respond, just nodded. *I will find her again*, he promised himself. *And I'll tell her that I love her back.*

><del>+</del>◆+<del></del>O<del></del>◆+<del>+</del>◄

The jets were able to make good time and they arrived in Ottawa just ahead of Bumani's crop duster plane. When they landed, Dylan and Andrew were whisked to the CSIS central offices. Phones were ringing incessantly and large radar screens pinpointed the incoming airplane. The countdown had begun as to when Canadian soil would be reached. Men and women tapped away at their keyboards, each looking intent on their job.

Andrew climbed down the short stairway and shrugged out of his jacket. He approached the terminal that had several men crowded around it. "Has any contact been made with the pilot?"

The technician sitting below him at the desk shook his head. "No. We've made several attempts though."

Andrew leaned toward his station. "Let me try."

He took over a small microphone headset and called out the plane's identifying information twice with no response. He tried a different tactic. "Sam, it's Andrew. If you are the only one who can hear me, tap the mike twice." Everyone in the room waited breathlessly. After a few moments, they heard two distinct taps. Andrew smiled and clenched his fist. "Okay. You should know that both the American and Canadian governments are listening in. Is Bumani with you? Tap twice for yes." Again they heard two distinct taps. "He's not on the pilot's headset though, correct?" Two more taps.

Andrew put down the microphone. He turned to the director of the CSIS who was standing next to him. "We've got her ears. What do you want to say to her?"

Bud Stewart was a small man, an analyst who'd worked his way up in the agency. He had a tic in his cheek that Andrew only saw when Bud was nervous or unsure. It was going a mile a minute right now. "Does she know where they're going?"

Andrew took a deep breath. "We know where she's going. London, Ontario."

Bud looked at Andrew through his thick lenses, and blinked. Andrew wanted to shake him and tell him to get hold of himself. The Director of National Defense joined in. "Ask her if she can land the plane safely," he said authoritatively, his height dwarfing both Andrew and Bud. Bud nodded.

"Can you land the plane safely without any of the weapon being deployed?" Andrew asked. There was no response. "Sam, are you still there?" Silence. All in the room seemed to hold their breath as they waited, to no avail.

The Director of National Defense shook his head. "I've got to report to the Solicitor General in ten minutes. The Prime Minister wants an update on the situation. What do we have to tell him?"

"The Americans want to shoot it down," Bud supplied. "But one of their agents is aboard."

"We can't support shooting it down until we know that agent is safe," Andrew said urgently, wanting to give Sam every benefit of the doubt.

"What if she's joined the terrorists?" The National Defense Director queried, shaking his head. "We can't risk infecting a nation with biological weapons."

"She hasn't joined the terrorists," Andrew said adamantly.

"Are you one hundred percent sure?"

Andrew took a deep breath and mentally counted to ten. "Nothing is ever one hundred percent sure, sir."

"Well we can't base our threat assessment on a hunch that you might have. I've got to make my report to the Prime Minister. Call me when there's news." The director walked away, his shoes snapping on the floor.

Bud put his hand on Andrew's shoulder. "You've got a feeling about this?"

Andrew nodded.

"They're approaching Newfoundland. We've got to make a decision."

"Let me talk to her one more time, Bud," Andrew implored.

"The Americans aren't giving us much time," Bud said as he handed the microphone back to Andrew. "They're deploying their fighter jets with orders to shoot. They think it's too close to their airspace and too much of a risk, so you better hurry because at this point, the Prime Minister would probably agree with the Americans and err on the side of caution."

Andrew took it, his eyes grateful. "Sam, it's Andrew. I want you to know they won't let you reach land. You're going to be shot down. If there's anything you can do, you've got to do it now. They're deploying the fighter jets as we speak." His voice was sad. "Sam, I don't think anything's been done yet that can't be fixed. Let's get you safely on the ground and talk about it."

Silence met his pleas.

Andrew put down the microphone, but it began to crackle. "Andrew," a female voice said clearly. "I just want you to know I'm sorry."

He put the microphone back to his mouth. "Sam, what's going on?"

Those in the room stopped what they were doing and the microphone was put on speakers. They could hear a male voice saying, "we're so close, don't do this. Don't make me kill you."

"You will die anyway, Jimon. You have failed." Sam's voice was clear.

"I am the most powerful man on earth," Jimon shrieked. "You will do as I say. This plane will land and the world will be at my mercy." As if he had grabbed the headset, his voice came clearly over the speakers. "I will win."

The speakers fell silent and the buzz of the headset dashed their hopes.

"Sam, Sam," Andrew called into the microphone.

After a few moments, that seemed like an eternity, the radar man announced that they'd lost the plane. "It's just disappeared," he reported.

"She crashed the plane," Andrew breathed. "Do we have any ships in the area? American or Canadian?" he asked. "Do we have their last location?"

The man two rows in front of them was frantically typing. "Yes, we have a ship in the area, the Trudeau, and we also have their last location."

"Well, let's get busy. We've got to recover that plane and hope there were survivors." Andrew said. "Maybe she parachuted out."

Andrew began to pace and Dylan took his arm. "Listen it might be hours before we know anything. Let's get out of here and grab something to eat."

Andrew looked at him like he was crazy. "I'm staying right here until I know what happened to Sam and that plane." He grabbed his coat. "Where's the director? I want to see for myself."

Dylan followed him. "Are you going to try to get on a plane or something?"

There was no answer and Dylan just followed the determined man before him. Within minutes Andrew had them a seat on a search helicopter and they were winging their way toward Newfoundland. "Is there any word yet?" Andrew shouted to the pilots, trying to be heard over the engines.

"No, sir, not yet," the younger pilot replied.

Andrew sat back in his seat, his chin resting on his hand. "Did you hear her last words to me Dylan?" he asked.

"Not really."

"She said she was sorry." He dropped his head to his chest. "I hope she made it."

The pilot leaned back and shouted to Andrew. "They've found the wreckage site," he reported. "They're looking for survivors."

"Do they know there is a biological weapon aboard?" Dylan asked.

"Affirmative. They're taking all the precautions," he was told.

When they reached the area the helicopter was instructed to land on the Canadian ship. Almost as soon as the helicopter landed Andrew was unbuckled and scrambling off. He met the captain of the ship and asked for an update.

"We have recovered one survivor, sir, a woman. She's in the infirmary being treated for shock. The other passenger did not survive, but we recovered his remains," the captain reported.

"What about the biological weapon being stored on the plane and the antidote to it?" Dylan asked.

"The biological weapon was in containers that were not breached, and all personal effects have been logged," the captain replied. "If it was there, we've got it." He looked Andrew in the eye. "The pilot obviously did some fancy flying. She was just barely able to parachute out in time and was able to make sure her passenger did not."

"So what's next?" Andrew asked.

"The Americans are sending a convoy for the weapon and their agent and we've been instructed to take everything to the Naval Air Station in Keflavik, Iceland," the captain said.

Andrew sighed. "At least the Americans will be able to study Tracin now, add it to their arsenal and have the antidote to it, eh?" He clapped Dylan on the back. "Well, never mind about that. It was a job well done."

Dylan agreed. "What will happen to Sam?"

"She'll be treated for her injuries, then turned over to the U.S." The captain saluted. "If you'll excuse me I've got to inform the Solicitor General."

"I hope she's okay," Andrew murmured. "I'm going to see her."

Andrew left Dylan standing on the launch pad. He watched his old friend's retreating back. He was glad the mission was over and everyone was safe, including Sam. It was easy to see that Andrew cared for her and Dylan wanted only the best for Andrew.

Within two hours Dylan and Andrew were being escorted back to Ottawa. "How's Sam?" Dylan asked.

"She'll be okay," Andrew told him. "Obviously she'll have some problems to work through with her government, but she really thought she was doing the right thing." Andrew looked thoughtful for a moment. "That's the crazy thing about this business. The rules have changed so much with fighting terrorism that it's hard to know what the right thing is anymore."

Dylan was silent, but that was exactly why he was getting out of the business. Because he knew it wasn't the right thing for him anymore. He didn't know exactly what the right thing was, but he knew what it wasn't. When they landed they were hurried back to the main office and were subjected to a lengthy debriefing. Both men were completely exhausted when they were finally free to go.

"Are we fit enough to drive?" Dylan asked as he walked out with Andrew. "We need to get out of here and get some rest. It's been a long couple of days."

"Yeah. At least Bud was able to explain things to the right people and we got the U.S. President's wife and father home safe and sound. Not to mention retrieving the biological weapon and a U.S. agent." He grunted. "Saved the world again," he laughed. "I definitely could use a shower and bed. The jet lag is starting to set in I'm afraid." He took one last look at the building behind him, then walked toward the double doors that led outside. "Can I drop you somewhere?"

"Don't worry about me," Dylan said. "I'll find my own way home."

"I've no doubt about that." They strode out of the building, handing in their identification tags and heading for the parking lot. "I'll see you back in Toronto," Andrew said.

"I'm handing in my resignation," Dylan reminded him.

"That's right," Andrew said, raking his hands through his hair. "Are you sure you want to do that?"

"Yes, I'm sure," Dylan replied, rubbing his ribs that were starting to hurt again. "I'm ready for that new direction in my life."

"Well, we'll still keep in touch," Andrew said.

"No you won't," Dylan smiled and hugged his old friend gingerly, careful of his injuries. "Thanks for everything, Andrew. There's just no words to say what you've meant to me over the years."

"Same here," Andrew pulled back and took his hand. "You've been like a son to me and I'm going to miss you."

Dylan swallowed twice. "Stay safe, Andrew."

"You, too. I'm going to miss you."

"I'll miss you, too." His voice was unsteady, but he held his emotions in, squeezing Andrew's arm and walking away, knowing he probably wouldn't see him again. Facing forward, he knew he was ready to meet the challenges a new career would bring him, and hopefully a new life with Elizabeth if she would have him. And if he could find her.

Chapter Twenty

D ylan sat in his grandpa's overstuffed armchair, rubbing his temples. The last three weeks had been emotionally draining. He'd come home to find that his grandfather had suffered another heart attack and wasn't expected to live. Dylan had practically lived in the intensive care unit at the hospital spending as much time with his grandpa as possible. From the few conversations they'd had, Dylan had made sure his grandfather had known how much he loved him. And in the quiet moments he told his grandpa about his new beliefs— that their relationship was eternal and they would see each other in the hereafter. Once, when he thought his grandfather was sleeping, he'd told him about eternal marriage and how he planned to find Elizabeth. His grandfather had startled him by squeezing his hand and motioning for him to take the oxygen mask off. Dylan looked around at the nurses, then complied.

"Make sure you get me married to your grandma for eternity," he rasped. "Just in case you Mormons are right." He winked at Dylan, then closed his eyes as the oxygen alarms started to go off, bringing the nurses running. That had been his last conversation with him, and he'd died the next day.

The funeral preparations had been difficult for Dylan. It was so hard to believe that his grandfather was actually gone, when just a few months before he'd been a relatively healthy vibrant man, helping Dylan cope with being shot and coming close to death himself. The funeral itself was in a beautiful cathedral, but the priest had barely known his grandfather and seemed unsure of what to say. His sister Avaeri got up and played a beautiful flute solo, that reverberated through the high ceilings, the sound winging its way to heaven as a tribute to the grandfather they loved. After Grandpa's best friend Arthur gave a beautiful eulogy, they proceeded to the cemetery where Grandpa was buried beside his wife, Abigail.

Dylan was reflective, mostly concentrating on trying to comfort his father who was taking it really hard. The neighbors and even a few ward members all stopped by to visit, with a casserole or dessert in their arms. The family had been surprised that people they barely knew from another religion would take the time to pay their respects, but they had accepted it graciously. It helped Dylan's father to be around friends and loved ones and hear all their memories of Grandpa George. It seemed to get everyone through the ordeal. He had lived a full life and the memories proved it.

They decided to put off going through his things for a few days after the funeral, but his grandfather's attorney had made an appointment with them to go over his will immediately. Dylan was dreading it, doling out his grandfather's material goods seemed so insignificant in the face of losing his beloved grandpa. When they arrived at the law offices, Mr. Dubray made them feel very comfortable. When they had all been seated, he pulled out a large file.

"I'll just read the will word for word, then we can go over your questions afterward," he instructed. He began to read all the legal mumbo jumbo, and his nasal voice was grating on Dylan's nerves. Practically squirming in his chair, he was just about to excuse himself when he heard his name mentioned. At first he thought he hadn't heard right.

"Could you repeat that please?" Dylan had asked.

The attorney looked at him over his glasses. "Certainly. I bequeath to my grandson Dylan Robert Campbell all of my liquid cash assets. I know I can entrust this money to him." Then he read the amount again and Dylan's mouth dropped open in amazement at the seven-figure sum he had received.

"I can't believe he's giving me that much money," Dylan muttered. His mother reached over and touched his arm as the attorney continued. Dylan hardly heard the attorney dividing the family jewelry between his sisters and seemed dazed when it was over.

The attorney asked for questions, but the family was silent. "I know it is a lot to take in, but I will be here and take you through the probate process. If you think of anything, please feel free to call." He stood and passed out his card to everyone.

"You're awfully quiet," his mom said, as they walked out of the office. Connie Campbell had always been the type of mother in tune with her children's feelings. Today was no exception.

He took her small hand in his, remembering all the comfort her hands had given him as a small boy, bandaging his scrapes and wounds and hugging him better. She always seemed to be able to soothe him—even now. He looked in her expectant face, her short brown hair tucked behind her ears, her soft brown eyes behind her glasses waiting for his answer. "It's a lot to take in, Mom," he replied. "What was Grandpa thinking?"

"That you'd do the right thing. That he loved you. At least that's what I think." She patted his arm. "Let's go home. Are you coming by or going to your apartment?"

"No, I'll follow you home in my car," he said. He waved goodbye to the rest of his family, then took the McDonald/ Cartier freeway to his parents' modest home on Richmond Hill. He stayed in his car for a few minutes, letting the events at the attorney's office sink in. When he finally went inside, his sisters had pulled out all the family pictures and were reminiscing about all the camping and fishing fun they'd had with Grandpa. Dylan stood there for a moment listening, then went into the den and there he sat contemplating what he was going to do next. He was getting a headache thinking about it and was just about to go home when his father joined him.

"What's going through your mind, son?" his dad asked. Dennis Campbell was the opposite of his wife. Although he was a loving father, he generally had a hard time reading what his children were thinking. Dylan watched his dad sit down on the couch, his shoulders slumped. He was looking older than Dylan ever remembered. He wore glasses now, and most of his hair was gone. Usually a smile was lighting up his face, but today was not the day for smiles. Dylan could see his father's weariness at the day's events and wished he could help shoulder the burden of grief his father was carrying.

Dylan looked his father straight in the eye. "I don't know, Dad. That's an awful lot of money." He leaned forward. "Not that I couldn't use it, since I am technically unemployed right now." He sighed. "I'd give it all back just to have Grandpa here."

"He wanted you to have it, Dylan, and he wanted you to do some good with it. He trusted you and was so proud of how you lived your life." His dad's eyes filled with tears. "He loved you."

"I know," Dylan's own eyes filling with tears. "He lived a good life and he's with Grandma now. They probably are having such a great time catching up right now."

His dad furrowed his brow. "What do you mean?"

"You know how Grandma loved to talk anyone's ear off. She had a lot to catch Grandpa up on, that's all," Dylan replied.

"Do you really think they're together?" his dad asked softly.

"I know they are, Dad." Dylan said with conviction. "Relationships that are made on this earth don't end here. They continue on."

"I'd like to believe that."

Dylan stood and went over to stand beside his father. "You can believe it Dad. I know it's true."

Dennis Campbell looked up at his son, seeing the

earnestness in his expression. "I think I'm ready to learn about your new beliefs, son. They've certainly given you a new outlook on life." He stood and hugged Dylan. "I love you and I'm glad you're home safe."

"Me, too," Dylan said, hugging his dad fiercely. Having the gospel had been a great comfort to him and he wanted that for his family. Perhaps the time was right.

>─+─◆─O─◆+─<

The next few weeks were a whirlwind. Dylan's family began the missionary discussions and it seemed to be going well. His parents were well-versed in the Bible, believed in God, and had researched many other religions in the past. His mother was especially interested in the account of the First Vision. She had always believed that the heavens were not closed to man, so when the missionaries told her how God the Father and his Son, Jesus Christ had appeared to the boy Joseph, she was really excited. His father had mostly concentrated on the idea of temples and of sealing families together for eternity. But both were progressing well and his sisters and their husbands had also joined in the discussions.

Dylan had been busy. He began his search for Elizabeth, and had gone back to the CSIS office in Toronto to make his resignation official. While there, he was called in to the director's office.

"You sure about this resignation?" Bud Stewart asked the question gruffly, but Dylan knew that was all for show. He was a great boss and really cared about his agents.

Dylan nodded his head. "I'm just going in a different direction."

Bud sat down and chuckled. "That sounds like it's right out of some manual or something. We're going to miss you around here. You're one of the best."

"Thanks. I'll miss some things about the place." He rubbed

the scar under his collarbone. "But I won't miss everything."

Bud put his briefcase on the table and took out a file. "I got a briefing on what happened with the pilot of that plane."

Dylan leaned forward expectantly. "Yeah?"

"She was taken into custody at Keflavik, Iceland as well as the virus and its antidote. Last I heard she was still being debriefed, but had confessed that she was the mole and it was she who had leaked the information. She felt like she had a good reason though—to win Bumani's trust and stop him. She used her field agent's reports to stay one step ahead of the CIA, then leaked information on several operations to deflect attention away from Bumani and help him trust her even more. It was her opinion that she had endangered the few to save mankind from the real threat that Bumani posed." He stopped and read further down the page. "Apparently the U.S. government is still deciding if any charges should be filed against her, since the biological weapon and its antidote were recovered."

Dylan leaned back in his chair. The news hadn't been unexpected, but he had hoped for some information regarding Elizabeth. "What about her field agent on the mission?"

"Right now they're concentrating on analyzing the plane's contents and wreckage site, but there's a rumor going around that they're also analyzing that field agent who'd been exposed. Apparently antibodies have been produced in her body." He slapped the file closed. "The United States wouldn't confirm that report however and everything was classified."

Dylan stood, keenly feeling the disappointment. He wondered how Elizabeth was and what they were really doing to her. He missed her and wished there was a way to contact her. He'd used all the resources he had to find her, but had failed so far. He didn't have her last name, he only knew her alias, Elizabeth Spencer. Of course, the CIA couldn't confirm or deny an agent by that name and wouldn't provide any information beyond that. He'd tried going through back channels, but got nothing, since the mission they'd been on had been classified top secret. Even Andrew had tried to pull a few strings, but it was as if she'd disappeared off the face of the planet. Dylan was crushed.

He cleared his desk, handed in his passwords and identification, and was just about to step out of the building when Amber, Bud's secretary rushed after him. "Dylan, I've got something for you." She handed him a file folder. "The chief thought you might want to have some of the pictures from your trip that looked personal."

He took the folder from her and put it in the box he was carrying. "Thanks, Amber. You've been a wonderful secretary."

She blushed. "We'll all miss you. Take care of yourself."

Dylan thanked her and nodded, making his way to the parking garage. Looking back, he was sad to close this chapter in his life, but was also looking forward to the future. Returning home, he was anxious to start re-evaluating his life and forming a new direction. First on his list was to spend more time with his family and get to know them again. He felt like he'd missed out on a lot with all his trips and what his job had required of him.

His first night home, Melissa had invited him over to dinner, but before they could even sit down, her water had broken and she'd gone into labor. Eric had rushed her to the hospital and within six hours Dylan had become an uncle when Melissa gave birth to a beautiful baby girl they named Kristen. When Dylan had held her for the first time, she'd yawned so delicately up at him and his heart had melted. She was the most beautiful baby he'd ever seen and while he enjoyed being an uncle, he knew he wanted to be a father more.

When Avaeri and her new husband Nathan came to visit the baby, they oohed and aahed over her, cuddling each other and dreaming of their own children they'd have someday. Dylan watched them, happy to see them in love, but it made him long for Elizabeth and what they'd shared.

He'd gone home and laid in his bed, wondering where his life was going. He slipped out and got on his knees, pouring his heart out to his Heavenly Father. He stayed on his knees for a long time, thinking, praying and waiting for an answer. And then it came. It was such a quiet, small bolt of lightning, he couldn't describe it, but he had his answer. He went to the box he'd collected from the CSIS offices and took out the file folder that Amber had given him. He glanced through the pictures and found the one he was looking for. It was of a little boy outside a hospital room waiting to hear whether his mother would live or die. He knew what he was going to do.

The next morning he called his grandfather's attorney and asked if anyone there had experience with forming non-profit organizations. The secretary had referred him to Courtney Willis. "She's top-notch in that area," he was assured.

The secretary rang him through to her office. "Yes," she answered crisply.

"Hello, this is Dylan Campbell. I'm told you're the attorney to talk to if you're thinking of forming a non-profit organization."

"Well, that depends on the type, Mr. Campbell." He could hear papers rustling in the background.

"I realize you must be very busy. Is it possible I could meet you for lunch somewhere?" Dylan asked.

"My schedule is completely full today, sir. Perhaps you could make an appointment for tomorrow and we'll discuss your intent." Her voice was cool and businesslike.

At first Dylan was put off by her manner, but he agreed to meet her tomorrow and made the appointment. When he arrived the next morning, he was surprised when Courtney greeted him at the door of her office. From her voice on the phone he had imagined an older woman with her hair pulled back tightly in a bun, no makeup, perhaps bearing a little extra weight. Courtney was the complete opposite. She was young, probably late twenties/early thirties, her long blonde hair reaching just past her shoulders. Her business suit was modest, a gray jacket over a white blouse with just a small amount of lace at the collar. Her skirt was just above the knee, but plainly showed she carried no extra weight.

"Hello, Mr. Campbell, it's nice to meet you." She held out her hand in greeting, her broad smile showed white, straight teeth. He wondered if she'd worn braces.

"Hello," he replied, realizing he'd been staring, and a flush crept up his neck.

She motioned him into her office. "Please sit down. What can I do for you?"

He sat, but couldn't get comfortable and kept shifting in his chair, a hard back that wasn't very comfortable, but looked right at home in her ultra-modern office with furniture in odd shapes. "I'm thinking of forming a non-profit organization to help relieve the suffering in Uganda. I've recently returned from a business trip there and seen first-hand the extreme need. Then when my grandfather died, he left me a substantial amount of money. I think this would be the perfect use for it."

She steepled her fingers in front of her. "It can be quite costly to form a non-profit," she said, but quickly smiled. "But you've definitely come to the right place. I can take you through the process." She went to her files and pulled out a thick one. "There is a lot of paperwork, however."

He nodded. "I thought as much."

They began poring over what would be needed and Dylan immersed himself in the work. He met with Courtney several times a week and when the will was through probate and the money released they were ready to go. Dylan had been impressed with her knowledge of the law and willingness to help from the beginning. When the Foundation was in place, Dylan called his family together for a family meeting at his parent's house.

When everyone was seated, Dylan strode to the middle

of the room. "I've called you all here today to make an announcement. I've decided on what to do with Grandpa's money." He paused for effect. "I have formed the George Campbell Relief Foundation so that I can use the money to help the suffering in Uganda." His voice softened. "I visited there and saw first-hand the children who need medical supplies and families who need fresh water. Even adults that need clothing and food. I think I can really make a difference."

His family was silent, then all began to chatter at once. "How can we help? Will you go to Uganda? What can we do?"

Dylan held up his hand. "You can all help and I'll be grateful for it," he assured them all. "I don't know if I'll go to Uganda anytime soon. I want to amass some supplies before I do." His eyes were shining. "It's so wonderful to be able to serve others and I'm grateful for a family that taught me the importance of service. Thanks for being such a great family."

Dylan's mother came to stand beside him. "We have an announcement for you, too." She looked around and everyone nodded. "While you've been so busy, we finished the missionary lessons and have all accepted the challenge to be baptized." Dylan stood and hugged his mother, then hugged his sisters and father.

"I can't believe it," he said smiling. "I really am so grateful for such a great family."

Avaeri laughed. "You already said that."

"He can keep on saying it," his father chimed in. "It's true. And we're going to be an eternal family."

Dylan sat down, watching his family laugh together. Life could not be more wonderful. If only he could have found Elizabeth, but he hadn't, and with no other recourse he'd have to move on and try to put her out of his mind. He knew without a doubt that it would be the most difficult thing he'd ever had to do.

Chapter Twenty-One

Over the next several months Dylan and Courtney spent many long hours together putting the Foundation in order to get entrance into Uganda. It had helped that Dylan had some government contacts from his service in the CSIS to smooth the way. Once the foundation was in place, they were even able to work with the Latter-Day Saint Charities, a foundation the LDS church had formed and the Red Cross. Both organizations were grateful for his government connections that were helping to get medical and school supplies into Kampala without the middle men who sometimes took the supplies for their own profit. From their work with Latter-Day Saint Charities he had found out that Courtney was LDS. He was a little surprised because some of her attitudes toward modesty and church attendance didn't reflect her membership.

When they realized they had a common religion, and were spending so much time together anyway, Courtney had asked him to dinner one night. He didn't have anything better to do, so he'd agreed. Since then, they'd practically spent every evening together, talking about the foundation and their plans for the future. Dylan never mentioned Elizabeth, somehow holding her memory too special to be discussed.

This particular night they'd gone to the CN Tower for a tour and to see the spectacular view, then gone on to dinner. Dylan's curiosity got the better of him, so he decided to ask her about her views on her church membership. "Why do you work on Sunday?"

Courtney shrugged delicately. "I'm busy building a practice and a reputation for myself. I don't see clients or anything."

"Don't you have a calling in your ward?"

"I think the bishop understands that at this point in my life I can't handle a Sunday calling. When I'm older I'll probably take one."

Dylan cut the steak in front of him, contemplating what she'd said. "But doesn't the Lord need you to build up his kingdom?"

Courtney leaned forward and took his hand. "I'm sure that because you're a new member you feel on fire with the gospel. I've been a member all my life. It's different for me."

"Do you have a testimony? How is it different?" Dylan asked doggedly, feeling like this was important for him to know.

"Can we talk about something else? I'd rather not argue with you." She slid close to him. "I guarantee you don't want to argue with me. I am an attorney you know." She reached up and kissed him on the cheek. "Let's not ruin the evening, okay?"

Dylan dropped it, but knew it would come up again. He needed to know where she stood.

"So are you excited at the thought of going back to Africa? I can't wait, myself, since I've never been there," Courtney said, changing the subject.

Dylan smiled, his thoughts on Kampala. "It is so beautiful there and so rich with culture. You'd be amazed at the people and what they've been through, but still have the strength to continue and teach their heritage to their children." His eyes became far away. "There was this little boy in a hospital waiting to see if his mother would die or not. I spoke with him and told him I'd pray for him and he seemed so mature for his age, and yet still had hope that a prayer might work for his mother. That's what motivated me to start the foundation." He stopped talking, remembering the day he'd met Balondemu, took Elizabeth to lunch and laughed with her. She made everyone around her want to laugh with her.

Courtney ran her hand in front of his face. "Hey, where did you go?"

He jerked his mind back to the present. "Just thinking, I guess."

"Well, did the mother die?"

"I don't know. I never saw them again after that." He sipped his water.

"Why were you at the hospital anyway?" She smoothed her short skirt, then looked up at him for his answer. Her blue eyes were clear like glacial ice and he knew she had a stubborn streak in her.

"You know I can't answer that. It's classified." He smiled. "Let's talk about something else, okay?" repeating her earlier statement.

"Maybe we're all talked out tonight," she said, wiping her mouth on her napkin and standing. He started to stand with her but she held up her hand. "Dylan, I think we both need to take a step back and see where we stand. I'm falling in love with you, but I'm not sure you feel the same." She grabbed her purse and Dylan could see tears starting to pool in her eyes. "I want to be part of your life, but sometimes I feel that you're only letting me see parts of you and I want to see the whole of you." She turned and took a tissue out of her purse and wiped her eyes. "Call me in a few days and we'll talk again. I just need some time by myself."

Dylan stood, but she waved him back. "I have my own car," she said as she left. He watched her leave, then paid for their dinner. He walked outside and got into his car, slowly driving toward the suburbs to his apartment in Scarborough. He drove without thinking, his thoughts on Courtney's accusation that he wasn't letting her in. It was true, he acknowledged. He had only let Courtney see parts of him. She was an excellent conversationalist, she was beautiful, but he was not in love with her. He knew his heart was reserved for Elizabeth, but he had no idea if he would ever see her again. His head told him to move on, to try harder with Courtney, but his heart wasn't in it. Her outburst tonight had shown him that he was hurting her and he didn't want to do that.

He drove into his apartment building's parking garage, alarmed his car and went upstairs. Unlocking his apartment door, he went inside and flicked on the lights. He checked his answering machine for messages, then flopped down on the sofa. They were supposed to be leaving in a few days to a conference that Courtney had set up. If all went well at the conference they could accompany their first shipment of supplies to Uganda.

Courtney had steered him into the fund-raising aspect of having a non-profit and he'd been very successful in getting some large donations. She'd set up the conference in Waterton, a resort in the province of Alberta, to schmooze some big donors. Apparently she was giving him until then to think things over and he needed to use every minute. He needed the chance to sort out his feelings. He felt that he was being tried and tested, knowing he was doing right, but having everything go wrong.

He went into his bedroom and got ready for bed, taking out his scriptures, the privilege of actually being able to hold them in his hand and read them a profound pleasure. He flipped them open, looking for a particular scripture. After several minutes he finally found it. "For it must needs be, that there is an opposition in all things. If not so . . . righteousness could not be brought to pass, neither wickedness, neither holiness, nor misery, neither good nor bad." Because of his trials, the suffering he'd witnessed and was now trying to alleviate, he understood better the plan of salvation. Without the trials he wouldn't know what happiness was, and "men are that they might have joy." He wanted to experience joy, the question was would he find it with Courtney?

He put his scriptures away and lay on his bed thinking. He

fell asleep with his thoughts, his dreams filled with a beautiful woman with long brown hair. She smiled and held her arms out to him, speaking his name. He awoke in the morning refreshed, but as the memory of his dream came back to him, he felt guilty, feeling somehow that he was betraying Courtney. But they weren't married, so that couldn't be true. Yet, Courtney had confessed that she was in love with him, so that should mean something shouldn't it?

Perhaps he'd been going about it wrong. He should be counting his blessings, not his trials. He was very blessed and made up his mind to concentrate on that. Courtney could be counted as a blessing, helping him with his foundation, a project dear to his heart, and giving him her love. He wouldn't just throw that away without giving it a chance. Making a decision to put Elizabeth out of his mind and give a life with Courtney a chance, he whistled softly as he dialed her number.

"Hello?" she answered.

"Courtney, it's Dylan."

"Yes?" she answered, her voice cool.

"I've called to ask for your forgiveness, and to see if you could find it in your heart to give me another chance."

"Do you mean it?" she asked. "I don't want your pity or anything given to me out of guilt."

"It is not out of pity or guilt. I truly want to see if we could ever have anything beyond friendship," he said. Going over to his mantle, he fingered the picture of Balondemu, knowing that his experience in Africa could never be truly far from his thoughts. But he wouldn't spend the rest of his life wishing for a woman he couldn't have.

"Well there's a Maple Leafs game tonight. Would you like to go?" she asked, her voice soft and shy, something he'd never heard from her before.

"I'd love to. Can I pick you up around six?"

"I'll be ready," she said and hung up the phone. Dylan put down the picture of the little African boy and closed his eyes.

His head told him he'd made the right decision and he hoped so. It would not be easy to forget about Elizabeth and all that they'd shared. But he had no other choice.

Chapter Twenty-Two

Dylan sat on his perch on the shores of Waterton Lake aimlessly skipping rocks. He knew he should be dressing for dinner with Courtney, but wanted to be alone for a moment longer. He stood up and brushed off his pants. Looking up at the spectacular Prince of Wales hotel standing sentinel over the lake, he remembered an ancient palace and the woman who had shared that view with him.

He shook his head, knowing he was breaking his promise to himself not to think of Elizabeth, to put her out of his mind. His head demanded he move on, that Elizabeth was lost to him, but his heart told him he'd never find anyone else like her. Yet, he had made up his mind to follow reason one last time. *Give it a shot with Courtney*, he told himself for the millionth time. Tonight he was going to concentrate on her. She was loving and tried so hard to make him see how good they were together. He ticked off her good points in his mind. She had made the last few months since his grandfather's death bearable, her vivaciousness was contagious, she was LDS, she was in love with him and he sternly told himself he would concentrate on all of her good qualities tonight.

He made the climb up the hill to the hotel, where he changed his clothes to a navy blue suit, with a burgundy and gray tie, then went to sit in the lobby, slowly sipping some hot chocolate while he waited for her.

They were here in Waterton for a conference and fund-raiser and had decided to stay an extra two days to sightsee.

It was a beautiful place, with boating, hiking, and quaint little shops. He'd especially like Cameron Falls and the serenity it offered. He looked up from his cup as Courtney entered the room and walked to his table. She was beautiful in a simple black dress that brushed just past her knees, the starkness of the black highlighting the blondeness of her hair. When she reached the table she bent over to kiss him on the cheek.

"Have you been waiting long?"

"No," he replied, standing up to help her with her chair.

When he had settled down in his chair, she reached across the table and took his hand. "Isn't the view incredible?" she asked, looking through the large window at the lights from the boats dancing in the harbor.

"It's amazing. I'm sort of sorry our trip is coming to an end."

"Me, too." Courtney sat back in her chair and Dylan ordered her a hot chocolate as well. "So how did we end up this weekend? Were you able to charm all the big donors?"

Chuckling, Dylan shook his head. "You know me too well. Of course. We have enough to take several loads of food, blankets and medicine." His eyes were twinkling. "And deliver it all personally."

Courtney took her drink in her hands, a satisfied smile on his face. "You've gotten everything you wanted."

Briefly Elizabeth's face flashed across his thoughts. "Not everything," he murmured. His time in Kampala was never far from his thoughts, not only because of Elizabeth but also because of the extreme poverty that he had witnessed. It had been appalling and using his grandfather's money to help those in need had satisfied his innermost soul. Just to see clothing and blankets given to the orphans, or food and medicine delivered to the hospital would be gratifying. Traveling to Uganda to deliver some of the supplies himself was exciting and he wanted to see the country again. Perhaps he'd even look up Nabulungi and see if Ojore had made it home.

He sipped his drink, and could feel Courtney's eyes on him, questioning him, wondering where his thoughts were. He put it down and stood up, motioning toward the dining room. "Are you ready to eat?"

She nodded, but didn't say anything. The atmosphere was charged and Dylan could feel the change in Courtney's demeanor. He mentally kicked himself again and promised to put Elizabeth and their time in Kampala out of his thoughts. He maneuvered Courtney through the crowd, his hand at her back as they made their way toward the dining room. But before he could even apologize to her or start a conversation, he saw a familiar brown ponytail just in front of them. He was stunned for a moment, then dropped Courtney's arm and gently pushed his way toward the woman. Turning her around and hugging her, he closed his eyes. "Elizabeth," he said.

As he opened his eyes and looked down at the frightened woman in his arms he knew he'd made a big mistake. He backed up hastily. "I am so sorry," he said, his face flaming red. "I thought you were someone else."

She backed away from him, her eyes wide. "You shouldn't be so friendly mister," she managed to say before joining her party in the dining room. Courtney came to stand at his side, staring at him as if he had two heads.

"What was that all about?" she asked.

"I thought she was someone I knew, but she wasn't," Dylan explained lamely. He watched the woman go to her table and point him out to the people who were seated. His face flushed again. "Maybe we should go somewhere else and eat."

Courtney looked over at the woman and took Dylan's arm as he led her back to the lobby and outside. They walked down the sloping road, their shoes crunching in the gravel. It reminded him of Kampala road, the stars above him, nature all around him. But it was not Elizabeth beside him.

"Do you want to tell me about her?" Courtney asked softly.

Dylan shook his head. "It wouldn't be fair to you," he said finally.

"I figured out that you weren't in love with me, because whenever we talk about Uganda, you get that faraway look in your eye and I know you're thinking about someone else. It just took me a while to realize you were not only thinking about the country but also a person. The woman you love I'd venture to guess," she said, patting his arm. "It's okay. I mean, I won't say I'm not disappointed. I had hoped to change your mind, but you can't force what's not there."

He took her hand and led her to a small bench where they sat down. "I'm so sorry, Courtney. I really do think you're wonderful. It's just a matter of timing."

"You're sweet to say that, Dylan. I think you're pretty wonderful, too, but tell me about her. I really want to know who stole your heart."

He watched the lights of the marina flicker off the water in Emerald Bay and it reminded him of the ferry in Greece and how the blue of the Mediterranean had matched the blue in Elizabeth's dress. Her long hair blowing in the wind, her smile and laughter as she bought the T-shirt that said, "I Love Greece." But what he remembered most was their goodbye, when she said she loved him. The ache of losing her was almost more than he could bear. "Her name is Elizabeth. I met her when she was an aide at a private hospital in Kampala." He turned to Courtney. "I haven't been able to find her, but I haven't been able to forget her." He took her hand and squeezed it. "I really did try to, you know."

Courtney stood and he stood with her. "I hope you find Elizabeth, Dylan. You deserve all the happiness in the world." She hugged him, and they walked slowly back to the hotel. "I want you to know after spending all this time with you, I've been thinking about my commitment to the gospel." She looked shyly at him. "I've made some changes and I plan to do more."

Dylan stopped and turned her to him. "I'm so glad, Courtney. But I doubt it had anything to do with me."

"It truly did," she said softly, her eyes shining.

"Don't cry," he begged. "Please don't cry because of me."

"I'm fine," she replied, waving his concern away. "I'll be fine. You go to Uganda. If you ever reconsider, you give me a call. You know where to find me."

Dylan watched her go the last few feet to the hotel. She was a wonderful woman, but she was right. You can't force what's not there. His heart seemed lighter and he went to his own room to pack. It was going to be a long night, but the pressure he'd put on himself was gone. Lately, he'd been reliving every memory he had of Elizabeth in his dreams—her face and the sound of her voice, carrying the memory of how she felt in his arms. The dream always ended with her saying his name and holding her hands out to him. But he always awoke and realized it was just a dream. Tonight would be no different, except he wouldn't feel that he was being untrue to Courtney. With that situation taken care of, he was ready to go back to Africa.

After several long flights and layovers, Dylan finally arrived at the Entebbe airport in Kampala. It was a strange feeling of homecoming as he got off the plane and walked through the airport to collect his bags. The country still seemed the same, hot and humid, the people were friendly, but guarded. He caught a hotel shuttle with Abdul the driver behind the wheel and two other Africans behind him. It was an enjoyable ride, albeit a little bumpy, through the center of town.

Kampala was a bustling city with a varied skyline of skyscrapers. The small patches of grass in between buildings sometimes reached all the way down to the small corrugated metal-walled shops which looked like they'd been hastily put together the day before. It was a country full of constant juxtaposition, but somehow he felt comfortable here. It was obvious that he was the one who had changed and it was all so clear now—his true mission in life, his need to serve the people here. The shuttle dropped him off at the Mamba Point Guesthouse, just a few minutes away from the core of the city in the Nakasero area. It was strange to him to be traveling like a tourist, but it gave him a feeling of controlling his own destiny.

The owners of the guesthouse, Guido and Fiona, greeted him as he checked in. It was a small guesthouse, looking more like a large two-story house back in Canada. But it had a pool and was clean, and with twenty hours of traveling behind him, Dylan was ready for bed.

When he awoke it was dark and his stomach was rumbling. He went outside and down the street to the adjacent Mamba Point Restaurant. After a great meal that filled his stomach, he started to walk into Kampala. He passed several familiar buildings and found himself on the path to the Mulago hospital. When he got there, he stood in the moonlight, looking at the courtyard, the stone bench and feeling all the memories those objects evoked in him. Elizabeth. He couldn't forget her. He stood for a few minutes longer, then made his way back to his hotel.

The next morning he was busy organizing and gathering the supplies. After several phone calls, he was on his way in one of the trucks, headed to several private hospitals in the city. The last stop was Mulago. In the aftermath of Bumani's death, his brother who'd owned the hospital had fled the country and a very sweet and honest man named Edward Fie had taken over. Dylan jumped out of the truck and greeted the little African man who was obviously waiting for them.

"Mr. Fie, I'm Dylan Campbell," he said.

"Mr. Campbell, it is a great pleasure to meet you." Mr. Fie shook his hand vigorously. "We are so grateful to you today."

Dylan opened the back of the truck which made a loud clanging noise. "It is wonderful to be able to help where I can." The truck driver joined them and they began unloading boxes of supplies. Mr. Fie directed them to the basement of the hospital and Dylan experienced a feeling of déjà vu. It was the same room that Bumani had used to store the materials for the making of Tracin. He smiled as he went inside. That was all behind him now.

When they were finished unloading, Mr. Fie asked if they'd like a tour of the building. Dylan accepted, never even hinting that he'd been there before. He wanted to see where he'd spent time with Elizabeth. It was the next best thing to being with her.

He followed Mr. Fie up the same uneven stairs with peeling paint to the floor where Elizabeth had worked. He opened the doors and saw a large crowd of people milling around. Mr. Fie turned to say something to him, but Dylan had already walked two steps ahead of him. A long brown ponytail was several feet in front of him and he almost involuntarily called out her name, before his humiliating experience of mistaken identity in Waterton came crashing back to him. He must have made a sound however, because the next few moments were in slow motion for him as she turned, her brown eyes staring, her mouth wide in a half-smile and just like in his dreams, Elizabeth held her hands out to him, calling his name.

Chapter Twenty-Three

He hugged her close, the feel of her in his arms, the smell of her hair, everything was familiar. "I can't believe I found you," he breathed. "I've been looking for you for six months!"

Elizabeth's arms were tight around his neck, but he didn't know if his shortness of breath was from that or from the fact that she stood before him.

"I'm so glad you're here," she said, her eyes wet. "I can't believe it, but you really are." She reached up to touch his face, her thumb lingering across the cleft in his chin.

He leaned down and touched his lips to hers, the depth of his emotion for her transferred in the kiss. "I love you," he whispered, as they broke apart. She was about to say something to him, when applause broke out. The couple turned to find most of the medical aides on the ward watching them, smiling and clapping.

"Thank you," Elizabeth said loudly. To Dylan, she said simply, "I think we need some privacy. Let's go into the lounge."

Dylan nodded and took her hand, waving briefly to those aid workers which were still watching them. As they entered the lounge, he held out a metal chair for her. She sat down and he took the chair next to her. He pointed to the T-shirt she was wearing, the one she had bought in Heraklion that showed the bull-leaping fresco and declared, "I Love Greece."

"I see you haven't forgotten all about me," he said. "I still have my shirt, too. It helped to wear it and feel close to you."

He took both her hands in his, still amazed that she was here and he could touch her. After a moment he settled back in his chair, but still held on to one of her hands, unwilling to break the contact. "So what happened after we left Greece?" he asked.

"They took me to Langley. I was able to listen in and find out what happened with Sam. Then they took me to be tested, since I'd been exposed to the virus. They wouldn't even tell me what they were looking for, it was all classified." She leaned across the table to envelop Dylan's hand with both of hers. "I wondered if you were looking for me."

He put his free hand at her back and pulled her closer until their foreheads were touching. "I tried everything, but all I had was your alias. And you're right, everything was classified, including your identity, whereabouts, everything." He sat back and ran his hand through his hair. "I even tried to go through back channels, but got nothing. I had all but given up."

"I'm glad you didn't," Elizabeth said softly. "I want to tell you something." She bowed her head for a moment. "What happened in Greece really affected me," she started.

"Me, too," Dylan interrupted.

She smiled. "When you prayed for me, it was such an intense experience. I really felt something. At first I thought that maybe it was just intense because I was going to die, but then on the tarmac before you left you said that I could find that feeling in the LDS Church." She stopped for a moment, and leaned closer to him. "I fought it for a while. But when I was going through the testing, I had a lot of time to think. So I decided to see if what you said was true."

Dylan listened, hoping with all his heart that what she was about to say to him, was what he thought it was.

"I investigated the Church, met the missionaries, took the discussions, and you were right. The feeling I experienced in Greece was there. I could pray to my Heavenly Father and feel the light that I always thought you had." Tears began to form in her eyes. "I was baptized four months ago. I quit the CIA and came back here to Africa to help ease the suffering. I felt needed here and led here." She got up and turned to face him, the only thing between them was the table. "I hoped that you would come back here to find me, and you did."

Dylan stood beside her, coming around the table to tenderly kiss her. "I couldn't believe that I was dumb enough not to ask you what your last name was so I could find you. I would have been able to be with you months ago if I had." Elizabeth started to say something, but he put his fingers to her lips. "I never want to be separated from you again. And I want you to have a last name that I can remember, so would you mind terribly if we got married and you took my last name?" He got down on one knee, still holding her hand. "Elizabeth, would you do me the honor of becoming Elizabeth Campbell, my wife?"

Elizabeth nodded then kneeled next to him. "Your last name is Campbell?" she said. "I thought it was Fields."

He blinked, then squeezed her hand. "Yes, it's Campbell. Do you like Fields better?"

"No, Campbell is fine." She looked thoughtful.

Dylan impatiently stifled a smile. "Elizabeth, I promise to love you and honor you for the rest of my life and all eternity, and I know all of our children will be proud to have the Campbell name. Will you please marry me and make me the happiest man on the face of the earth?"

"Yes, a thousand times yes." They embraced, hugging each other tightly before breaking apart. Dylan couldn't keep his eyes off her, the reality of her in front of him was hard to take in. Tears were rolling down her cheeks, but she was smiling. He wiped them away, his fingers lingering on her face. "Are those happy tears I hope?" She nodded. After a few moments, Dylan helped her to her feet. "I love you," he repeated again. "I'll never let you go."

She smiled back. "You can't get rid of me now." She grabbed his hand and started for the door. "I have a surprise for you."

"What's that?"

She didn't say anything but led him to a nurses station down the hall. Nabulungi was there, with Serapio standing behind her. "Mr. Fields," she said. "You came back! I knew you would," she glanced at Elizabeth. "You were right, miss."

Elizabeth blushed. "How are you today, Serapio?"

He held out a large basket. "Fine. We're here to bring lunch to Papa."

"Papa?" Dylan asked, his eyebrows raised.

Nabulungi came around the table and hugged Dylan. "You brought my husband back to me." She drew back. "I can never thank you enough."

"Ojore made it home then," he smiled, very pleased.

"Yes, I did," a large voice boomed behind him, and Dylan was enveloped in another tight hug. "Thanks to you."

"Ojore," Dylan slapped him on the back. "I'm so glad to see you back where you belong."

He stepped back and put his arm around Elizabeth. "Did you ever imagine that we'd all be here together?"

"I hoped it would be that way," Elizabeth said. She looked around the group. "Dylan asked me to marry him and I said yes." She smiled and accepted their congratulations. "I'd like you all to be at the wedding."

"What temple will you be married in?" Nabulungi asked. "Probably South Africa I imagine."

"How do you know about temples?" Dylan asked, astonished.

"That's my other surprise," Elizabeth laughed. "Do you remember when you left, some missionaries had brought Nabulungi the Book of Mormon? She read it, took the discussions and was also baptized. That's how I met her, at the Kabowa branch."

Now it was Dylan's turn to give Nabulungi a hug. "Congratulations," he said, his voice sincere. "I am so happy for you."

"Thank you," she said shyly. "When Ojore returned, he told me of meeting you and of your testimony of the book. I wondered why you hadn't shared that with me?"

"I was on a government assignment and wasn't supposed to give out personal information about myself," Dylan said sheepishly. "I'm sorry. I really wanted to, since I was a new member myself then, and I desperately wanted to tell you my testimony of the book, but couldn't. I'm really sorry."

"Well, your testimony in prison made Ojore want to read it, to find out more about what the man who saved him believed." She looped her arm through his. "He was also baptized." Her face clouded over. "It was a more difficult process for him since he was a fugitive. He had to go to the government and ask for a pardon. We were very scared that he would be thrown back in prison, but we prayed often and relied on our new faith in the Lord that He knew what was best."

Ojore finished for her. "We were very blessed. I received my pardon and was able to find employment at the hospital. I have my family back." He drew Nabulungi and Serapio into his arms. "We are very blessed indeed," he repeated.

Elizabeth snuggled into Dylan's arm. "I want to be married in the South Africa temple," she announced. "After living a life where you think only from moment to moment and have to live for today since there might not be a tomorrow, I am thrilled at the thought of spending eternity with you and seeing a whole other perspective." She put her hand on Dylan's chest, her eyes shining as she looked at him. "I love you."

"I love you too," he replied. "I will be honored to be your husband."

The adults were barely able to contain their tears at the tender confessions of love, when Serapio held out the basket. "Is it lunch yet? I am very hungry."

The adults laughed. "Please join us for lunch," Nabulungi invited. "I have enough for everyone."

They took the basket out to the courtyard, passing the

bench where Dylan and Elizabeth had sat so many months ago, wondering if they would see each other again. So much had happened to bring them to this point. Dylan slipped his arm around Elizabeth and squeezed it. She had agreed to become his wife! Everything he had ever dreamed of was about to come true.

They found a large tree and small patch of grass and sat down to unload the basket. She had filled it with chicken, fruit and bread, and everyone ate their fill. "So what brings you back to Africa, despite the obvious?" Ojore asked, nodding his head toward Elizabeth.

Dylan smiled. "My grandfather passed away."

"Oh, Dylan, I'm so sorry," Elizabeth interrupted.

"Thanks." He leaned over and gave her a small kiss. "He left me a large amount of money, and at first, I didn't know what to do with it. But then the inspiration came and I started a foundation to help the people of Uganda. I'm here accompanying a shipment actually."

Elizabeth's eyes were wide. "You wouldn't happen to be talking about The George Campbell Relief Foundation would you?"

"Yes, that's our foundation. Why?"

"The hospital was struggling. We thought we might have to close down, but at the very last minute, the Campbell foundation came through and gave us enough supplies to keep us afloat," Elizabeth explained.

"I thought I would lose my job and we would have to go north to our son," Ojore said. "And it was you who saved us again."

Dylan waved off the praise. "I know I was inspired by the Lord. It was in his plan all along."

He stood and brushed off his pants, holding out his hand for Elizabeth. "Will you walk awhile with me?" She nodded and stood with him. "Thank you for the lunch Nabulungi. It was the best food I've tasted in a long time."

"You're welcome. I will save your room for you in the village if you would like to stay with us," Nabulungi invited.

"Definitely," Dylan accepted immediately. "I'll move my things over tonight. See you then."

They waved and started to walk slowly back to the hospital. Elizabeth put her arm around him, laying her head on his shoulder. "I can't believe it's real. I've dreamed about this moment for so long."

"Me, too," Dylan agreed. They walked slowly past the marketplace, the vendors and shop owners anxious for business. "Come on," Dylan said suddenly, taking her hand and darting through the crowd.

"Hey," Elizabeth protested, laughing. "Where are we going?"

Dylan didn't reply, just kept on walking. When he stopped short in front of a man painting, the tears began to form in Elizabeth's eyes. "Oh Dylan."

They stood before the man who had painted the Savior in such a real and life-like way. He was still there, painting, but this time his portraits showed the Savior holding a child. The artist glanced up at them, then straightened. "I remember you," he said excitedly. "You bought my painting for your lady."

"Yes, I did," Dylan confirmed. "Where is your son?"

The artist grinned, his chest puffing out. "I was able to save enough money to send him to school," he said proudly.

"That's wonderful," Elizabeth said warmly.

"Do any of my new paintings interest you?" he said pointing to several. "I will paint anything you want."

Dylan could not take his eyes off of the picture of the Savior gazing down into the eyes of the small child. "I like this one," he said. "How much?"

"Two dollah," the man pronounced.

Elizabeth smiled. "Are you going to dicker with him?"

"Not today," Dylan replied, handing the man several bills. "You deserve every penny and more."

The artist took the painting and gave it to Elizabeth. "He has watched over you."

Elizabeth smiled up at Dylan. "Yes, he has." She held the painting close to her and they turned to go. "Do you remember what you told me when you bought me the first painting?" she asked Dylan.

"Not really," he replied.

"You told me that you didn't know all the answers, but that you knew God had a plan for us. I didn't know if I believed you then, but I believe you now."

He turned her around and looked down into her laughing brown eyes. "I love you, future Mrs. Elizabeth Campbell. Do you think God planned on that?"

"Absolutely," Elizabeth laughed before reaching up to kiss him.

Epilogue

Dylan sat in the South Africa temple on a small, simply upholstered pew, his father, Dennis and Ojore beside him, as they waited for their wives to join them. It had been a busy eight months since Dylan had asked Elizabeth to marry him, her work as a medical aide and his with the foundation keeping them occupied until this day had finally arrived. They had chosen to be married in Africa, since that was where they lived and worked, but also where they had fallen in love. It was a small ceremony, attended only by Nabulungi, Ojore, Dylan's parents and his sisters. Serapio and Elizabeth's family were waiting outside for them.

"I'm so happy for you, son, we all love Elizabeth," Dennis patted him on the knee.

"Thanks, Dad." Dylan stood. "I wonder what could be taking so long?"

Ojore laughed. "You will get used to waiting for your wife."

"Remember this moment, son. She's going to walk through that door in her wedding gown and it will be a moment to tell your grandchildren about," his father advised.

Dylan sat back down and stared at the door, memorizing the grain. He couldn't wait to see his wife! After several minutes the door opened and Dylan looked up expectantly. All else was forgotten when Elizabeth walked through it, her face glowing with happiness, looking beautiful in her simple, white temple dress. Nabulungi and Dylan's mother, Connie, followed close behind.

Dylan strode to Elizabeth and kissed her. "Hello, Mrs. Campbell."

"Hello, Mr. Campbell." She snuggled into his arms. "It's finally official and feels so good to hear."

Dylan's mother touched his shoulder. "Elizabeth's family is waiting outside." Dylan nodded and took Elizabeth's arm to escort her outside. It was a beautiful late afternoon, the sun low in the sky, the temperatures cooling slightly. A perfect day to be married.

They walked down the small hallway that led outside to the temple grounds to meet Elizabeth's family. At first Elizabeth's parents and brother had been surprised and frustrated that not only was she marrying someone they'd never met, but she was getting married in a place where they couldn't witness it. But after meeting Dylan several times and seeing how happy Elizabeth was, they'd finally given their blessing.

They walked into the lobby, and her parents stood from the elegant, but tasteful wingback chairs they had been waiting in. They opened their arms and Dylan and Elizabeth stepped into them. "Congratulations," her mother murmured, stepping back to adjust Elizabeth's veil, the tears evident in her eyes. "I'm so happy for you."

"Thanks, Mom," Elizabeth said, delicately wiping at her own eyes. "I love you so much and I'm so glad you were able to be here for me."

"Take good care of my girl," Elizabeth's father admonished Dylan, patting him on the back.

"Don't worry sir, I will," Dylan agreed.

They chatted for a few moments before going outside to pause for several pictures on the grounds. When they turned a corner of the temple, Dylan stopped. His mouth fell open in complete surprise at who was standing before him.

"Andrew!" he said. "What are you doing here?"

"I wanted to congratulate you in person." Andrew Blythe looked at Elizabeth, then came forward to offer her a hug. "You got a good man here," he said.

"I know," Elizabeth replied, looking up at her new husband.

"How did you know I was getting married today?" Dylan asked incredulously. "I wasn't able to get through to you and I left no message."

"I am an officer in the Canadian Security Intelligence Service. I have my ways," Andrew said, winking. "You should know that. Is there any chance at all that I could convince you to come back to the agency?" he asked Dylan.

"No way," Dylan said quickly. "Let me introduce you to my parents," he turned to look for them, but they were a distance behind, chatting with Nabulungi and Ojore.

"Didn't think you'd come back, but I had to ask." Andrew looked at his watch. "I'm sorry I can't stay longer but duty calls. Be happy, you two."

"I wish you could stay for the celebration afterward, but thanks for coming Andrew," Dylan said. "You've always been there for me."

"I always will be, you remember that." Andrew looked at them for a moment, and hugged them again before walking away. Dylan watched him go.

"Do you miss working for the agency?" Elizabeth asked.

"No. I'm grateful that it led me to you, but I knew that wasn't what I wanted to do for the rest of my life." He took her hand and led her to a small stone bench that stood in front of some spectacular landscaping. "I've never felt more fulfilled than having the opportunity to help ease the suffering here in Africa." He cupped her chin and tilted it toward him. "Besides, deciding to partner up with you was the best decision I ever made."

She laughed. "I think *I* decided we could be partners, not the other way around." Her brow furrowed. "I always wondered why you didn't have a partner on that mission."

"I was waiting for you," he said, running his fingers through her hair, drawing her face closer to him and looking deeply into the dancing brown eyes that he loved. "Partners?"

"Partners?" she said mildly, her eyebrows raised. "We're more than partners now, we're eternal companions." She grinned, then lifted her lips to seal the sentiment with a kiss.

The African sun was beginning to set, the rays reaching down to touch the couple, illuminating the beginning of their new life together. They had been on the edge of darkness and danger, facing insurmountable odds, but they had overcome it all and could now enjoy the light and happiness that came from the love of the gospel, the love of their Heavenly Father, and the love they had for each other.

About the Author

Julie Coulter Bellon is originally from Canada and loves incorporating her native country with its complexities into her writing. This book also uses many of the settings she visited while vacationing in the beautiful city of Athens and on the islands of Greece. Julie and her husband Brian are the parents of six children and her greatest joy is being a mother. She graduated from Brigham Young University with a Bachelor's degree in Secondary Education—English teaching, and she currently teaches a high school journalism course for BYU Continuing Education. Julie serves as the Chairman of the Library Board in her community so she always has an excuse to be near books.

When she's not busy being a mom, teaching, serving in the community or writing, you will find her browsing through bookstores to add to her book collection, at the library borrowing books, or reading the treasures she's found.